FATHERS AND SONS

FATHERS AND SONS

Ivan S. Turgenev

WORDSWORTH CLASSICS

This edition published 1996 by
Wordsworth Editions Limited
Cumberland House, Crib Street
Ware, Hertfordshire SG12 9ET

ISBN 1 85326 286 2

Typeset by Antony Gray
Printed and bound in Great Britain by
Mackays of Chatham plc, Chatham, Kent

INTRODUCTION

Ivan Turgenev lived largely in Baden-Baden and Paris and developed a sensibility and literary technique peculiarly akin to those of contemporary Western European writers. He was the first of the great authors of nineteenth-century Russia to make a name for himself outside his own country, and his novels, which illuminate the political, social and philosophical preoccupations of the day by focusing on individual lives, became extremely influential. Conrad, Galsworthy, Virginia Woolf and George Moore are all indebted to Turgenev, and Henry James particularly admired his supreme artistic rigour and control of the elusive novel form.

Turgenev's fourth novel, *Fathers and Sons* was first published in March of 1862. It is a story of universal significance that presents a revelation of humanity through depiction of contemporary Russian life. Turgenev conveys a striking vision of the ubiquitous clash between generations, focusing on the conflict between the younger members of the Russian intelligentsia who became prominent after the Crimean War, and the older intellectuals who, though sympathetic to the need for reform, were fundamentally committed to both the political and aesthetic ideals of Western civilisation, and gave no quarter to talk of revolution.

Objectivity was Turgenev's great gift, and though he himself clearly identifies with the 'fathers' of the novel, he has been much lauded for his discerning portrayal of a 'son' in the character of Bazarov. The novel was conceived during a visit to Ventnor on the Isle of Wight where Turgenev was struck by the personality of a young Russian doctor. He used attributes of this Dr Paulov, of the famous Russian critic Dobrolyubov and of the radical journalist Preobrazhensky to create the character of the first 'nihilist' hero of Western fiction.

Turgenev consciously gave even the minor figures in his novels a thoroughly sound background, building up details with punctilious attention. Virginia Woolf notes in *A Writer's Diary* that Turgenev kept a journal for Bazarov in which everything was recorded from his point of view. Seen in a variety of settings, Bazarov, the self-reliant, radical free-thinker with a wealth of potential, is indisputably the most memorable of all Turgenev's heroes and became a prototype for many other novelists. He repudiates everything that cannot be explained by the laws of natural science, striving for reality rather than negation, and he embodies the spirit of revolution. Bazarov is contrasted most sharply with Pavel Petrovich, conservative uncle of his friend Arkady, but towards the end of the novel the emphasis shifts.

Turgenev's tender presentation of fatherhood and of the profound affection between old and young which is shown to be an elementary part of life as the fates of individuals are inevitably interwoven, supersedes the theme of the generation gap. Despite his scrupulous impartiality, Turgenev's admiration for the new man personified by Bazarov is clearly tinged with fear and sometimes dislike. Ultimately the novel upholds the eternal values that the fathers (and particularly Turgenev) prized: paternal love, the continuity of family ties, friendship, passion, art, traditionalism, individualism and religion are justified.

A grand master of style, Turgenev writes a meticulous prose which can be daunting to the translator. An autographed manuscript of *Fathers and Sons* reveals much reworking and refining, and illustrates Turgenev's delight in both dramatic dialogue and the most precise use of language. Charles James Hogarth's translation is both lucid and fluent and retains the author's original emphases.

It is essentially Turgenev's practice of showing rather than telling, his ability to 'state the obvious and let the reader do the rest', as Virginia Woolf says, that makes his work so attractive to the Western reader. *Fathers and Sons* is in many respects a very specific novel set in a precise historical time, yet it has a tragic dimension that extends its implications and gives it an enduring relevance.

Ivan Sergeyevich Turgenev was born in 1818 at Orel in central Russia where he grew up on his family estate at Spasskoye. He graduated from the University of St Petersburg in 1837 and moved to Berlin to study classical languages, literature and philosophy. He returned to Russia in 1841 expecting to teach philosophy but found that the government had removed the subject from the syllabus. After an interlude of idleness, Turgenev took a minor post in the civil service for a couple of years before devoting himself to literature.

He published some poetry in 1838, but his first literary success was with the prose pieces, Hunter's Notes, which appeared between 1847 and 1851. In 1850 his mother died and he inherited a large fortune. That year saw the publication of his most famous and critically acclaimed play, A Month in the Country. *An article that Turgenev published in 1852 on the death of Gogol led to his being imprisoned for a month. He was subsequently banished to his estate where he wrote a series of novels and short stories, among them* Rudin *(1856),* Asya *(1858),* A Nest of Gentlefolk *(1859),* First Love *(1860) and* On the Eve *(1860).* Fathers and Sons *appeared in 1862 and was harshly criticised by Russian conservatives and radicals alike for its portrayal of Bazarov. Disenchanted, Turgenev left Russia in 1863, only returning from his self-imposed exile for brief visits.*

In 1843 he had met and fallen in love with Pauline Garcia Viardot, a singer married to the French writer, Louis Viardot. He loved her for the rest of his life, and though she never returned his feelings, she allowed him to follow her and her husband as they moved about Europe. He lived largely in Baden-Baden and Paris, publishing his next novel, Smoke, *in 1867. This attacked both Russian factions and was another bone of public contention, causing a rift with Dostoyevsky. Much of Turgenev's life was beset with literary disputes, though he was reconciled with both Dostoyevsky and Tolstoy before his death from cancer at Bougival in 1883. He is buried at Volkovo Cemetery in St Petersburg.*

FURTHER READING

Gilbert Phelps, *The Russian Novel in English Fiction*, London 1956
Richard Freeborn, *Turgenev, the Novelist's Novelist. A Study*, Oxford 1960
Leonard Schapiro, *Turgenev: His Life and Times*, New York 1978
David Lowe: *Turgenev's* Fathers and Sons, 1983

Chapter 1

'WELL, PETER? Cannot you see them yet?' asked a *barin** of about forty who, hatless, and clad in a dusty jacket over a pair of tweed breeches, stepped on to the verandah of a posting-house on the 20th day of May, 1859. The person addressed was the *barin's* servant – a round-cheeked young fellow with small, dull eyes and a chin adorned with a tuft of pale-coloured down.

Glancing along the high road in a supercilious manner, the servant (in whom everything, from the turquoise ear-ring to the dyed, pomaded hair and the mincing gait, revealed the modern, the rising generation) replied:

'No, *barin*, I cannot.'

'Is that so?' queried the *barin*.

'Yes,' the servant affirmed.

The *barin* sighed, and seated himself upon a bench. While he is sitting there with his knees drawn under him and his eyes moodily glancing to right and left, the reader may care to become better acquainted with his personality.

His name was Nikolai Petrovitch Kirsanov, and he owned (some fifteen versts from the posting-house) a respectable little property of about two hundred souls (or, as, after that he had apportioned his peasantry allotments, and set up a 'farm,' he himself expressed it, a property 'of two thousand *desiatini*†'). His father, one of the generals of 1812, had spent his life exclusively in military service as the commander, first of a brigade, and then of a division; and always he had been quartered in the provinces, where his rank had enabled him to cut a not inconspicuous figure. As for Nikolai Petrovitch himself, he was born in Southern Russia (as also was his elder brother, Paul – of whom presently), and, until his fourteenth year, received his education amid a circle of hard-up governors, free-and-easy aides-de-camp, and sundry staff and regimental officers. His mother came of the family of the Koliazins, and, known in maidenhood as Agathe, and subsequently as Agathoklea Kuzminishna Kirsanov, belonged to the type of 'officer's lady.' That is to say, she wore pompous mobcaps and rustling silk dresses, was always the first to approach the cross in church, talked volubly and in a loud tone, of set practice admitted her sons to kiss her

* Gentleman or squire.
† A *desiatin* is equivalent to 2.86 acres and just larger than a hectare.

hand in the morning, and never failed to bless them before retiring to rest at night. In short, she lived the life which suited her. As the son of a general, Nikolai Petrovitch was bound – though he evinced no particular bravery, and might even have seemed a coward – to follow his brother Paul's example by entering the army; but unfortunately, owing to the fact that, on the very day when there arrived the news of his commission, he happened to break his leg, it befell that, after two months in bed, he rose to his feet a permanently lamed man. When his father had finished wringing his hands over the mischance, he sent his son to acquire a civilian education; whence it came about that Nikolai, at eighteen, found himself a student at the University of St Petersburg. At the same period his brother obtained a commission in one of the regiments of Guards; and, that being so, their father apportioned the two young men a joint establishment, and placed it under the more or less detached supervision of Ilya Koliazin, their maternal uncle and a leading tchinovnik.* That done, the father returned to his division and his wife, and only at rare intervals sent his sons sheets of grey foolscap (scrawled and re-scrawled in flamboyant calligraphy) to which there was appended, amid a bower of laborious flourishes, the signature 'Piotr Kirsanov, Major-General.' In the year 1835 Nikolai Petrovitch obtained his university degree; and in the same year General Kirsanov was retired for incompetence at a review, and decided to transfer his quarters to St Petersburg. Unfortunately, just as he was on the point both of renting a house near the Tavritchesky Gardens and of being enrolled as a member of the English Club, a stroke put an end to his career, and Agathoklea Kuzminishna followed him soon afterwards, since never had she succeeded in taking to the dull life of the capital, but always had hankered after the old provincial existence. Already during his parents' lifetime, and to their no small vexation, Nikolai Petrovitch had contrived to fall in love with the daughter of a certain tchinovnik named Prepolovensky, the landlord of his flat; and since the maiden was not only comely, but one of the type known as 'advanced' (that is to say, she perused an occasional 'Science' article in one newspaper or another), he married her out of hand as soon as the term of mourning was ended, and, abandoning the Ministry of Provincial Affairs to which, through his father's influence, he had been posted, embarked upon connubial felicity in a villa adjoining the Institute of Forestry. Thence, after a while, the couple removed to a diminutive, but in every way respectable, flat which could boast of a spotless vestibule and an icy-cold drawing-room; and thence, again, they migrated to the country, where

* Civil servant.

they settled for good, and where, in due time, they had born to them a son Arkady. The existence of husband and wife was one of perfect comfort and tranquillity. Almost never were they parted from one another, they read together, they played the piano together, and they sang duets. Also, she would garden or superintend the poultry-yard, and he would set forth a-hunting, or see to the management of the estate. Meanwhile Arkady led an existence of equal calm and comfort, and grew, and waxed fat; until, in 1847, when ten years had been passed in this idyllic fashion, Kirsanov's wife breathed her last. The blow proved almost more than the husband could bear – so much so that his head turned grey in a few weeks. Yet, though he sought distraction for his thoughts by going abroad, he felt constrained, in the following year, to return home, where, after a prolonged period of inaction, he took up the subject of Industrial Reform. Next, in 1855, he sent his son to the University of St Petersburg, and, for the same reason, spent the following three winters in the capital, where he seldom went out, but spent the greater part of his time in endeavouring to fraternise with his son's youthful acquaintances. The fourth winter, however, he was prevented by various circumstances from spending in St Petersburg; and thus in the May of 1859 we see him – greyheaded, dusty, a trifle bent, and wholly middle-aged – awaiting his son's homecoming after the elevation of the latter (in Nikolai's own footsteps) to the dignity of a graduate.

Presently either a sense of decency or (more probably) a certain disinclination to remain immediately under his master's eye led the servant to withdraw to the entrance gates, and there to light a pipe. Nikolai Petrovitch, however, continued sitting with head bent, and his eyes contemplating the ancient steps of the verandah, up which a stout speckled hen was tap-tapping its way on a pair of splayed yellow legs, and thereby causing an untidy, but fastidious-looking, cat to regard it from the balustrade with marked disapproval. Meanwhile the sun beat fiercely down, and from the darkened interior of a neighbouring granary came a smell as of hot rye straw. Nikolai Petrovitch sank into a reverie. 'My son Arkady a graduate!' – the words kept passing and repassing through his mind. Again and again he tried to think of something else, but always the same thought returned to him. Until eventually he reverted to the memory of his dead wife. 'Would that she were still with me!' was his yearning reflection. Presently a fat blue pigeon alighted upon the roadway, and fell to taking a hasty drink from a pool beside the well. And almost at the instant that the spectacle of the bird caught Nikolai Petrovitch's eye, his ear caught the sound of approaching wheels.

'They are coming, I think,' hazarded the servant as he stepped forward through the gates.

Nikolai Petrovitch sprang to his feet, and strained his eyes along the road. Yes, coming into view there was a *tarantass*,* drawn by three stagehorses; and in the *tarantass* there could be seen the band of a student's cap and the outlines of a familiar, well-beloved face.

'Arkasha, Arkasha!' was Kirsanov's cry as, running forward, he waved his arms. A few moments later he was pressing his lips to the sun-tanned, dusty, hairless cheek of the newly-fledged graduate.

* A species of four-wheeled carriage.

Chapter 2

'YES, BUT FIRST give me a rub down, dearest Papa,' said Arkady in a voice which, though a little hoarsened with travelling, was yet clear and youthful. 'See! I am covering you with dust!' he added as joyously he returned his father's caresses.

'Oh, but that will not matter,' said Nikolai Petrovitch with a loving, reassuring smile as he gave the collar of his son's blue cloak a couple of pats, and then did the same by his own jacket. Thereafter, gently withdrawing from his son's embrace, and beginning to lead the way towards the inn yard, he added: 'Come this way, come this way. The horses will soon be ready.'

His excitement seemed even to outdo his son's, so much did he stammer and stutter, and, at times, find himself at a loss for a word. Arkady stopped him.

'Papa,' he said, 'first let me introduce my good friend Bazarov, who is the comrade whom I have so often mentioned in letters to you, and who has been kind enough to come to us for a visit.'

At once Nikolai Petrovitch wheeled round, and, approaching a tall man who, clad in a long coat with a tasselled belt, had just alighted from the *tarantass*, pressed the bare red hand which, after a pause, the stranger offered him.

'I am indeed glad to see you!' was Nikolai Petrovitch's greeting, 'I am indeed grateful to you for your kindness in paying us this visit! Alas, I hope that, that – But first might I enquire your name?'

'Evgenii Vasiliev,' replied the other in slow, but virile, accents as, turning down the collar of his coat, he revealed his face more clearly. Long and thin, with a high forehead which looked flattened at the top and became sharpened towards the nose, the face had large, greenish eyes and long, sandy whiskers. The instant that the features brightened into a smile, however, they betokened self-assurance and intellect.

'My dearest Evgenii Vasiliev,' Nikolai Petrovitch continued, 'I trust that whilst you are with us you will not find time hang heavy upon your hands.'

Bazarov gave his lips a slight twitch, but vouchsafed no reply beyond raising his cap – a movement which revealed the fact that the prominent convolutions of the skull were by no means concealed by the superincumbent mass of indeterminate-coloured hair.

'Now, Arkady,' went on Nikolai Petrovitch as he turned to his son, 'shall we have the horses harnessed at once, or should you prefer to rest a little?'

'Let us rest at home, Papa. So pray have the horses put to.'

'I will,' his father agreed. 'Peter! Bestir yourself, my good fellow!'

Being what is known as a 'perfectly trained servant,' Peter had neither approached nor shaken hands with the young *barin*, but contented himself with a distant bow. He now vanished through the yard gates.

'Though I have come in the *koliaska*,' said Nikolai Petrovitch, 'I have brought three fresh horses for the *tarantass*.'

Arkady then drank some water from a yellow bowl proffered by the landlord, while Bazarov lighted a pipe, and approached the ostler, who was engaged in unharnessing the stagehorses.

'Only two can ride in the *koliaska*,' continued Nikolai Petrovitch; 'wherefore I am rather in a difficulty to know how your friend will – '

'Oh, he can travel in the *tarantass*,' interrupted Arkady. 'Moreover, do not stand on any ceremony with him, for, wonderful though he is, he is also quite simple, as you will find for yourself.'

Nikolai Petrovitch's coachman brought out the horses, and Bazarov remarked to the ostler:

'Come, bestir yourself, fat-beard!'

'Did you hear that, Mitiusha?' added another ostler who was standing with his hands thrust into the back slits of his blouse. 'The *barin* has just called you a fat-beard. And a fat-beard you are.'

For answer Mitiusha merely cocked his cap to one side and drew the reins from the back of the sweating shafts-horse.

'Quick now, my good fellows!' cried Nikolai Petrovitch. 'Bear a hand, all of you, and for each there will be a glassful of vodka.'

Naturally, it was not long before the horses were harnessed, and then father and son seated themselves in the *koliaska*, Peter mounted the box of that vehicle, and Bazarov stepped into the *tarantass*, and lolled his head against the leather cushion at the back. Finally the cortège moved away.

Chapter 3

'To THINK that you are now a graduate and home again!' said Nikolai Petrovitch as he tapped Arkady on the knee, and then on the shoulder. 'There now, there now!'

'And how is Uncle? Is he quite well?' asked Arkady – the reason for the question being that though he felt filled with a genuine, an almost childish delight at his return, he also felt conscious of an instinct that the conversation were best diverted from the emotional to the prosaic.

'Yes, your uncle is quite well. As a matter of fact, he also had arranged to come and meet you, but at the last moment changed his mind.'

'Did you have very long to wait?' continued Arkady.

'About five hours.'

'Dearest Papa!' cried Arkady as, leaning over towards his father, he imprinted upon his cheek a fervent kiss. Nikolai Petrovitch smiled quietly.

'I have got a splendid horse for you,' he next remarked. 'Presently you shall see him. Also, your room has been entirely repapered.'

'And have you a room for Bazarov as well?'

'One shall be found for him.'

'Oh – and pray humour him in every way you can. I could not express to you how much I value his friendship.'

'But you have not known him very long, have you?'

'No – not very long.'

'I thought not, for I do not remember to have seen him in St Petersburg last winter. In what does he most interest himself?'

'Principally in natural science. But, to tell the truth, he knows practically *everything*, and is to become a doctor next year.'

'Oh! So he is in the Medical Faculty?' Nikolai Petrovitch remarked; after which there was silence for a moment.

'Peter,' went on Nikolai, pointing with his hand, 'are not those peasants there some of our own?'

Peter glanced in the direction indicated, and saw a few waggons proceeding along a narrow by-road. The teams were bridleless, and in each waggon were seated some two or three *muzhiks* with their blouses unbuttoned.

'Yes, they are some of our own,' Peter responded.

'Then whither can they be going? To the town?'

'Yes – or to the tavern.' This last was added contemptuously, and with a wink to the coachman that was designed to enlist that functionary's sympathy: but as the functionary in question was one of the old school which takes no share in the modern movement, he stirred not a muscle of his face.

'This year my peasants have been giving me a good deal of trouble,' Nikolai Petrovitch continued to his son. 'Persistently do they refuse to pay their tithes. What ought to be done with them?'

'And do you find your hired workmen satisfactory?'

'Not altogether,' muttered Nikolai Petrovitch. 'You see, they have become spoilt, more's the pity! Any real energy seems quite to have left them, and they not only ruin my implements, but also leave the land untilled. Does estate-management interest you?'

'The thing we most lack here is shade,' remarked Arkady in evasion of the question.

'Ah, but I have had an awning added to the north balcony, so that we can take our meals in the open air.'

'But that will give the place rather the look of a villa, will it not? Things of that sort never prove effectual. But oh, the air here! How good it smells! Yes, in my opinion, things never smell elsewhere as they do here. And oh, the sky!'

Suddenly Arkady stopped, threw a glance of apprehension in the direction of the *tarantass*, and relapsed into silence.

'I quite agree with you,' replied Nikolai Petrovitch. 'You see, the reason is that you were born here, and that therefore the place is bound to have for you a special significance.'

'But no significance can attach to the place of a man's birth, Papa.'

'Indeed?'

'Oh no. None whatsoever.'

Nikolai Petrovitch glanced at the speaker, and for fully half a verst let the vehicle proceed without the conversation between them being renewed. At length Nikolai Petrovitch observed:

'I cannot remember whether I wrote to tell you that your old nurse, Egorovna, is dead.'

'Dead? Oh, the poor old woman! But Prokovitch – is *he* still alive?'

'He is so, and in no way changed – that is to say, he grumbles as much as ever. In fact, you will find that no *really* important alterations have taken place at Marino.'

'And have you the same steward as before?'

'No; I have appointed a fresh one, for I came to the conclusion that I could not have any freed serfs about the place. That is to say, I did not feel as though I could trust such fellows with posts of responsibility.'

Arkady indicated Peter with his eyes, and Nikolai Petrovitch therefore subdued his voice a little. 'He? Oh, *il est libre, en effet*. You see, he is my valet. But as regards a steward, I have appointed a *miestchanin*,* at a salary of 250 roubles a year, and he seems at least capable. But' – and here Nikolai Petrovitch rubbed his forehead, which gesture with him always implied inward agitation – 'I ought to say that, though I have told you that you will find no alterations of importance at Marino, the statement is not strictly true, seeing that it is my duty to warn you that, that – ' Nikolai Petrovitch hesitated again – then added in French: 'Perhaps by a stern moralist my frankness might be considered misplaced; yet I will not conceal from you, nor can you fail to be aware, that always I have had ideas of my own on the subject of the relations which ought to subsist between a father and his son. At the same time, this is not to say that you have not the right to *judge* me. Rather, it is that at my age – Well, to put matters bluntly, the girl whom you will have heard me speak of – '

'You mean Thenichka?' said Arkady.

Nikolai Petrovitch's face went red.

'Do not speak of her so loudly,' he advised. 'Yes, *she* is living with us. I took her in because two of our smaller rooms were available. But of course the arrangement must be changed.'

'Why must it, Papa?'

'Because this friend of yours is coming, and also because – well, it might make things awkward.'

'Do not disturb yourself on Bazarov's account. He is altogether superior to such things.'

'Yes, so you say; but the mischief lies in the fact that the wing is so small.'

'Papa, Papa!' protested Arkady. 'Almost one would think that you considered yourself to blame for something; whereas you have *nothing* to reproach yourself with.'

'Ah, but I have,' responded Nikolai Petrovitch. His face had turned redder than ever.

'No, you have *not*, Papa,' repeated Arkady with a loving smile, while adding to himself with a feeling of indulgent tenderness for his good, kind father, as well as with a certain sense of 'superiority': 'Why is he making these excuses?'

'I beg of you to say no more,' he continued with an involuntary feeling of exultation in being 'grown up' and 'emancipated.' As he did so Nikolai Petrovitch glanced at him from under the fingers of the hand

* A member of the trading or shopkeeping class.

which was still rubbing his brows. At the same moment something seemed to give his heart a stab. Mentally, as before, he blamed himself.

'Here our fields begin,' he observed after a pause.

'I see,' rejoined Arkady. 'And that is our forest in front, I suppose?'

'It is so. Only, only – I have sold it, and this year it is to be removed.'

'Why have you sold it?'

'Because I needed the money. Moreover, the land which it occupies must go to the peasants.'

'What? To the peasants who pay you no tithes?'

'Possibly. But someday they will pay me.'

'I regret the forest's loss,' said Arkady, and then resumed his contemplation of the landscape.

The scenery which the party were traversing could not have been called picturesque, for, with slight undulations, only fields, fields, and again fields, stretched to the very horizon. True, a few patches of copse were visible, but the ditches, with their borderings of low, sparse brushwood, recalled the antique land-measurement of Katherine's day. Also, streams ran pent between abruptly sloping banks, hamlets with dwarfed huts (of which the blackened roofs were, for the most part, cracked in half) stood cheek by jowl with crazy grinding-byres of plaited willow, empty threshing-floors had their gates sagging, and from churches of wood or of brick which stood amid dilapidated graveyards the stucco was peeling, and the crosses were threatening at any moment to fall. As he gazed at the scene Arkady's heart contracted. Moreover, the peasants encountered on the road looked ragged, and were riding sorry nags, while the laburnum trees which stood ranged like miserable beggars by the roadside had their bark hanging in strips, and their boughs shattered. Lastly, the lean, mud-encrusted cows which could be seen hungrily cropping the herbage in the ditches were so 'staring' of coat that the animals might just have been rescued from the talons of some terrible, death-dealing monster; and as one gazed at those weak, pitiful beasts, almost one could fancy that one saw uprisen from amid the beauty of spring, the pale phantoms of Winter – its storms and its frost and its snow.

'Evidently this is not a rich district,' reflected Arkady. 'Rather, it is a district which gives one the impression neither of abundance nor of hard work. Yet can it be left as it is? No! Education is what we need. But how is that education to be administered, or, for that matter, to be introduced?'

Thus Arkady. Yet, even as the thought passed through his mind, Spring seemed once more to regain possession of her kingdom, and everything around him grew golden-green, and trees, shrubs, and herbage started to wave and glimmer under the soft, warm breath of the vernal zephyrs, and larks took to pouring out their souls in endless, ringing strains, and siskins, circling high over sunken ponds, uttered their cry, then skimmed the hillocks in silence, and handsome black rooks stalked among the tender green of the short corn-shoots, or settled among the pale-white, smokelike ripples of the young rye, whence at intervals they protruded their heads.

Arkady gazed and gazed; and gradually, as he did so, his late thoughts grew dimmer and disappeared, and, throwing off his travelling-cloak, he peered so joyously, with such a boyish air, into his father's face that Nikolai Petrovitch bestowed upon him yet another embrace.

'We have but little further to go now,' he remarked. 'In fact, when once we have topped that rise the house will come into view. And what a time we are going to have together, Arkasha! For you will be able to help me with the estate (if you care to, that is to say?), and you and I will draw nearer to one another, and make one another's better acquaintance.'

'We will!' cried Arkady. 'And what splendid weather for us both!'

'Yes; specially for your homecoming is spring in all its glory. Yet I am not sure that I do not agree with Pushkin where he says, in *Eugène Onegin*:

> How sad to me is your coming,
> O spring, spring, season of love!

'Arkady,' shouted Bazarov from the *tarantass*, 'please send me a match or two, for I have nothing to light my pipe with.'

Instantly Nikolai Petrovitch ceased quoting poetry, and Arkady (who had listened with considerable surprise, though also with a certain measure of sympathy, to his father) hastened to produce from his pocket a silver matchbox, and to dispatch the same by the hand of Peter.

'In return, would you care to have a cigar?' called Bazarov.

'I should,' replied Arkady.

The result was that when Peter returned to the *koliaska* he handed Arkady not only the matchbox, but also a fat black cigar. This Arkady lit at leisure, and then proceeded to diffuse around him so strong and acrid an odour of tobacco that Nikolai Petrovitch (a non-smoker from birth) found himself forced to avert his nose (though he did this covertly, for fear of offending his son).

A quarter of an hour later the vehicles drew up at the steps of a new wooden mansion, painted grey, and roofed with red sheet-iron. The mansion was Marino, or Novaia Sloboda, or, to quote the peasants' name, 'Bobili Chutor.'

Chapter 4

THERE ISSUED on to the verandah to greet the arrivals no throng of household serfs – only a solitary girl of twelve. Presently, however, she was joined by a young fellow much resembling Peter, but dressed in a grey livery coat to which embossed, silver-gilt buttons were attached. This was Paul Kirsanov's valet. In silence he opened the door of the *koliaska*, and unhooked the apron of the *tarantass*; whereupon the three gentlemen alighted, passed through a dark, bare hall (the face of a young woman peered at them for a moment from behind a door), and entered a drawing-room upholstered in the latest fashion.

'So here we are at home again!' exclaimed Nikolai Petrovitch, taking off his cap, and shaking back his hair. 'Let us have supper, and then for bed, bed!'

'Yes, something to eat would undoubtedly be welcome,' remarked Bazarov as, yawning, he seated himself upon a sofa.

'Quite so; I will have supper served at once.' Nikolai Petrovitch, for no apparent reason, tripped over his own feet. 'And here comes Prokofitch,' he added.

As he spoke entered a man of about sixty who, white-haired, and of thin, swarthy features, was wearing a cinnamon-coloured tail-coat with brass buttons and a crimson collar. He smiled with delight as he approached and shook hands with Arkady. Then, with a bow to the guest, he retired to the doorway, and folded his hands behind his back.

'So here is the young master, Prokofitch!' said Nikolai Petrovitch. 'He is home at last. And how, think you, is he looking?'

'Very well, very well,' the old man said with another smile. The next moment, however, he knit his shaggy brows, and suggested: 'Shall I lay the table?'

'If you please, if you please.' Nikolai Petrovitch turned to Bazarov. 'Before supper,' he said, 'would you care to go to your room?'

'I thank you, no. But please have my trunk conveyed thither, and also this wrap.' And Bazarov divested himself of his cloak.

'Certainly. Prokofitch, take the gentleman's cloak.'

The old butler received the garment gingerly, held it well away from him with both hands, and left the room on tiptoe.

'And you, Arkady?' continued Nikolai Petrovitch. 'Do you not wish to go to your room?'

'Yes; for a wash I should be thankful,' was Arkady's reply as he moved towards the door. At that moment it opened to admit a man of medium height who was dressed in a dark English suit, a fashionably low collar, and a pair of patent leather boots. This was Paul Petrovitch Kirsanov. Although forty-five, he had close-cropped grey hair of the sheen of new silver, and his sallow, unwrinkled face was as clear-cut and regular of outline as though carved with a light, fine chisel. Still retaining traces of remarkable comeliness, his bright, black, oblong eyes had a peculiar attraction, and his every well-bred, refined feature showed that symmetry of youth, that air of superiority to the rest of the world which usually disappears when once the twenties have been passed.

Drawing from his trouser pocket a slender hand the long, pink nails of which looked all the slenderer for the snowy whiteness of the superimposed cuff and large opal sleeve-link, he offered it to his nephew; after which, this prefatory European 'handshake' over, he thrice kissed Arkady in the Russian fashion – that is to say, touched his nephew's cheek with his perfumed moustache, and murmured: 'I congratulate you.'

Next Nikolai Petrovitch presented to him Bazarov. Inclining his supple figure with a faint smile, Paul Petrovitch this time did not offer his hand. On the contrary, he replaced it in his pocket.

'I was beginning to think that you never meant to arrive,' he said with an amiable hoist of his shoulders and a display of some beautiful white teeth. 'What happened to you?'

'Nothing,' replied Arkady, 'except that we lingered a little. For the same reason are we as hungry as wolves; so pray tell Prokofitch to be quick, Papa, and I shall be back in a moment.'

'Wait; I will go with you,' added Bazarov as he rose from the sofa; and the two young men left the room together.

'Who is your guest?' asked Paul Petrovitch.

'A friend of Arkady's, and, according to Arkady's showing, a man of intellect.'

'He is going to stay here?'

'He is.'

'A long-haired fellow like that?'

'Certainly.'

In that particular direction Paul Petrovitch said no more, but, tapping the table with his finger-nails, added:

'*Je pense que notre Arkady s'est dégourdi.** And in any case I am

* 'I think that our friend Arkady has acquired some polish.'

pleased to see him back again.'

At supper little was said. In particular did Bazarov scarcely speak, though he ate heartily; and only Nikolai Petrovitch proved garrulous as he related various incidents in what he termed his 'agricultural life,' and gossiped of forthcoming administrative measures, committees, deputations, the need of introducing machinery and other such topics.

For his part, Paul Petrovitch paced the room (he never took supper), and sipped a glassful of red wine, and occasionally interjected some such remark – rather exclamation – as 'Ah!' or 'Oh, ho!' or 'H'm!' Arkady's contribution consisted of a little St Petersburg gossip, even though, throughout, he was conscious of a touch of that awkwardness which overtakes a young man when, just ceased to be a boy, he returns to the spot where hitherto he has ranked as a mere child. In other words, he drawled his phrases unnecessarily, carefully avoided the use of the term 'Papasha,'* and, once, even went so far as to substitute for it the term 'Otety'† – though, true, he pronounced it with some difficulty. Lastly, in his excessive desire to seem at his ease, he helped himself to more wine than was good for him, and tasted some of every brand. Meanwhile Prokofitch chewed his lips, and never removed his eyes from his young master.

Supper over, the company dispersed.

'A queer fellow is that uncle of yours,' Bazarov said to Arkady as, clad in a dressing-gown, he seated himself by his friend's bed, and sucked at a short pipe. 'To think of encountering such elegance in the country! He would take a prize with his finger-nails.'

'You do not know him yet,' said Arkady. 'In his day he was a leading lion, and sometime or another I will tell you his history. Yes, many and many a woman has lost her head over his good looks.'

'Then I should think that he has nothing to live on save memories,' observed Bazarov. 'At all events there is no one *here* for him to enslave. I looked him over tonight, and never in my life have beheld a collar of such marvellous gloss, or a chin so perfectly shaven. Yet such things can come to look ridiculous, do not you think?'

'Yes – perhaps they can. But he is such an excellent fellow in himself!'

'Oh, certainly – a truly archangelic personage! Your father, too, is excellent; for though he may read foolish poetry, and though his ideas on the subject of industry may be few, his heart is in the right place.'

'He is a man with a heart of gold.'

'Nevertheless, did you notice his nervousness tonight?'

* Dear Papa.   † Father.

Arkady nodded as though to himself such a weakness was a perfect stranger.

'Curious indeed!' commented Bazarov. 'Ah, you elderly Romanticists! You over-develop the nervous system until the balance is upset. Now, good-night. In my room there is an English washstand, yet the door will not shut! But such things (English washstands I mean) need to be encouraged: they represent "progress." '

And Bazarov departed, while Arkady surrendered himself to a sensation of comfort. How pleasant was it to be sinking to sleep in one's comfortable home, and in one's own familiar bed, and under a well-known coverlet worked by loving hands – perhaps those of his good, kind, tireless old nurse! And at the thought of Egorovna he sighed, and commended her soul to the Heavenly Powers. But for himself he did not pray.

Soon both he and Bazarov were asleep; but certain other members of the household there were who remained wakeful. In particular had Nikolai Petrovitch been greatly excited by his son's return; and though he went to bed, he left the candle burning, and, resting with his head on his hands, lay thinking deeply.

Also, his brother sat up in his study until nearly midnight. Seated in an ample armchair before a corner where a marble stove was smouldering, he had effected no alteration in his costume beyond having exchanged his patent leather boots for a pair of heelless, red felt slippers. Lastly, he was holding, though not reading, the latest number of *Galignani*, and his eyes were fixed upon the stove, where a quivering blue spurt of flame kept alternately disappearing and bursting forth again. Whither his thoughts were wandering God only knows; but that they were not meandering through the past alone was proved by the fact that in his expression there was a concentrated gloom which is never in evidence when a man's mind is occupied with memories and no more.

Finally, seated on a chest in a small room at the back of the house, and wearing a blue dressing-jacket and, thrown over her dark hair, a white scarf, was the girl Thenichka. As she sat there she kept listening, and starting, and gazing towards an open door which at once afforded a glimpse of an infant's cot and admitted the sound of a sleeping child's respiration.

Chapter 5

NEXT MORNING Bazarov was the first to awake and go out of doors.

'Ah,' thought he to himself as he gazed about him, 'this is *not* much of a place to look at.'

When apportioning allotments to his peasantry, Nikolai Petrovitch had found himself forced to exclude from the new 'farm' four *desiatins* of level, naked land, and upon this space had built himself a house, quarters for his servants, and a homestead. Also, he had laid out a garden, dug a pond, and sunk two wells. But the young trees had fared badly, very little water had risen in the pond, and the wells had developed a brackish taste. The only vegetation to attain robust growth was a clump of lilacs and acacias, under the shade of which the household was accustomed to take tea or to dine. Within a few minutes Bazarov had traversed all the paths in the garden, visited the stables and the cattlesheds, and made friends with two young household serfs whom he happened to encounter, and with whom he set forth to catch frogs in a marsh about a verst from the manor.

'For what do you want frogs, *barin*?' asked one of the lads.

'To make them useful,' replied Bazarov (who possessed a peculiar gift for winning the confidence of his inferiors, even though he never cozened them, but, on the contrary, always treated them with asperity). 'You see I like to open them, and then to observe what their insides are doing. You and I are frogs too, except that we walk upon our hind legs. Thus the operation helps me to understand what is taking place in ourselves.'

'And what good will that do you?'

'This. That if you should fall sick, and I should have to treat you, I might avoid some mistakes.'

'Then you are a doctor?'

'I am.'

'Listen to that, Vasika! The *barin* says that you and I too are frogs. My word!'

'I don't like frogs,' remarked Vasika, a barefooted boy of seven with a head as white as tow, and a costume made up of a grey blouse and a stiff collar.

'*Why* don't you like them?' asked Bazarov. 'Do you think they will bite you? Nay! Into the water, my young philosophers!'

Nikolai Petrovitch too had left his bed, and, on going to visit Arkady, found him fully dressed; wherefore father and son proceeded to repair to the terrace, and there seated themselves under the shade of the awning. Amid nosegays of lilac, a tea-urn was simmering on a table by the balustrade, and presently there appeared upon the scene also the damsel who, on the previous night, had met the arrivals on the verandah. She announced in shrill tones:

'Theodosia Nikolaevna is not very well this morning, and cannot come to breakfast. So she has told me to ask you whether you will pour out tea for yourselves, or whether she is to send Duniasha?'

'I will pour it out myself,' Nikolai Petrovitch replied with some haste. 'Will you have cream or lemon in your tea, Arkady?'

'Cream,' he replied. After a pause he continued:

'Papasha – '

Nikolai Petrovitch glanced confusedly in his direction.

'Yes?' said he.

Arkady lowered his eyes.

'Pardon me if my question should seem to you indiscreet,' he began, 'but, owing to your frankness of last night, I am emboldened to return it. You will not take offence, will you?'

'Oh no! Pray go on.'

'Then I feel encouraged to ask you whether it – whether it is because I am here that she – that is to say, Thenichka – has not joined us at breakfast?'

Nickolai Petrovitch slightly averted his face.

'It may be so,' he said at length. 'At all events, I presume that – that she prefers, she prefers – in fact, that she is shy.'

Arkady glanced at his father.

'But why should she be shy?' he enquired. 'In the first place, you know my views' (he uttered the words with no little complacency), 'and, in the second place surely you cannot suppose that I would by a hair's breadth intrude upon your life and your habits? No; sure am I that never could you make a bad choice; and if you have asked this girl to reside under your roof, that is tantamount to saying that she has well deserved it. In any case, moreover, it is not for a son to summon his father to judgement – least of all for me, who possess a father like yourself, a father who has never restricted his son's freedom of action.'

At first Arkady's voice had trembled a little, since not only did he feel that he was doing the 'magnanimous,' but also he knew that he was delivering something like a 'lecture' to his father; but such an effect does the sound of his own voice exercise upon a human being that towards the end Arkady pronounced his words firmly, and even with a certain degree of *empressement*.

'I thank you, Arkady,' Nikolai Petrovitch said faintly as his fingers began their customary perambulation of his forehead. 'Nor is your conjecture mistaken, for if this girl had not deserved the invitation, I should not, of course, have – in other words, as you imply, this is no frivolous whim on my part. Nor need I have spoken of the matter, were it not that I desired you to understand that she might possibly have felt embarrassed at meeting you on the very day after your arrival.'

'Then let *me* go and meet *her*,' exclaimed Arkady with another access of 'magnanimity' as he sprang from his chair. 'Yes, let *me* go and explain to her why she need not shun me.'

Nikolai Petrovitch also rose.

'Arkady,' he began, 'pray do me a favour. Hitherto I had not warned you that – '

But, without listening to him, Arkady darted from the terrace. For a moment or two Nikolai Petrovitch gazed after him – then, overcome with confusion, relapsed into a chair. His heart was beating rapidly. Whether or not he was picturing to himself a strangeness of future relations with his son; whether he was imagining that, had his son refrained from interfering, the latter might have paid him more respect in future; whether he was reproaching himself for his own weakness – it is difficult to say what his thoughts were. Probably in them there was a combination of the feelings just indicated, if only in the form of apprehensions. Yet those apprehensions cannot have been deeply rooted, as was proved by the fact that, for all the beating of his heart, the colour had not left his face.

Soon hasty footsteps were heard approaching, and Arkady reappeared on the terrace.

'I have made her acquaintance!' he shouted with a kindly, good-humoured, triumphant expression. 'That Theodosia Nikolaievna is not well today is a fact; but also it is a fact that she is going to appear later. And why did you not tell me that I had a little brother? Otherwise I should have gone and kissed him last night, even as I have done this moment.'

Nikolai Petrovitch tried to say something – to rise and to make an explanation of some sort; but Arkady cut him short by falling upon his neck.

'What is this? Again embracing?' said Paul Petrovitch behind them.

As a matter of fact, neither father nor son was ill-pleased to see him appear, for, however touching such situations may be, one may be equally glad to escape from them.

'At what are you surprised?' asked Nikolai Petrovitch gaily.

'Remember that I have not seen Arkesha for several centuries – at all events, not since last night!'

'Oh, I am not surprised,' said Paul Petrovitch. 'On the contrary, I should not mind embracing him myself.'

And Arkady, on approaching his uncle, felt once more upon his cheek the impression of a perfumed moustache. Paul Petrovitch then sat down to table. Clad in an elegant morning suit of English cut, he was flaunting on his head a diminutive fez which helped the carelessly folded tie to symbolise the freedom of a country life. At the same time, the stiff collar of the shirt (which was striped, not white, as best befitted a matutinal toilet) supported with its usual rigour an immaculately shaven chin.

'Well, Arkady?' said he. 'Where is your new friend?'

'Out somewhere. He seldom misses going for an early morning walk. But the great thing is to take no notice of him, for he detests all ceremony.'

'So I have perceived.' And with his usual deliberateness Paul Petrovitch began to butter a piece of bread. 'Will he be staying here very long?'

'Well, as long as he may care to stay. As a matter of fact, he is going on to his father's place.'

'And where does his father live?'

'Some eighty versts from here, in the same province as ourselves. I believe he has a small property, and used to be an army doctor.'

'H'm! Ever since last night I have been asking myself where I can have heard the name before. Nikolai, do you remember whether there was a doctor of that name in our father's division?'

'Yes, there used to be.'

'Then that doctor will be this fellow's father. H'm!' And Paul Petrovitch twitched his moustache. 'What exactly is your Bazarov?' he enquired of Arkady.

'What *is* he?' Arkady repeated smiling. 'Do you really want me to tell you what he is, Uncle?'

'If you please, my nephew.'

'He is a Nihilist.'

'A what?' exclaimed Nikaloi Petrovitch, while even Paul Petrovitch paused in the act of raising a knife to the edge of which there was a morsel of butter adhering.

'A Nihilist,' repeated Arkady.

'A Nihilist?' queried Nikolai Petrovitch. 'I imagine that that must be a term derived from the Latin *nihil* or "nothing." It denotes, I presume, a man who – a man who – well, a man who declines to accept *anything*.'

'Or a man who declines to *respect* anything,' hazarded Paul Petrovitch as he re-applied himself to the butter.

'No, a man who treats things solely from the critical point of view,' corrected Arkady.

'But the two things are one and the same, are they not?' queried Paul Petrovitch.

'Oh no. A Nihilist is a man who declines to bow to authority, or to accept any principle on trust, however sanctified it may be.'

'And to what can that lead?' asked Paul Petrovitch.

'It depends upon the individual. In one man's case it may lead to good; in that of another, to evil.'

'I see. But we elders view things differently. We folk of the older generation believe that without principles' (Paul Petrovitch pronounced the word softly, and with a French accent, whereas Arkady had pronounced it with an emphasis on the leading syllable) – 'without principles it is impossible to take a single step in life, or to draw a single breath. *Mais vous avez changé tout cela.* God send you health and a general's rank, Messieurs Nihil – how do you pronounce it?'

'Ni – hi – lists,' said Arkady distinctly.

'Quite so (formerly we had Hegelists, and now they have become Nihilists) – God send you health and a general's rank, but also let us see how you will contrive to exist in an absolute void, an airless vacuum. Pray ring the bell, brother Nikolai, for it is time for me to take my cocoa.'

Nikolai Petrovitch did as requested, and also shouted for Duniasha; but, instead of the latter, there issued on to the terrace Thenichka in person. A young woman of twenty-three, she was pale, and gentle-looking, with dark eyes and hair, a pair of childishly red, pouting lips, and delicate hands. Also, she was clad in a clean cotton gown, a new blue kerchief was thrown lightly over her rounded shoulders, and she was carrying in front of her a large cup of cocoa. Shyly she placed the latter before Paul Petrovitch, while a warm, rosy current of blood suffused the exquisite skin of her comely face, and then she remained standing by the table, with lowered eyes and the tips of her fingers touching its surface. Yet, though she looked as though she were regretting having come, she looked as though she felt that she had a right to be there.

Paul Petrovitch frowned, and Nikolai Petrovitch looked confused.

'Good-morning, Thenichka,' the latter muttered.

'Good-morning,' she replied in a low, clear voice. Then she glanced askance at Arkady, and he smiled at her in friendly fashion. Finally she departed with a quiet step and slightly careless gait – the latter a peculiarity of hers.

Silence reigned on the terrace. For a while Paul Petrovitch drank his cocoa. Then he suddenly raised his head, and muttered:

'Monsieur Nihilist is about to give us the pleasure of his company.'

True enough, Bazarov could be seen stepping across the flowerbeds. On his linen jacket and trousers was a thick coating of mud, to the crown of his ancient circular hat clung a piece of sticky marshweed, and in his hand he was holding a small bag. Also, something in the bag kept stirring as though it were alive. Approaching the terrace with rapid strides, he nodded to the company and said:

'Good-morning, gentlemen! Pardon me for being so late. I shall be back presently, but first my captures must be stowed away.'

'What are those captures?' Paul Petrovitch enquired. 'Leeches?'

'No, frogs.'

'Do you eat them? Or do you breed them?'

'I catch them for purposes of experiment,' was Bazarov's only reply as carelessly he entered the house.

'In other words, he vivisects them,' was Paul Petrovitch's comment. 'In other words, he believes in frogs more than in principles.'

Arkady threw his uncle a reproachful look, and even Nikolai Petrovitch shrugged his shoulders, so that Paul Petrovitch himself felt his *bon mot* to have been out of place, and hastened to divert the subject to the estate and the new steward.

Chapter 6

BAZAROV, RETURNING, seated himself at the table, and fell to drinking tea. The brothers contemplated him in silence. Arkady glanced covertly from his father to his uncle, and back again.

'Have you walked far this morning?' at length Nikolai Petrovitch enquired.

'To a marsh beside an aspen coppice. By the way, Arkady, I flushed five head of woodcock. Perhaps you would like to go and shoot them?'

'Then you yourself are no sportsman?'

'No.'

'That is to say, you prefer physics to anything else?' This from Paul Petrovitch.

'Yes, I prefer physics – in fact, the natural sciences in general – to anything else.'

'Well, I am told that the *Germanics* have made great strides in that department?' (Paul Petrovitch used the term 'Germanics' instead of 'Germans' ironically, but no one noticed it.)

'True,' was Bazarov's careless reply. 'In fact, the Germans are, in the same respect, our masters.'

'You think highly of the Germans?' Paul Petrovitch's tone was now studiously polite, for he was beginning to feel irritated with the man – his aristocratic nature could not altogether stomach Bazarov's absolute lack of ceremony, the fact that this doctor's son not only knew no diffidence, but actually returned snappish and reluctant answers, and infused a *brusquerie* akin to rudeness into his tone.

'At least the savants of that part of the world have some energy in them,' retorted Bazarov.

'Quite so. And your opinion of our Russian savants is – well, perhaps less flattering?'

'It is, with your leave.'

'That constitutes a piece of laudable modesty on your part,' Paul Petrovitch observed with a slight hitch of his figure and a toss of his head. 'But how comes it about that Arkady has just told us that you recognise no authorities whatsoever? Do you not trust authorities?'

'Why should I? Is anything in the world trustworthy? Certainly, should I be told a fact, I agree with it, but that is all.'

'Oh! Then the Germans confine themselves solely to facts?' Paul

Petrovitch's face had now assumed an expression of detachment, as though he had suddenly become withdrawn to the ultimate heights of the empyrean.

'No, not all Germans,' replied Bazarov with a passing yawn. Clearly he had no mind to continue the controversy. Meanwhile Paul Petrovitch glanced at Arkady as much as to say: 'Admit that your friend has beautiful manners!'

'For my own part,' he continued, ostentatiously, and with an effort, 'I, a fallible mortal, do *not* favour the Germans. Of course, I am not including in that category the *Russo*-Germans, who, as we know, are birds of passage. Rather, it is the Germans of Germany proper whom I cannot abide. Once upon a time they used to produce men like Schiller and like – what's his name? – Goethe: for both of which authors my brother has a marked predilection. But now the German nation has become a nation solely of chemists and materialists.'

'A good chemist is worth a score of your poets,' remarked Bazarov.

'Quite so.' Paul Petrovitch hitched his eyebrows a little, as though he had come near to falling asleep. 'Er – I take it then that you decline to recognise art, but believe only in science?'

'I have told you that I believe in nothing at all. What after all, is science – that is to say, science in the mass? A science may exist, even as a trade or a profession may exist; but with regard to science in the mass, there is no such thing.'

'Very good. And, with regard to such other postulates as usually are granted in human affairs, the attitude which you adopt is negative in the same degree?'

'What is this?' suddenly countered Bazarov. 'Is it an examination in tenets?'

Paul Petrovitch turned pale, and Nikolai Petrovitch thought it time to intervene in the dispute.

'Nay, we will debate the subject later,' he said. 'And then, while recognising your views, good Evgenii Vasilitch, we will state our own. Individually speaking, I am delighted that you should be interested in the natural sciences. For instance, I am told that recently Liebig* has made some surprising discoveries in the matter of the improvement of soils. Consequently you might be able to help me in my agricultural labours, and to give me much useful advice.'

'Always I shall be at your service, Nikolai Petrovitch,' replied Bazarov.

---

* Justus Freiherr von Liebig (1803–73), the great German chemist – in particular, the founder of agricultural chemistry.

'But what has Liebig to do with us? First the alphabet should be learnt before we try to read books. We have not even reached the letter A.'

'You are a Nihilist – that is plain enough,' reflected Nikolai Petrovitch; while aloud he added: 'Yet allow me to seek your occasional assistance. Brother Paul, I believe it is time that we interviewed our steward.'

Paul Petrovitch rose from his chair.

'Yes,' he said, without looking at anyone in particular, 'it is indeed a terrible thing to have lived five years in the country, and to have stood remote from superior intellects! If one is *ab origine* a fool, one becomes so more than ever, seeing that, however much one may try not to forget what one has learnt, there will dawn upon one, sooner or later, the revelation that one's knowledge is all rubbish, that sensible men have ceased to engage in such futilities, and that one has lagged far behind the times. But, in such a case, what is one to do? Evidently the younger generation know more than we do.'

And, slowly turning on his heel, he moved away as slowly, with Nikolai Petrovitch following in his wake.

'Does Paul Petrovitch always reside here?' asked Bazarov when the door had closed upon the pair.

'Yes, he does. But look here, Evgenii. You adopted too sharp a tone with my uncle. You have offended him.'

'What? Am I to fawn upon these rustic aristocrats, even though their attitude is one purely of conceit and subservience to custom? If such be Paul Petrovitch's bent, he had better have continued his career in St Petersburg. Never mind him, however. Do you know, I have found a splendid specimen of the water beetle *dytiscus marginatus*. Are you acquainted with it? I will show it you.'

'Did I not promise to tell you his history?' observed Arkady musingly.

'Whose history? The water beetle's?'

'No; my uncle's. At least you will see from it that he is not the man you take him for, but a man who deserves pity rather than ridicule.'

'I am not prepared to dispute it. But how come you to be so devoted to him?'

'Always one ought to be fair.'

'The connection I do not see.'

'Then listen.'

And Arkady related the story to be found in the following chapter.

Chapter 7

'LIKE HIS BROTHER, Paul Petrovitch Kirsanov received his early education at home, and entered the Imperial Corps of Pages. Distinguished from boyhood for his good looks, he had, in addition, a nature of the self-confident, quizzical, amusingly sarcastic type which never fails to please. As soon, therefore, as he had received his officer's commission, he began to go everywhere in society, to set the pace, to amuse himself, to play the rake, and to squander his money. Yet these things somehow consorted well with his personality, and women went nearly mad over him, while men called him "Fate," and secretly detested him. Meanwhile he rented a flat with his brother, for whom, in spite of their dissimilarity, he had a genuine affection. The dissimilarity in question lay, among other things, in the fact that, while Nikolai Petrovitch halted, had small, kindly, rather melancholy features and narrow black eyes, and was of a disposition prone to reading omnivorously, to bestirring himself but little, and to feeling nervous when attending social functions, Paul Petrovitch never spent a single evening at home, but was renowned for his physical dexterity and daring (he it was who made gymnastics the rage among the gilded youth of his day), and read, at most, five or six French novels. Indeed, by the time that he reached his twenty-eighth year Paul had risen to be a captain, and before him there seemed to lie a brilliant career; but everything suddenly underwent a change, as shall be related forthwith.

'Among the society of St Petersburg of that period there was accustomed to appear, and to disappear, at irregular intervals a certain Princess R. whose memory survives to this day. Though wedded to a highly placed and very presentable (albeit slightly stupid) husband, she had no children, and spent her time between making unexpected visits abroad and unexpected returns to Russia. In short, she led a very curious life, and the world in general accounted her a coquette, in that she devoted herself to every sort of pleasure, and danced at balls until she could dance no more, and laughed and jested with young men whom she received before dinner in the half-light of a darkened drawing-room. Yet, strangely enough, as the night advanced she would fall to weeping and praying and wringing her hands, and, unable to rest, would pace her room until break of day, or sit huddled, pale and cold, over the Psalter. But no sooner would daylight have appeared than she would once more become a woman of the world, and drive, and laugh, and chatter, and fling herself upon anything which seemed to offer any sort of distraction. Also, her power to charm was extraordinary; for though no one could have called her a beauty (seeing that the one good feature of her face lay in her eyes – and even then it was not the small, grey eyes themselves which attracted, but the glance which they emitted), she had hair of the colour and weight of gold which reached to her knees. That glance! – it was a glance which could be careless to the point of daring or meditative to the point of melancholy; a glance so enigmatical that, even when her tongue was lisping fatuous nonsense, there gleamed in her aspect something intangible and out of the common. Finally, she dressed with exquisite taste.

'This woman Paul Petrovitch met at a ball; and at it he danced a mazurka with her. Yet, though, during the dance, she uttered not a single word of sense, he straightway fell in love with her, and, being a man accustomed to conquests, attained his end in this case also. Yet, strangely enough, the facility of his triumph in no way chilled him, but led him on to become more and more resolutely, more and more painfully, attached, and that though she was a woman in whom, even after she had made the great surrender, there still remained something as immutably veiled, as radically intangible, as before – something which no one had yet succeeded in penetrating. What was in that soul God alone knows. Almost would it seem as though she were subservient to a mysterious force of which the existence was absolutely unknown to her, but which sported with her as it willed, and whose whims her mentality was powerless to control. At all events, her conduct constituted a series of inconsistencies, and even the few letters which she wrote to Paul Petrovitch – missives which would undoubtedly have aroused her husband's suspicions had he seen them – were written to a man who was practically a stranger to her. And in time her love began to be succeeded by fits of despondency; she ceased to smile and jest with the lover whom she had selected, and looked at him, and listened to his voice, with reluctance. In fact, there were moments – for the most part, unexpected moments – when this reluctance bordered upon chill horror, and her face assumed a wild, corpse-like expression, and she would shut herself up in her bedroom, whence her maid, with ear glued to the keyhole, would hear issue sounds as of dull, hopeless sobbing. Paul Petrovitch himself frequently found that, when returning home after one of these tender interviews, there was naught within his breast save the bitter, galling sensation which comes of final and irrevocable failure. "What more could I want?" he would say to himself in his bewilderment; yet always he spoke with an aching heart.

'It happened that on one occasion he gave her a ring having a stone carved in the figure of the Sphinx.

' "What?" she exclaimed. "Do you offer me the Sphinx?"

' "I do," he replied. "The Sphinx is yourself."

' "I?" she queried with a slow lift of her enigmatical eyes. "You are indeed flattering!"

'With the words went the ghost of a smile, while her eyes looked stranger than ever.

'Even during the time that the Princess loved him things were difficult for Paul Petrovitch; but when she cooled in her affection for him (as soon happened) he came near to going out of his mind. Distracted with jealousy, he allowed her no rest, but followed her to such an extent that at length, worn out with his persistent overtures, she betook herself on a tour abroad. Yet even then Paul Petrovitch listened to neither the prayers of his friends nor the advice of his superior officers, but, resigning his commission, set out on the Princess's track. Thus four years were spent in hunting her down, and losing sight of her again: and though, throughout, he felt ashamed of his conduct, and disgusted with his lack of spirit, all was of no avail – her image, the baffling, bewitching, alluring image which ever flitted before his eyes, had implanted itself too deeply in his breast. At last – it was at Baden – the pair once more came together; and though it seemed that never had she loved him as she did now, before a month was over another rupture had occurred, and, this time, a final one, as, with a last flicker, the flame died down and went out. True, that the parting would come he had foreseen; yet still he sought to be friends with her (as though friendship with such a woman could have been possible!), and only the fact that she quietly withdrew from Baden, and thenceforth studiously avoided him, baffled his purpose. Returning to Russia, he endeavoured to resume his former mode of life: but neither by hook nor crook could he regain the old rut. As a man with a poisoned system wanders hither and thither, so did he drive out, and retain all the customs of a society *habitué*. Nay, he could even have boasted of two or three new conquests. But no. What he wanted was obtainable neither through himself nor others, since his whole power of initiative was gone, and his head gradually growing grey. To sit at his club, to consume his soul in jaundice and *ennui*, to engage in bachelor disputes which failed to interest him – such was now become his sole occupation. And, as we know, it is an occupation which constitutes the worst of signs. Nor, for that matter, seems he to marriage to have given a thought.

'Thus ten years elapsed in colourless, fruitless pursuits. Yet Paul found time pass swiftly, indeed, with amazing swiftness, for nowhere in the world does it fly as it does in Russia (in prison only is its passage said to be still swifter); wherefore there came at length a night when, while dining at his club, he heard that the Princess was dead – that she had died in Paris in a state bordering upon insanity. Rising from the table, he fell to pacing the rooms of the club with a face like that of a corpse, and only at intervals halting to watch the tables of the card-players; until, his usual time for returning home having arrived, he departed. Soon after he had reached his flat there was delivered for him a package containing the ring which he had given to the Princess. The Sphinx on it was marked with a mark like the sign of the cross, and enclosed also was a message to say that through the cross had the enigma become solved.

'These things took place just at the time (early in '48) when Nikolai Petrovitch had lost his wife, and removed to St Petersburg; and since, also, the period of Nikolai's marriage had coincided with the earlier days of Paul's acquaintance with the Princess, Paul had not seen his brother since the day when the latter had settled in the country. True, on returning from abroad, Paul had paid Nikolai a visit with the intention of staying with him for a couple of months, as a congratulatory compliment on his happiness; but the visit had lasted a week only, since the difference in the position of the two brothers had been too great, and even now, though that difference had diminished somewhat, owing to the fact that Nikolai Petrovitch had lost his wife, and Paul Petrovitch his memories (after the Princess's death he made it his rule to try and forget her) – even now, I say, there existed the difference that, whereas Nikolai Petrovitch could look back upon a life well spent, and had a son rising to manhood, Paul Petrovitch was still a lonely bachelor, and, moreover, entering upon that dim, murky period when regrets come to resemble hopes, and hopes are beginning to resemble regrets, and youth is fled, and old age is fast approaching. To Paul Petrovitch that period was particularly painful, in that, in losing his past, he had lost his all.

' "I shall not invite you to come to Marino," were Nikolai Petrovitch's words to his brother. "Even when my wife was alive, you found the place tedious; and now it would kill you."

' "Ah, but in those days I was young and foolish and full of vanity," replied Paul Petrovitch. "Even though I may not have grown wiser, at least am I quieter. So, if you should be willing, I will gladly come and make your place my permanent home."

'For answer Nikolai Petrovitch embraced him; and though a year and a half elapsed before Paul Petrovitch decided to carry out his intention, once settled on the estate, he has never left it – no, not even during the three winters spent by Nikolai Petrovitch with his son in St Petersburg. Meanwhile he has taken to reading books – more especially English books, and, in general, to ordering his life on the English pattern. Rarely, also, does he call upon his neighbours, but confines his excursions, for the most part, to attending election meetings, where, as a rule, he holds his tongue, but occasionally amuses himself by angering and alarming the older generation of landowners with Liberal sallies. From the representatives of the younger generation he holds entirely aloof. Yet both parties, though they reckon him haughty, accord him respect. They do so because of his refined, aristocratic manners, and of what they have heard concerning his former conquests, and of the fact that he dresses with exquisite taste, that he always occupies the best suites in the best hotels, that he dines sumptuously every day, that once he took dinner with the Duke of Wellington at the Court of Louis Philippe, that invariably he takes about with him a silver *nécessaire* and a travelling bath, that he diffuses rare and agreeable perfumes, that he is a first-rate and universally successful whist-player, and that his honour is irreproachable. The ladies too look upon him as a man of charming melancholy: but with their sex he has long ceased to have anything to do.

'You see, then, Evgenii,' wound up Arkady, 'that you have judged my uncle very unfairly. Moreover, I have omitted to say that several times he has saved my father from ruin by making over to him the whole of his money (for they do not share the estate), and that he is always ready to help anyone, and, in particular, that he stands up stoutly for the peasants, even though, when speaking to them, he pulls a wry face, and, before beginning the interview, scents himself well with eau-de-Cologne.'

'We all know what nerves like his mean,' remarked Bazarov.

'Perhaps so. Yet his heart is in the right place; nor is he in any way a fool. To myself especially has he given much useful advice, especially on the subject of women.'

'Ah, ha! "Scalded with milk, one blows to cool another's water." That is a truism.'

'Finally and to put matters shortly,' resumed Arkady, 'he is a man desperately unhappy, not one who ought to be despised.'

'*Who* is despising him?' exclaimed Bazarov. 'All that I say is that a man who has staked his whole upon a woman's love, and, on losing the throw, has turned crusty, and let himself drift to such an extent as to become good for nothing – I say that such a man is not a man, a male creature, at all. He is unhappy, you say; and certainly you know him better than I do; but it is clear also that he has not yet cleansed himself of the fool. In other words, certain am I that, just because he occasionally reads *Galignani*, and because, once a month, he saves a peasant from distress for debt, he believes himself really to be a man of action.'

'But think of his upbringing!' expostulated Arkady. 'Think of the period in which he has lived his life!'

'His upbringing?' retorted Bazarov. 'Why, a man ought to *bring himself* up, even as I had to do. And with regard to his period, why should I, or any other man, be dependent upon periods? Rather, we ought to make periods dependent upon *us*. No, no, friend! Sensuality and frivolity it is that are at fault. For of what do the so-called mysterious relations between a man and a woman consist? As physiologists, we know precisely of what they consist. And take the anatomy of the eye. What in it justifies the guesswork whereof you speak? Such talk is so much Romanticism and nonsense and unsoundness and artificiality. Let us go and inspect that beetle.'

And the two friends departed to Bazarov's room, where he had already succeeded in creating a medical-surgical atmosphere which consorted well with the smell of cheap tobacco.

Chapter 8

AT HIS BROTHER'S INTERVIEW with the steward (the latter was a tall, thin man of shifty eyes who to every remark of Nikolai's replied in an unctuous, mellifluous voice: 'Very well, if so it please you'), Paul Petrovitch did not long remain present. Recently the system of estate-management had been reorganised on a new footing, and was creaking as loudly as an ungreased cartwheel or furniture which has been fashioned of unseasoned wood. For the same reason, though never actually giving way to melancholy, Nikolai Petrovitch often indulged in moodiness and sighing, for the reason that it was clear that his affairs would never prosper without money, and that the bulk of the latter had disappeared. As for Arkady's statement that frequently Paul Petrovitch had come to his brother's assistance, it had been perfectly true, for on more than one occasion had Paul been moved by the sight of his brother's perplexity to walk slowly to the window, to plunge a hand into his pocket, to mutter, *'Mais je puis vous donner de l'argent,'* and, lastly, to suit the action to the word. But on the day of which we are speaking Paul had no spare cash himself; wherefore he preferred to remove himself elsewhere, and the more so in that the *minutiæ* of estate-management wearied him, and that he felt certain that, though powerless to suggest a better way of doing business than the present one, he knew at least that Nikolai's was at fault.

'He is not sufficiently practical,' would be his reflection. 'He lets these fellows cheat him right and left.'

On the other hand, Nikolai had a high opinion of Paul's practicality, and always sought his advice.

'I am a weak, easy-going fellow,' he would say, 'and have spent the whole of my life in retirement; whereas you cannot have lived in the world for nothing – you know it well, and have the eye of an eagle.'

To this Paul Petrovitch would make no reply: he would merely turn away without attempting to undeceive his brother.

After leaving Nikolai Petrovitch's study, Paul traversed the corridor which separated the front portion of the house from the rear, and, on reaching a low doorway, halted in seeming indecision, tugged at his moustache for a moment, then tapped with his knuckles upon the panels.

'Who is there?' replied Thenichka from within. 'Pray enter.'

'It is I,' said Paul Petrovitch as he opened the door.

Springing from the chair on which she had been seated with her baby, she handed the latter to the nurse-girl (who at once bore it from the room), and hastened to rearrange her bodice.

'Pardon me for having disturbed you,' said Paul Petrovitch without looking at her, 'but my object in coming here is to ask you (for I understand that you are sending in to the town today) if you would procure me a little green tea for my own personal use.'

'I will,' replied Thenichka. 'How much ought I to have ordered?'

'I think that half a pound will suffice. But what a change!' he went on glancing around the room with an eye which included also in its purview Thenichka's features. 'It is those curtains that I am referring to,' he explained on seeing that she had failed to grasp his meaning.

'Yes – those curtains. They were given me by Nikolai Petrovitch himself, and have been hung a long while.'

'But it is a long time, remember, since last I paid you a visit. The room looks indeed comfortable, does it not?'

'Yes, thanks to Nikolai Petrovitch's kindness,' whispered Thenichka.

'And you find things better here than in the wing?' continued Paul Petrovitch politely – also, without the least shadow of a smile.

'I do.'

'And who is lodged in the wing in your place?'

'The laundry women.'

'Ah!'

Paul Petrovitch relapsed into silence, while Thenichka thought to herself: 'I suppose he will go presently.' So far from doing so, however, he remained where he was, and she had to continue standing in front of him with her fingers nervelessly locking and unlocking themselves.

'Why have you had the little one taken away?' at length he enquired. 'I love children. Pray show him to me.'

Thenichka reddened with confusion and pleasure; and that though Paul Petrovitch was accustomed to make her nervous, so seldom did he address her.

'Duniasha!' she cried (Duniasha she addressed, as she did everyone in the house, in the second person plural*). 'Bring Mitia here, and be quick about it! But first put on his clothes.' With that she moved towards the door.

'Never mind, never mind,' said Paul Petrovitch.

'But I shall soon be back.' And she disappeared.

Left alone, Paul looked about him with keen attention. The small,

---

* Used, as in French, in formal speech or that of a person addressing a social superior.

low room in which he was waiting was clean and comfortable, and redolent of balm, camomile, and furniture polish. Against the walls stood straight-backed, lyre-shaped chairs which the late General had purchased during the period of the Polish campaign; in one corner stood a bedstead under a muslin coverlet, with, flanking it, a large, iron-clamped, convex-lidded chest; in the opposite corner burnt a lamp before a massive, smoke-blackened *ikon* of Saint Nikolai the Miracle Worker – the Saint's halo suspended by a red riband, and a tiny china egg resting on his breast; on the window-sills were ranged some carefully sealed jars of last year's jam, which filtered the light to green, and of which the parchment covers were inscribed, in Thenichka's large handwriting, 'Gooseberry' – a jam of which Nikolai Petrovitch was particularly fond; from the ceiling hung, by a long cord, a cage containing a short-tailed siskin which kept up such a perpetual twittering and hopping that its cage rocked to and fro as it sang, and stray hemp seeds came pattering lightly to the floor; on the wall space above a small chest of drawers hung a few poorly executed photographs of Nikolai Petrovitch in various attitudes (the work of a travelling photographer); alongside these photographs hung a very unsuccessful one of Thenichka herself, since it revealed nothing but an eyeless face peering painfully from a dark frame; and, lastly, above the portrait of Thenichka hung a picture of Ermolov in a big cloak and a portentous frown – the latter directed principally towards a distant mountain range of the Caucasus, while over the forehead of the portrait dangled a silken pincushion in the shape of a shoe.

For five minutes or so there came from the adjoining room a sound as of rustling and whispering. From the chest of drawers Paul Petrovitch took up a greasy, dog's-eared volume of Masalsky's *The Strielitsi*, and turned over a few of its pages. Suddenly the door opened, and Thenichka entered with Mitia, whom she had now vested in a red robe and beaded collar, while his little head had been brushed, and also his face washed. Though he was breathing stertorously, and wriggling his whole body about, and twitching his tiny arms after the manner of all healthy children, the dainty robe had had its effect, and his face was puckered with delight. Also, Thenichka had tidied her own hair, and rearranged her bodice – well enough though she would have done as she was. For, in all the world, is there a more entrancing spectacle than that of a young, handsome mother with, in her arms, a healthy child?

'What a little beauty!' Paul Petrovitch exclaimed indulgently as he tickled Mitia's double chin with the tip of his forefinger. The baby fixed its eyes upon the siskin, and smiled.

'This is Uncle,' said Thenichka as she bent over the boy and gave

him a gentle shake. For fumigating purposes Duniasha deposited upon
the window-sill a lighted candle, and, beneath it, a two-kopeck piece.

'How old is he?' asked Paul Petrovitch.

'Six months. On the eleventh of this month he will be seven.'

'No, eight, will he not, Theodosia Nikolaievna?' timidly corrected
Duniasha.

'No, seven.'

Here the infant crowed, fixed his eyes upon the chest in the corner,
and suddenly closed his five tiny fingers upon his mother's mouth and
nose.

'The little rascal!' she said, without, however, freeing her features
from his grasp.

'He is very like my brother,' commented Paul Petrovitch.

'Whom else should he be like?' she thought.

'Yes,' he continued, half to himself. 'Undoubtedly I see the likeness.'
He gazed pensively, almost mournfully, at the young mother.

'This is Uncle,' again she said to the child: but this time she said it
under her breath.

'Oh, here you are, Paul!' cried Nikolai Petrovitch from behind them.

Paul Petrovitch faced about and knit his brows. But so joyously, and
with such a grateful expression, was his brother regarding the trio that
Paul could only respond with a smile.

'He is a fine little fellow, this baby of yours,' the elder brother
observed. Then, glancing at his watch, he added: 'I came here merely
to arrange about the purchase of some tea.' With which he assumed an
air of indifference, and left the room.

'He came here of his own accord, did he?' was Nikolai Petrovitch's
first enquiry.

'Yes, of his own accord,' the girl replied. 'He just knocked at the door
and entered.'

'And what of Arkasha? Has he too been to see you?'

'No, Nikolai Petrovitch. By the way, might I return to the rooms in
the wing of the house?'

'Why do you want to?'

'Because they suit me better than these.'

'I think not,' said Nikolai Petrovitch, rubbing his forehead with an
air of indecision. 'Before there was a reason for your being there, but
that reason no longer exists.'

'Good-morning, little rascal!' was his next remark as, with a sudden
access of animation, he approached and kissed the baby's cheek. Then,
bending a little, he pressed his lips to Thenichka's hand – a hand,

against the red of Mitia's robe, as white as milk.

'Why have you done that, Nikolai Petrovitch?' she murmured with downcast eyes. Yet when she raised them, their expression, as she glanced from under her brows and smiled her caressing, but slightly vacant, smile, was charming indeed!

Of the circumstances of Nikolai Petrovitch's first meeting with Thenichka the following may be related. Three years ago it had fallen to his lot to spend a night at an inn in a remote country town; and, while doing so, he had been struck with the cleanliness of the room assigned him, and also with the freshness of the bed-linen. 'Clearly,' he had thought to himself, 'the landlady must be a German.' But, as it had turned out, she was not a German, but a Russian of about fifty, well-dressed, and possessed both of a comely, intelligent countenance and of a refined manner of speaking. When breakfast was over, he had had a long conversation with her, and conceived for her a great liking. Now, as fate would have it, he had just removed to his new house, and, owing to a reluctance to continue keeping bonded serfs, was on the look-out for hired domestics; while she, for her part, was in despair over the question of the hard times, which caused only a limited number of visitors to resort to the town. In the end, therefore, Nikolai Petrovitch proposed to her to come to his house as house-keeper; and to this proposal, (since her husband was dead, and her family consisted only of a young daughter named Thenichka) she eventually agreed. Accordingly, within two weeks Arina Savishna (such was the new housekeeper's name) arrived at Marino with her child, and took up her abode in the wing of the new manor-house; nor was it long before she had put the place to rights. To Thenichka, however, then a girl of sixteen, she never referred; and few people even caught a glimpse of the maiden, since she lived a life so modest and retired that only on Sundays could Nikolai Petrovitch contemplate the delicate profile of her face in an aisle of the parish church. More than a year thus elapsed.

But one morning Arina entered his study, bowed to him as usual, and requested him to be so good as to come and help her with her daughter, one of whose eyes had been injured with a spark from the stove. It so happened that, like most men of sedentary habit, Nikolai Petrovitch had picked up a smattering of medicine – nay, he had even compiled a list of homoeopathic remedies for one and another emergency; wherefore he hastened to order Arina to produce the sufferer. As soon as she heard that the *barin* had sent for her, Thenichka turned very nervous, but followed her mother as in duty bound; whereupon Nikolai Petrovitch led her to the window, took her head in his hands, and, after an inspection of the red, inflamed eye, wrote out a prescription for a lotion, compounded the stuff himself, and, lastly, tore off a portion of his handkerchief, and showed her how best the eye could be bathed. Meanwhile Thenichka listened attentively, and then tried to leave the room. 'But the idea of going away without kissing the *barin*'s hand, foolish one!' cried Arina; whereupon, in lieu of offering the girl his hand, Nikolai Petrovitch felt so embarrassed that in the end he himself kissed her bent head at the spot where the hair lay parted. Soon Thenichka's eye healed, but the impression produced upon Nikolai Petrovitch did not pass away so quickly. Continually there flitted before him a pure, tender, timidly upturned face; continually he could feel between the palms of his hands soft coils of hair; continually appearing to his vision there would be a pair of innocent, half-parted lips between which a set of pearl-like teeth flashed back the sunlight. Consequently he began to observe the girl more in church, and to try to engage her in conversation. But shyness always overcame her, and, on one occasion when she happened to meet him on a narrow path through a rye field, she turned aside, and plunged into the mass of tall grain and undergrowth of cornflowers and wormwood. Yet, despite her endeavours to escape, his eye discerned her head amid the golden mesh of cornblades, and he called to her, as she gazed at him with wild eyes:

'Good-morning, Thenichka! I shall not hurt you.'

'Good-morning, *barin*!' she whispered in reply, but did not leave her retreat.

As time went on, however, she grew more accustomed to his presence; and by the time that she was beginning really to get over her bashfulness, her mother died of cholera. Here was a dilemma indeed! For what was to be done with the young Thenichka, who had inherited her mother's love of orderliness, and also her mother's good sense and natural refinement? In the end, she was so young and lonely, and Nikolai Petrovitch was so good-hearted and modest, that the inevitable came about. The rest need not be related.

'So my brother has been to you?' he enquired again. 'You say that he just knocked at the door and entered?'

'Yes, he just knocked at the door and entered.'

'Good! Now, hand me Mitia.'

And Nikolai Petrovitch fell to tossing the baby up and down towards the ceiling – a proceeding which greatly delighted the little one, but as greatly disquieted the mother, who, at each upward flight, stretched her hands in the direction of the infant's naked toes.

Meanwhile Paul Petrovitch returned to his study, of which the walls were lined with a paper of red wild roses, and hung with weapons; the floor was covered with a striped Persian carpet; and the furniture, consisting of a Renaissance bookcase in old black oak, a handsome writing-table, a few bronze statuettes, and a stove, was constructed, for the most part, of hazelwood, and upholstered in dark-green velvet. Stretching himself upon a sofa, he clasped his hands behind his head, and remained staring at the ceiling. Did presently the thoughts which were passing through his mind need to be concealed even from the walls, seeing that he rose, unhooked the heavy curtains from before the windows, and replaced himself upon the sofa?

Chapter 9

THE SAME DAY also saw Bazarov make Thenichka's acquaintance. This was when he was walking in the garden with Arkady, and discussing the question of why certain trees in the garden, especially oaks, had not prospered as they might have done. Said he:

'You ought to plant the place with as many silver poplars as you can, and also with Norwegian firs – limes too, if loam should first be added. For instance, the reason why this clump has done so well is that it is made up of lilacs and acacias, of which neither require much room. But hullo! There is someone sitting there!'

The persons seated in the arbour were Thenichka, Duniasha, and little Mitia. Bazarov halted, and Arkady nodded to Thenichka as to an old acquaintance. Then the pair passed on again, and Bazarov enquired of his companion:

'Who was she?'

'To whom are you referring?'

'You know to whom. My word, she *is* good-looking!'

Arkady explained, with a touch of embarrassment, the identity of Thenichka.

'Ah!' Bazarov remarked. 'Then your father has not at all bad taste. Indeed, I commend it. But what a young dog he is! I too must be introduced.'

And he turned back in the direction of the arbour.

'Evgenii!' exclaimed Arkady nervously as he followed his friend. 'For God's sake be careful what you do!'

'You need not be alarmed. I know what is what. I am no rustic.'

And, approaching Thenichka, he doffed his cap.

'Allow me to introduce myself,' he said with a polite bow. 'I am a friend of Arkady's, and a perfectly harmless individual.'

Rising from her seat, Thenichka gazed at him in silence.

'Oh, and what a fine baby!' he continued. 'Pray do not disturb yourself. Never yet have I cast upon a child an evil spell. But why are his cheeks so red? Is he cutting teeth?'

'Yes,' replied Thenichka. 'He has now cut four of them, and the gums are a little swelled.'

'Then let me see them. Do not be afraid. I am a doctor.'

With that he took the baby into his arms, and both Thenichka and Duniasha were astonished at the fact that it made no resistance, showed no fear.

'I see,' he continued. 'Well, everything is going right with him, and he will have plenty of teeth. Nevertheless, should he in any way ail, please let me know. Are you yourself well?'

'Yes, thank God!'

' "Thank God," say I too, for health on the part of the mother is the chief point of all. And you?' he added, turning to Duniasha. The latter, ultra-prim of demeanour in the drawing-room, and ultra-frivolous of behaviour in the kitchen, answered with a giggle.

'Well, you *look* all right. Here! Take your hero back again.'

He replaced the baby in Thenichka's arms.

'How quiet he has been with you!' she exclaimed under her breath.

'Always children are quiet with me,' he remarked.

You see. I know how to handle them.'

'And *they* know when people are fond of them,' put in Duniasha.

'True,' assented Thenichka. 'Though it is seldom that Mitia will go to anyone's arms but mine.'

'Would he come to me?' ventured Arkady, who, until now standing in the background, at this moment came forward towards the arbour. But on his attempting to wheedle Mitia to his arms, the infant threw back its head, and started to cry – a circumstance which greatly perturbed Thenichka.

'Another time – when he has come to be more used to me,' said Arkady indulgently. And the two friends departed.

'What is her name?' asked Bazarov.

'Thenichka – Theodosia,' replied Arkady.

'And her patronymic?'

'Nikolaievna.'

'*Bene!* What I like about her is her total absence of shyness. True, that is a *trait* which some might have condemned in her, but I say, "What rubbish!" For why need she be bashful? She is a mother, and therefore justified.'

'I agree,' said Arkady. 'And my father – '

'Also is justified,' concluded Bazarov.

'No, I do not agree in that respect.'

'You do not altogether welcome a superfluous heir?'

'For shame, Evgenii!' cried Arkady heatedly. 'How can you impute such motives? What I mean is that my father is not justified from *one* point of view. That is to say, he ought to marry her.'

'Oh, ho!' said Bazarov quietly. 'How high and mighty we are getting! So you still attribute importance to the marriage rite? This I should not have expected of you.'

For some paces the friends walked on in silence. Then Bazarov continued:

'I have been inspecting your father's establishment. The cattle look poor, the horses seem broken-down, the buildings have a tipsy air, the workmen manifest a tendency to loaf, and I cannot yet determine whether the new steward is a fool or a rogue.'

'You are censorious today?'

'I am; and the reason is that these good peasants are cheating your father – exemplifying the proverb that "The Russian *muzhik* will break even the back of God." '

'Soon I shall have to agree with my uncle in his opinion that you think but poorly of Russia.'

'Rubbish! The Russian's very best point is that he holds a poor opinion of *himself*. Two and two make four. Nothing but that matters.'

'And is nature also rubbish?' queried Arkady with a musing glance at the mottled fields where they lay basking in the soft, kindly rays of the morning sun.

'Nature *is* rubbish – at least in the sense in which *you* understand her. She is not a church, but a workshop wherein man is the labourer.'

At this moment there came wafted to their ears the long-drawn strains of a violoncello, on which a sensitive, but inexperienced, hand was playing Schubert's *Erwartung*. Like honey did the voluptuous melody suffuse the air.

'Who is the musician?' asked Bazarov in astonishment.

'My father.'

'What? Your father plays the 'cello?'

'He does.'

'At his age?'

'Yes – he is only forty-four.'

Bazarov burst out laughing.

'Why do you laugh?' asked Arkady.

'Pardon me, but the idea that your father – a man of forty-four, a paterfamilias, and a notable in the county – should play the 'cello!'

And he continued laughing, though Arkady, for all his reverence for his mentor, failed to accomplish even a smile.

Chapter 10

DURING THE NEXT two weeks life at Marino pursued its normal course. Arkady took things easily, and Bazarov worked. In passing, it may be said that, for all his careless manner and abrupt, laconic speech, the latter had become an accepted phenomenon in the house. In particular had Thenichka so completely lost her shyness of him that one night she sent to awake him because Mitia had been seized with convulsions; whereupon Bazarov arrived, and, half-joking, half-yawning, according to his usual manner, helped her for two hours in the task of attending to the baby. Only Paul Petrovitch disliked the man with the whole strength of his soul, for he accounted him a proud, cynical, conceited plebeian, and suspected him not only of failing to respect, but even of holding in contempt, the personality of Paul Petrovitch Kirsanov. Also, Nikolai Petrovitch stood in slight awe of the young Nihilist, since he doubted the likelihood of any good accruing from Bazarov's influence over Arkady. Yet always he would listen with pleasure to Bazarov's discourses, and gladly attend the chemical or physical experiments with which the young doctor (who had brought a microscope with him) would occupy himself for hours at a stretch. On the other hand, in spite of Bazarov's domineering manner, all the servants had become attached to him, for they felt him to be less a *barin* than their brother; and in particular did Dunisha readily joke and talk with him, and throw him many meaning glances as she sped past in quail-like fashion, while Peter himself, though a man full of conceit and stupidity, with a forehead perpetually puckered, and a dignity which consisted of a deferential demeanour, a practice of reading journals syllable by syllable, and a habit of constantly brushing his coat; even Peter, I say, would brighten and strike an attitude when he was noticed by Bazarov. In fact, the only servant to disapprove of Bazarov was old Prokofitch, the butler, who looked sour whenever he handed the young doctor a dish, and called him a 'sharper' and a 'flaunter,' and declared that, for all his whiskers, Bazarov was no better than 'a dressed-up pig,' whereas he, Prokofitch, was practically as good an aristocrat as Paul Petrovitch himself.

In the early days of June, the best season of the year, the weather became beautiful. True, from afar there came threatenings of cholera, but to the local inhabitants such visitations had become a commonplace. Each day Bazarov rose early to set forth upon a tramp of some two or three versts; nor were those tramps undertaken merely for the sake of the exercise (he could not abide aimless expeditions), but, rather, for the sake of collecting herbs and insects. Sometimes, too, he would succeed in inducing Arkady to accompany him; and whenever this was the case the pair would, on the way back, engage in some dispute which always left Arkady vanquished in spite of his superior profusion of argument.

One morning the pair lingered considerably by the way, and Nikolai Petrovitch set out across the garden to meet them. Just as he reached the arbour, he heard their voices and brisk footsteps approaching, though he himself was invisible to the returning friends.

'You do not understand my father,' Arkady was saying.

Nikolai Petrovitch halted instead of revealing himself.

'Oh, he is a good fellow enough,' replied Bazarov. 'But also he is a man on the shelf, a man whose song has been sung.'

Though Nikolai Petrovitch strained his ears, he failed to catch Arkady's reply. So the 'man on the shelf' lingered for a minute or two – then walked slowly back to the house.

'For the past three days I have noted him reading Pushkin,' continued Bazarov. 'You ought to explain to him that no good can come of that, for he is no longer a boy, and ought to have shaken himself free of such fiddlesticks. Who would desire to be a Romanticist? Give him something *practical.*'

'For instance?'

'Let me consider. For a start, give him Büchner's* *Stoff und Kraft.*'

'Good!' Arkady's tone was approving. '*Stoff und Kraft* is at least written in a popular style.'

The same day Nikolai Petrovitch was sitting with his brother. At length he said:

'I find that you and I are men on the shelf, that our songs have been sung. Eh? And perhaps Bazarov is right. Yet I confess that one thing hurts me: and that is that, though I had hoped to draw nearer to Arkady, I am being left in the rear, and he is for ever marching ahead. No longer do he and I understand one another.'

'And why is he for ever marching ahead?' asked Paul Petrovitch indignantly. 'How comes he to stand at such a distance from us? The reason is simply the ideas which that precious "Nihilist" is putting into his head. For myself, I detest the fellow, and think him a charlatan. Also, I am certain that, in spite of his frogs, he is making no

* Ludwig Büchner (1824–99), German physician and materialist philosopher.

real progress in physics.'

'We ought not to say that, brother. For my own part, I look upon him as a man of culture and ability.'

'If so, a detestably conceited one.'

'Perhaps he *is* conceited,' Nikolai Petrovitch allowed. 'But then it would appear that nothing can be done without something of the kind. What I cannot make out is the following. As you know, I have done everything possible to keep up with the times – I have organised my peasantry, I have set up such a farm that throughout the province I am known as "Fine Kirsanov," persistently I read and educate myself, in general I try to march abreast of the needs of the day. Yet, though I do all this, I am now given to understand that my day is past and gone! And, brother, I do not say that I am not partially inclined to accept that view.'

'For what reason?'

'For the following. Today, as I was reading Pushkin (I think it was "The Gypsies" that I had lighted upon), there suddenly entered the room Arkady. Silently, and with an air of kindly regret, and as gently as a child, he withdrew the book from my hand, and laid before me another book – a German production of some kind. That done, he gave me another smile, and departed with my volume of Pushkin under his arm.'

'Good gracious! And what might be the book which he has given you?'

'This.'

Nikolai Petrovitch extracted from the tail pocket of his frock-coat a copy (ninth edition) of Büchner's well-known work.

Paul Petrovitch turned it over in his hands.

'H'm!' he grunted. 'Arkady does indeed seem solicitous for your education! Have you tried reading the book?'

'Yes.'

'And how do you like it?'

'Well, either I am a fool or the thing is rubbish. Of the two views, the former seems to me the most probable.'

'It is not because you have forgotten your German, I suppose?'

'Oh no. I understand the language perfectly.'

Again Paul Petrovitch turned over the book, and again he glanced at his brother from under his brows. A moment's silence ensued.

'By the way,' continued Nikolai Petrovitch with an evident desire to change the conversation, 'I have received a letter from Koliazin.'

'From Matvei Ilvitch?'

'From the same. It seems that he has just arrived at — for the purpose of carrying out the Revision* of the province, and he writes very civilly that, as our kinsman, he would be glad to see Arkady and you and myself.'

'Do you intend to accept his invitation?' asked Paul Petrovitch.

'I do not. Do you?'

'No. We have no need to drag ourselves fifty versts to eat blanc-mange. The good Mathieu wants to show off a little – that is all. He can do without us. But what an honour to be a Privy Councillor! Had I continued in the Service, continued hauling at the old tow-rope, I myself might have been Adjutant-General! As it is, I, like yourself, am on the shelf.'

'Yes, brother. Clearly it is time that we ordered our tombstones, and folded our hands upon our breasts.'

A sigh concluded Nikolai Petrovitch's speech.

'But *I* do not intend to give in so soon,' muttered his brother. 'There is first going to be a skirmish between that chirurgeon of Arkady's and myself. That I can see beyond a doubt.'

And, sure enough, the 'skirmish' occurred the same evening. Ready for battle as soon he repaired to the drawing-room for tea, Paul Petrovitch entered angrily, but firmly, and sat waiting for an excuse to advance upon the foe. Yet for a while that excuse hung fire, since Bazarov never said much in the presence of 'the old Kirsanovs,' and tonight was feeling out of spirits, and drank his tea in absolute silence. However, Paul Petrovitch was so charged with impatience that his wish was bound to attain fulfilment.

It happened that the conversation became turned upon a neighbour-ing landowner.

'He is just a petty aristocrat,' Bazarov drily remarked (it seemed that he and the landowner had met in St Petersburg).

'Allow me,' put in Paul Petrovitch, his lips quivering. 'In your view, do the terms "good-for-nothing" and "aristocrat" connote the same thing?'

'I said "*petty* aristocrat," ' replied Bazarov as he lazily sipped his tea.

'Quite so. Then I take it that you hold the same opinion of aristocrats as of "petty aristocrats"? Well, I may remark that your opinion is not mine. And to that I would add that, while I myself possess a reputation for Liberal and progressive views, I possess that reputation for the very reason that I can respect *real* aristocrats. For instance, my dear sir' (the latter term was so heatedly uttered that Bazarov raised his eyebrows), 'for instance, my dear sir, take the

* i.e. the census-taking of the serf population.

aristocracy of England. While yielding upon their rights not an iota, they yet know how to respect the rights of others. While demanding fulfilment of obligations due to themselves, they yet fulfil their own obligations. And for those reasons it is to her aristocratic caste that England stands indebted for her freedom. It is because the English aristocratic caste itself supports that freedom.'

'A tale which we have heard many times before!' commented Bazarov. 'But what are you seeking to prove?'

'I am seeking to prove this,' replied Paul Petrovitch. 'That without a certain sense of personal dignity, without a sense of self-respect (both of which senses are inborn in the true aristocrat), the social edifice, the *bien public*, cannot rest upon a durable basis. It is *personality* that matters, my dear sir: and the human personality requires to be as firm as a rock, in that there rests upon it the entire structure of society. For example, I know that you ridicule my customs, my dress, my fastidious tastes. Yet do those very things proceed from that sense of duty – yes, of duty, I repeat – to which I have just alluded. In other words, I may live in the depths of the country, yet I do not let myself go. For I respect in myself the man.'

'Allow me, Paul Petrovitch,' said Bazarov. 'You say that you respect yourself. Very good. Yet you can sit there with your hands folded! How will *that* benefit the *bien public*, seeing that inaction would scarcely seem to argue self-respect?'

Paul Petrovitch blanched a little.

'That is another question altogether,' he said. 'However, I do not feel called upon to explain the reason why I sit with my hands folded (according to your own estimable term). It will suffice merely to remark that in the aristocratic idea there is contained a *principle*, and that nowadays men who live without principles are as destitute of morality as they are of moral substance. The same thing did I say to Arkady on the day after his arrival, and I say it now to you. You agree with me, Nikolai, do you not?'

Nikolai Petrovitch nodded assent, while Bazarov exclaimed:

'The aristocratic idea, forsooth! Liberalism, progress, principles! Why, have you ever considered the vanity of those terms? The Russian of today does not need them.'

'Then what, in your opinion, does he need? To listen to you, one would suppose that we stood wholly divorced from humanity and humanity's laws; whereas, pardon me, the logic of history demands – '

'What has that logic to do with us? We can get on quite well without it.'

'How can we do so?'

'Even as I have said. When you want to put a piece of bread into your mouth do you need logic for the purpose? What have these abstractions to do with ourselves?'

Paul Petrovitch waved his hand in disgust.

'I cannot understand you,' he said. 'You seem to me to be insulting the Russian people. How you or anyone else can decline to recognise principles and precepts is a thing which passes my comprehension. For what other basis for action in life have we got?'

Arkady put in a word.

'Both I and Bazarov have told you,' he said, 'that we recognise no authority of any sort.'

'Rather, that we recognise no basis for action save the useful,' corrected Bazarov. 'At present the course most useful is denial. Therefore we deny.'

'Deny everything?'

'Deny everything.'

'What? Both poetry and art and – I find it hard to express it? – '

'I repeat, *everything*,' said Bazarov with an ineffable expression of *insouciance*.

Paul Petrovitch stared. He had not quite expected this. For his part, Arkady reddened with pleasure.

'Allow me,' interposed Nikolai Petrovitch. 'You say that you deny everything – rather, that you would, consign everything to destruction. But also you ought to construct.'

'That is not our business,' said Bazarov. 'First must the site be cleared.'

'Yes; for the present condition of the people demands it,' affirmed Arkady. 'And that demand we are bound to fulfil, seeing that no one has the right merely to devote himself to the satisfaction of his own personal egotism.'

With this last Bazarov did not seem altogether pleased, since the phrase smacked too much of philosophy – rather, of 'Romanticism,' as Bazarov termed that science, but he did not trouble to confute his pupil.

'No, no!' Paul Petrovitch exclaimed with sudden heat. 'I *cannot* believe that gentlemen of your type possess sufficient knowledge of the people to be rightful representatives of its demands and aspirations. For the Russian people is not what you think it to be. It holds traditions sacred, and is patriarchal, and cannot live without faith.'

'I will not dispute that,' observed Bazarov. 'Nay, I will even agree that you are right.'

'And, granting that I am right – '

'You have proved nothing.'

'Yes, proved nothing,' echoed Arkady with the assurance of a chess-player who, having foreseen a dangerous move on the part of his opponent, awaits the attack with expert composure.

'But how have I proved nothing?' muttered Paul Petrovitch, rather taken aback. 'Do you mean to say that you are opposed to, not in favour of, the people?'

'Good gracious! Do not the common folk believe, when it thunders, that the Prophet Elijah is going up to Heaven in his chariot? You and I do not agree with that? The point is that the people is Russian, and that I am the same.'

'Not after what you have just said! Henceforth must I decline to recognise you as any countryman of mine.'

With a sort of indolent *hauteur* Bazarov replied:

'With his own hand did my grandfather guide the plough. Ask, therefore, of your favourite peasant which of us two – you or myself – he rates most truly as his countryman. Why, you do not know even how to speak to him!'

'And you, while speaking to him, despise him.'

'Should he merit contempt, yes. Reprobate, therefore, my views as much as you like, but who told you that they have come to me fortuitously rather than been derived from the very national spirit of which you are so ardent an upholder?'

'Phaugh! We need you Nihilists, do we not?'

'Not ours is it to decide the need or otherwise, seeing that even a man like yourself considers that he has a use.'

'Gentlemen, gentlemen!' interposed Nikolai Petrovitch as he rose to his feet. 'I beg of you to indulge in no personalties!'

Paul Petrovitch smiled. Then, laying his hand upon his brother's shoulder, he forced him to resume his seat.

'Do not be alarmed,' he said. 'That very sense of dignity at which this gentleman pokes such bitter fun will keep me from forgetting myself.'

And he turned to Bazarov again.

'Do you suppose your doctrine to be a new one?' he continued. 'If so, you are wasting your time. More than once has the Materialism which you preach been mooted; and each time it has been proved bankrupt.'

'Another foreign term!' muttered Bazarov. He was now beginning to lose his temper, and his face had turned a dull, copperish tint. 'In the first place, we Nihilists preach nothing at all. For to preach is not our custom.'

'What, then, is your custom?'

'To proclaim facts such as that our civil servants accept bribes, that we lack highways, commerce, and a single upright judge, and that – '

'Of course, of course! In other words, you and yours are to act as our "censors" (I believe that to be the correct term?). Well, I agree with many of your censures, but – '

'Other tenets which we hold are that to chatter, and to do nothing but chatter, concerning our differences is not worth the trouble, seeing that it is a pursuit which merely leads to pettiness and doctrinairism; that beyond question are our so-called leaders and censors not worth their salt, seeing that they engage in sheer futilities, and waste their breath on discussions on art and still life and Parliamentarism and legal points and the devil only knows what, when all the time it is the bread of subsistence alone that matters, and we are being stifled with gross superstition, and all our commercial enterprises are failing for want of honest directors, and the freedom of which the Government is for ever prating is destined never to become a reality, for the reason that, so long as the Russian peasant is allowed to go and drink himself to death in a dram-shop, he is ready to submit to any sort of despoilment.'

'You have decided, then, you feel conscious, that your true *métier* is to apply yourselves seriously to nothing?'

'Even so,' came the sullen reply, for Bazarov had suddenly become vexed with himself for having exposed his mind with such completeness to this *barin*.

'You have decided merely to deny everything?'

'We have decided merely to deny everything.'

'And that you call Nihilism?'

'That we call Nihilism.' In Bazarov's repetition of Paul Petrovitch's words there echoed, this time, a note of pride.

Paul Petrovitch knit his brows.

'So, so!' he said in a voice that was curiously calm. 'Nihilism is designed to combat our every ill, and you alone are to act as our saviours and our heroes! Well, well! But in what consider you yourselves and your censorious friends to excel the rest of us? For you chatter as much as does everyone else.'

'No, no!' muttered Bazarov. 'At least we are not guilty of *that*, however we may err in other ways.'

'You do things, then? At all events, you are preparing to do things?'

Bazarov did not reply, although, in his excitement, Paul Petrovitch had started up and then quickly recovered his self-command.

'H'm!' continued Paul Petrovitch. 'With you to act is to demolish. But how is such demolition to benefit when you do not even know its purpose?'

'We demolish because we are a force,' interposed Arkady.

Paul Petrovitch stared – then smiled.

'And a force need render account to no one!' added Arkady with a self-conscious straightening of his form.

'Fool!' gasped Paul Petrovitch. Evidently he could contain himself no longer. 'Have you ever considered *what* you are maintaining with your miserable creed? Even an angel would lose patience! "A force," forsooth! You might as well say that the wild Kalmuck, or the barbaric Mongol, represents a force. What boots such a force? Civilisation and its fruits are what we value. And do not tell me that those fruits are to be overlooked, seeing that even the meanest *barbouilleur*,* the meanest piano-player who ever earned five kopecks a night, is of more use to society than you. For men of that kind at least stand for culture rather than for some rude, Mongolian propelling-power. Yes, you may look upon yourselves as "the coming race," yet you are fit but to sit in a Kalmuck shanty. "A force," foorsoth! Good and "forceful" sirs, I beg to tell you that you number but four men and a boy, whereas those others number millions, and are folk of the kind who will not permit such as *you* to trample upon their sacred beliefs, but will first trample upon your worthy selves.'

'Let them trample upon us,' retorted Bazarov. 'We are more in number than you think.'

'What? You really believe that you will succeed in inoculating the nation as a whole?'

'From a little candle,' replied Bazarov, 'there arose, as you know, the conflagration of Moscow.'†

'A pride almost Satanic in its nature, and then banter! And thus you would seek to attract our youth, *thus* you would attempt to win the inexperienced hearts of our boys! For sitting beside you is one of those very boys, and he is absolutely worshipping you!' (Upon this Arkady knit his brows, and averted his head a little.) 'Yes, the canker has spread far already. For instance, they tell me that in Rome our artists decline to enter the Vatican, and look upon Raphael as next-door to a fool, just because he is an "authority"! Yet those very artists are themselves so barren and impotent that their fancy cannot rise above "Girls at Fountains," and so forth, villainously executed! And such artists you account fine fellows, I presume?'

'Like those artists,' said Bazarov, 'I consider Raphael to be worth not a copper groat. And as for the artists themselves, I appraise them at about a similar sum.'

'Bravo, bravo!' cried Paul Petrovitch. 'Listen, O Arkady – listen to

* Scribbler.   † In 1812.

the way in which the young men of the present day ought to express themselves! Surely our youth will now rally to your side? For once upon a time they had to go to school, since they did not like to be taken for dunces, and therefore worked at their studies; but now they have but to say: "Everything in the world is rubbish," and, behold! the trick is done. They consider that delightful – and naturally! In other words, the blockheads of former days are become the Nihilists of the present.'

'Your self-sufficiency – I mean, your self-respect – is carrying you away,' Bazarov remarked nonchalantly (as for Arkady, his eyes had flashed, and his whole form was quivering with indignation). 'But our dispute has gone far enough. Let us end it. Whenever you may feel that you can point out to me a single institution in our family or our public life which does not call for complete and unsparing rejection, I shall be pleased to accept your view.'

'Of institutions of that kind I could cite you millions,' exclaimed Paul Petrovitch. 'For example, take the village commune.'

Bazarov's lips twisted themselves into a contemptuous smile.

'The village commune,' said he, 'is a subject which you would do better to discuss with your brother, since he is learning by experience the meaning of that commune, and of its circular guarantee, and of its enforced sobriety and other contrivances.'

'Take the family, then – yes, take the family, since at least among the peasantry it is still a surviving institution.'

'And that question, too, I should imagine were best not dissected by you in detail. But see here, Paul Petrovitch. Allow yourself a minimum of two days to think over these things (you will need quite that amount of time to do so); and cite to yourself in succession our various social conditions, and give them your best attention. Meanwhile Arkady and myself will go and – '

'Go and make sport of everything, I presume?'

'No, go and dissect frogs. Come, Arkady! *Au revoir*, gentlemen.'

And the two friends departed. Left alone, the brothers looked at one another.

'So,' at last said Paul Petrovitch, 'you see the young men of the day – you see our successors!'

'Our successors – yes,' re-echoed Nikolai Petrovitch despondently. Throughout the conversation he had been sitting simply on pins and needles; throughout it he had dared do no more than throw an occasional pained glance at Arkady. 'My brother, there came to me just now a curious reminiscence. It was of a quarrel which once I had with my mother. During the contest she raised a great outcry, and refused to listen to a single word I said; until at length I told her that for her to understand me was impossible, seeing that she and I came of different generations. Of course this angered her yet more, but I thought to myself: "What else could I do? The pill must have been a bitter one, but it was necessary that she should swallow it." And now *our* turn is come; now is it for us to be told by our heirs that we come of a different generation from theirs, and must kindly swallow the pill.'

'You are too magnanimous and retiring,' expostulated Paul Petrovitch. 'For my part, I feel sure that we are more in the right than these two youngsters, even though we may express ourselves in old-fashioned terms, and lack their daring self-sufficiency. Indeed, what a puffed-up crowd is the youth of today! Should you ask one of them whether he will take white wine or red, he will reply, in a bass voice, and with a face as though the whole universe were looking at him: "Red is my customary rule."'

'Should you like some more tea?' interrupted Thenichka, who had been peeping through the doorway, but had not dared to enter during the progress of the dispute.

'No,' was Nikolai Petrovitch's reply as he rose to meet her. 'So you can order the *samovar* to be removed.'

Meanwhile, with a brief '*Bon soir*,' Paul Petrovitch betook himself to his study.

Chapter 11

HALF AN HOUR LATER Nikolai Petrovitch sought his favourite arbour. Despondent thoughts were thronging through his brain, for the rift between himself and his son was only too evident. Also, he knew that that rift would widen from day to day. For nothing had he spent whole days, during those winters in St Petersburg, in the perusal of modern works! For nothing had he listened to the young men's discourses! For nothing had he been delighted when he had been able to interpolate a word into their tempestuous debates!

'My brother says that we are more in the right than they,' he reflected. 'And certainly I too can say without vanity that I believe these young fellows to stand at a greater distance from the truth than ourselves. Yet also I believe that they have in them something which we lack – something which gives them an advantage over us. What is that something? Is it youth? No, it is not youth alone. Is it that there hovers about them less of the *barin* than hovers about ourselves? Possibly!'

Bending his head, he passed his hand over his face.

'Yet to reject poetry!' he muttered. 'To fail to sympathise with art and nature!'

And he gazed around as though he were trying to understand how anyone could be out of sympathy with the natural world. Evening was just closing in, and the sun sinking behind a small aspen copse which, situated half a verst from the garden, was trailing long shadows over the motionless fields. Along the narrow, dark track beside the copse a peasant on a white pony was trotting; and though the pair were overshadowed by the trees, the rider was as clearly visible, even to a patch on his shoulder, as the twinkling legs of his steed. Piercing the tangled aspens, the sun's beams were bathing the trunks in so brilliant a glow that trunks and beams were one bright mass, and only the foliage on the boughs above formed a dusky blur against the lighter tints of the flame-coloured sky. Overhead bats were whirling; the wind had sunk to rest; a few late-homing bees were buzzing somnolently, sluggishly amid the lilac blossoms; and a pillared swarm of gnats was dancing over a projecting bough.

'O God, how fair!' was Nikolai's involuntary thought as his lips breathed a favourite couplet.

Suddenly he remembered Arkady and *Stoff und Kraft*; and though he continued to sit where he was, he quoted poetry no more, but surrendered his mind wholly to the play of his lonely, irregular, mournful thoughts. At all times he was a man fond of dreaming; and to this tendency his life in the country had added confirmation. To think of what only a short while ago he had been dreaming as he waited for his son on the post-house verandah! For since that hour a change had come about, and in the vague relations between himself and his son there had dawned a more definite phase. Next, he saw before him his dead wife. Yet he saw her, not as she had appeared to him during the later years of her life – that is to say, as a kindly, thrifty *châtelaine* – but as a young girl slim of figure and innocently enquiring of eye. Yes, there flitted before his vision a picture only of neatly plaited tresses falling over a childish neck. And he thought of his first meeting with her when, as a student, he had encountered her on the staircase leading to his suite of rooms. He remembered how, having accidentally brushed against her, he had stopped to apologise, but had only succeeded in muttering 'Pardon, *monsieur*'; whereupon she had bowed, and smiled, and fled as in sudden alarm – but only to turn, the next moment, at the bend of the staircase, to look swiftly back, and then, as swiftly, to blush, and assume a more demure demeanour. Ah, those first timid meetings, those half-spoken words, those bashful smiles, those alternate fits of rapture and despair, that courtship that was destined to be crowned with swooning joy! Whither was it all fled? True, she had become his wife, and had conferred upon him such happiness as falls to the lot of few men on earth; but ever the thought recurred to him, and recurred again: 'Why could those days of sweetness not have lasted for ever, so that we might have lived a life which should never have known death?'

He made no attempt to co-ordinate his thoughts. The predominant feeling in his mind was that he would give worlds to be able to connect himself with those blessed days by something stronger than the mere power of memory. He wanted to feel his Maria near him once more, to scent her dear breath. A curious mood had him in its grip.

'Nikolai Petrovitch!' came the voice of Thenichka from a spot somewhere in the vicinity. 'Where are you?'

As he heard the call, a feeling that was neither vexation nor shame passed over him. No comparison between his dead wife and Thenichka was possible, yet he gave a start, and felt a passing regret that Thenichka had seized *that* moment to seek him. For in some way did the sound of her voice bring back to him his grey hairs, his old age, all that constituted the present. So for an instant the enchanted world which he had just entered, and which he had just seen emerge from the misty waves of the past, quivered – then disappeared.

'I am here, Thenichka,' he called. 'Please go away. I will come presently.'

'Another reminder that I am a *barin*,' he reflected.

Thenichka retired, and suddenly he became aware of the fact that since the moment when he had sunk into a reverie nightfall had come. Yes, all around him there lay a motionless obscurity, with, gleaming amid it, as a small, pale blur, Thenichka's face. Rising, he started to return to the house, but his unstrung nerves could not calm themselves, and, glancing now at the ground, now towards the heavens where there swarmed myriads of twinkling stars, he fell to pacing the garden. He continued this pacing until he was almost worn out; for still did the vague, despondent, insistent sense of agitation refuse to leave his breast. Could Bazarov have divined his thoughts, how the Nihilist would have laughed! And even Arkady would have condemned him. For from the eyes of Nikolai Petrovitch – from the eyes of a man of forty-four who was the proprietor of an estate and a household – there were welling slow, uncalled-for tears. This was a hundred times worse than the 'cello-playing!

And still he continued his pacing, for he could not make up his mind to enter the peaceful, inviting retreat which beckoned to him so cheerfully with its lighted windows, and to leave the darkness of the garden, to forego the touch of fresh air upon his face, to throw off his present mood of sadness and emotion.

At a turn in the path he encountered Paul Petrovitch.

'What is the matter with you?' Paul enquired. 'You are looking as white as a ghost. Are you ill? Why not go to bed?'

Nikolai Petrovitch explained to him in a few words his frame of mind – then moved towards the house. Paul Petrovitch sauntered down towards the other end of the garden, and ever and anon, as he did so, indulged in wrapt contemplation of the heavens. Yet, save for the reflection of the starlight, there was nothing to be seen in his dark, handsome eyes; for he had not been born a Romanticist, and his drily fastidious, passionate, Frenchified, misanthropic soul was incapable of castle-building.

'I tell you what,' Bazarov said to Arkady the same night. 'A splendid idea has come into my head. You know that today your father said that a certain eminent relation had sent him an invitation which he had no-intention of accepting. Well, how would it be if you and I were to accept it, seeing that you too have been included in the honour? The weather has turned beautiful, and we might drive over and look at the town, and thus, incidentally, secure a few days' uninterrupted talk together.'

'Should you then return here?'

'No. I should go on to my father's. You see, he lives thirty versts away only, and it is a long time since last I saw either him or my mother. Moreover, the old folk deserve to be humoured a little, seeing that they have been very good to me – especially my father – and that I am their only son.'

'And shall you stay long?'

'No. Staying in that place is dull work.'

'Then pay us a second visit on your way back?'

'I will if possible. We will go, then, eh?'

'At your pleasure,' Arkady replied with a show of indifference. But, as a matter of fact, he was delighted with Bazarov's proposal; and only the thought that he must keep up his 'Nihilism' prevented him from manifesting his feelings.

So, the next day, the pair set out for the town of — ; while with one consent the youth of Marino broke into lamentations over their going, and Duniasha even went so far as to weep. Only their elders breathed more freely.

Chapter 12

THE TOWN OF — , whither our friends now proceeded lay under the dominion of one of those young, progressive, despotic provincial governors who afflict Russia in an unending sequence. As early as the first year of his rule this particular potentate had succeeded in quarrelling, not only with the President of the Provincial Council (who was a retired staff officer, a horse breeder, and an agriculturist), but also with his whole gubernatorial staff of *tchinovniks*: with the result that at the time of our story the commotion therefrom had attained a pitch which had just necessitated the sending down of a commissary empowered to hold an investigation. The Government's choice for this purpose had fallen upon Matvei Ilyitch Koliazin, the son of the Koliazin who had once acted as guardian to the brothers Kirsanov, and a man of the younger school – that is to say, a man who, though a little over forty, still aimed at attaining the dignity of a statesman, and having a breast covered with stars (including at least one of a foreign minor order), and who, also like the Governor whom he had come to examine, was accounted a Progressive, and held a high opinion of himself. Yet never did Matvei allow his boundless vanity to prevent him from affecting a stereotyped air of simplicity and good humour, or from listening indulgently to anything that might be said to him, or from cultivating so pleasant a laugh that everywhere he contrived to pass for 'not a bad sort of a fellow.' True, he could on important occasions (if I may quote the trite saying) 'make dust fly' ('Energy is indispensable for a State worker,' was a frequent saw of his – '*L'énergie est la première qualité d'un homme d'état*'); yet almost invariably did he end by being set down as a fool, while *tchinovniks* of more experience rode roughshod over him. Amongst other things, he had a custom of expressing a great respect for Guizot,* and also of striving to convince everyone that he (Koliazin) was not one of 'your men of routine, your retired bureaucrats,' but, rather, a man who noted 'every new and more important phenomenon of our social life.' In fact, such phrases he had at his finger ends, and also he studied (though with a sort of careless pomposity only) the development of contemporary literature. Lastly, it not seldom befell that, on meeting a street procession of students, he

* François Pierre Guillaume Guizot (1787–1874), the great French minister, ambassador, *littérateur* and educationalist.

would, though maturer of years than the majority of its members, add himself to its ranks. In short, only his circumstances and his epoch caused Matvei Ilyitch in any way to differ from those officials of the Alexandrine period who, before setting out to attend a reception at Madame Svietchin's* (then resident in St Petersburg), would read a few pages of Condillac's† works. Yet, though an adroit courtier, Matvei was a mere glittering fraud, since, save that he knew how to hold his own against all comers (though, certainly, that is a great achievement in life), he was, in all matters of State, a complete stranger to common sense.

On the present occasion he welcomed Arkady with all the *bonhomie*, all the jocosity, of an 'enlightened' bigwig. Nevertheless his face fell a little when he learned that the other relatives whom he had invited had preferred remaining in the country. 'Your father always was a queer fish,' he remarked as he parted the tails of a velvet 'cutaway.' And, having said this, he turned to a young *tchinovnik* in a tightly buttoned uniform, and asked him irritably what he wanted; at which onslaught the young *tchinovnik* (whose lips looked as though a confirmed habit of keeping their own counsel had gummed them permanently together) straightened himself with a sharp, apprehensive look at his superior. But, once Matvei had effected this 'settling' of his subordinate, the great man paid the little one no further attention.

In passing, I may observe that to most of our bigwigs is this species of 'settling' very dear, and that many are the expedients resorted to for its achievement. Particularly is the following method 'quite a favourite,' as the English say – in other words, much in request. Suddenly a given bigwig will cease to be able to grasp with his intelligence even the simplest sentence, and assume an air of abysmal density. For example, he will enquire what the day of the week may be, and be told (with great and stammering deference) that the day is, say, Friday.

'What?' will roar the bigwig with an air of being forced to strain his ears to the utmost. 'Eh? what do you say?'

'I–It is F–Friday, your E–E–Excellency.'

'Eh, what? Friday? What mean you by Friday?'

'Y–Your Excellency, F–Friday is, is – F–F–Friday is a day in the week.'

---

* Madame Svietchin (1782–1857), wife of the Russian General Svietchin. For more than forty years she maintained a famous salon.
† Etienne Bonnot de Mably de Condillac (1715–80), a French philosopher who based knowledge solely upon the physical senses.

'Come, come! You need not have taken so much time to tell me *that*.'

Matvei Ilyitch was just such a bigwig, although he called himself a Liberal.

'My good fellow,' he now continued to Arkady, 'I should advise you to go and leave your card upon the Governor. Of course you understand that my reason for counselling you to adopt this procedure is, not that I in any way hold with any bygone ideas about kow-towing to authority, but, rather, because the Governor is a good fellow, and I know that you would like to see a little society. For you too are not a bear, I hope? No? Well, the Governor is giving a grand ball the day after tomorrow.'

'And shall you be there?' asked Arkady.

'I shall, of course, receive tickets for it,' replied Matvei Ilyitch with an assumed air of regret. 'You dance, I presume?'

'I do – though very badly.'

'Never mind, never mind. There exists here plenty of good society, and it would never do for a young fellow like yourself to be a non-dancer. Again I say this, not because I in any way revere antiquated notions, nor yet because I think that intellect ought to go kicking its heels about, but because Byronism has become absurd – *il a fait son temps*.'

'But I belong to neither the Byronists nor – '

'Well, well! I will introduce you to some of our ladies – I myself will take you under my wing.' And Matvei Ilyitch smiled in a self-satisfied way. 'In fact, you shall have a gay time here.'

At this point a servant entered to announce the President of the Provincial Treasury. The latter, a mild-eyed veteran with wrinkles around his lips and a great love for nature, was accustomed to remark on summer days that 'of every little flower each little bee is now taking its toll.' So Arkady seized the occasion to depart.

He found Bazarov at the hotel where the pair were putting up, and had great difficulty in persuading him to join in the projected call upon the Governor.

'Well, well!' eventually said Bazarov. 'I have laid a hand upon the tow-rope, so it ill becomes me to complain of its weight. As we are here to inspect the local lions, let us inspect them.'

To the young men the Governor accorded a civil enough welcome, but neither bade them be seated nor set the example himself. A man in a perpetual hurry and ferment, he, on rising in the morning, was accustomed to don a tight uniform and stiff collar, and then to give himself up to such an orgy of orders-giving that he never finished a single meal. As the result, he was known throughout the province as

'Bardeloue' – in reference be it said, not to the great French preacher,* but to *burda*, fermented liquor. After inviting Arkady and Bazarov to the coming ball, the Governor, two minutes later, repeated the invitation as though he had never given it; while likewise he mistook the pair for brothers, and addressed them throughout as 'the Messieurs *Kaiserov*.'

Subsequently, as the pair were proceeding homewards, a man of small stature, and dressed in a 'Slavophil' costume, leapt from a passing *drozhki*, and, with a cry of 'Evgenii Vasilitch!' flung himself upon Bazarov.

'Is that you, Herr Sitnikov?' remarked Bazarov without even checking his stride. 'What chance brings you hither?'

'A pure accident,' was the other's reply as, turning to the *drozhki*, he signed to the coachman to follow at a foot's pace. 'You see, I had business to do with my father, and he invited me to pay him a visit.' Sitnikov hopped across a puddle. 'Also, on learning of your arrival, I have been to call at your place. '(True enough, on subsequently reaching the hotel, the two friends found awaiting them Sitnikov's visiting-card, with the corners turned down, and one side of it inscribed with his name in the French fashion, and the other with his name in Slavonic characters.)

'You are from the Governor's, I suppose?' continued the little man. 'I sincerely hope not, however.'

'Your hopes are vain.'

'Then I too, alas, must pay him my *devoirs*. But first introduce me to your friend.'

'Sitnikov – Kirsanov,' responded Bazarov without halting.

'Delighted!' minced Sitnikov as he stepped back, struck an attitude, and hurriedly doffed his super-elegant gloves. 'I have heard much of you, Monsieur Kirsanov. I too am an old acquaintance – I might even say, an old pupil – of Evgenii Vasilitch's. Through him it was that I came by my spiritual regeneration.'

Arkady glanced at Bazarov's 'old pupil,' and saw that he had small, dull, pleasant, nervous features; also that his narrow, sunken eyes expressed a great restlessness, and that his lips were parted in a perpetual smile of a wooden and ingratiating order.

'Do you know,' Sitnikov continued, 'when Evgenii Vasilitch first told me that we ought to ignore every species of authority I experienced a sense of rapture, I felt as though I had suddenly ripened. "Ah," I thought, "at last have I found my man!" By the way, Evgenii Vasilitch,

* Louis Bourdaloue (1632–1704), a professor in the Jesuit College of Bourges.

you *must* come and see a certain lady of my acquaintance – one who, beyond all others, is the person to understand you, and to look upon your coming as a red-letter event. Perhaps you have heard of her already?'

'No. Who is she?' asked Bazarov reluctantly.

'A Madame Kukshin – a Madame, I should say, *Evdoksia* Kuvshin. And she is not merely a remarkable character and a woman of light and leading; she is also representative of the *émancipée*, in the best sense of the word. But look here. How would it be if all three of us were to go and see her? She lives only two steps away, and she would give us luncheon. You have not lunched already, I presume?'

'No, we have not.'

'Then the arrangement would suit us all. By the way, she is independent, but a married woman.'

'Good-looking?' queried Bazarov.

'N-No – one could not exactly say that.'

'Then why ask us to go and see her?'

'Ah, ha! You *will* have your jest, I see. But remember that she will stand us a bottle of champagne.'

'The practicality of the man!'

Sitnikov gave a shrill giggle.

'Shall we go?' he added.

'I cannot decide.'

Here Arkady put in a word.

'We have come to inspect the local people,' he remarked, 'so let us inspect them.'

'True enough,' seconded Sitnikov. 'And, of course, *you* must come, Monsieur Kirsanov. We could not go without you.'

'What? Are all three of us to descend upon her?'

'What matter? She herself is an odd person.'

'And you say that she will stand us a bottle of champagne.'

'Yes; or even a bottle apiece,' asserted Sitnikov. 'I will go bail upon that.'

'Go bail with what?'

'With my head.'

'Your purse would have been better; but lead on.'

Chapter 13

THE VILLA IN WHICH Avdotia, or Evdoksia, Nikitishna Kukshin resided was one of the usual Moscow pattern, and stood in one of the recently consumed streets (for as we know, every fifth year sees each of our provincial capitals burnt to the ground) of the town of —. Beside the front door there hung (over a cracked, crooked visiting-card) a bell-handle, while in the hall the visitors were met by a female who constituted, not exactly a maidservant, but a mob-capped 'lady companion.' And it need hardly be added that these two phenomena, the bell-handle and the 'lady companion,' constituted clear evidence of the 'progressiveness' of the hostess's views.

On Sitnikov enquiring whether Avdotia Nikitishna were within, a shrill voice interrupted him from an adjoining room:

'Is that you, Victor? Pray enter.'

The female in the mob-cap disappeared.

'I have not come alone,' Sitnikov responded as, after an enquiring glance at Arkady and Bazarov, he divested himself of his greatcoat, and revealed thereunder a sort of sack jacket.

'Never mind,' the voice replied. '*Entrez, s'il vous plaît.*'

The young men did as bidden, and found themselves in a room which resembled a workshop rather than a parlour. On tables were piled promiscuous papers, letters and Russian magazines (most of the latter uncut); everywhere on the floor were to be seen gleaming the fag-ends of cigarettes; and on a leather-padded sofa a lady – youngish, flaxen-haired, and clad in a *négligée* soiled silk gown was lolling in a semi-recumbent position. About her stumpy wrists were clasped a large pair of bracelets, and over her head was thrown a lace mantilla. Rising, she draped her shoulders carelessly in a velvet tippet with faded ermine trimming, and, saying indolently, 'Good-day, Victor,' pressed Sitnikov's hand.

'Bazarov – Kirsanov,' he said in abrupt imitation of the former; whereupon she responded, 'How do you do?' and then added, as she fixed upon Bazarov a pair of large eyes between which glimmered a correspondingly small, pink, upturned nose: 'I have met you before.'

That said, she pressed his hand even as she had done Sitnikov's.

Bazarov frowned, for though the plain, insignificant features of the emancipated lady contained nothing actually to repel, there was something in their mien which produced upon the beholder the sort of unpleasant impression which might have inclined him to ask her: 'Are you hungry, or bored, or afraid? At all events what is it you want?' Also, like Sitnikov, she kept pawing the air as she spoke, and her every word, her every gesture, revealed such a lack of control as at times amounted to sheer awkwardness. In short, though she conceived herself to be just a simple, good-hearted creature, her bearing was of the kind to lead the beholder to reflect that, no matter what she did, it was not what she had intended to do, and that everything was done (to use the children's term) 'on purpose' – that is to say, non-simply and non-naturally.

'Yes, I have met you before, Bazarov,' she repeated (like many other contemporary females of Moscow and the provinces, she had adopted the fashion of calling men by their surnames alone on first introduction). 'Will you have a cigar?'

'I thank you,' interposed Sitnikov (who had deposited his person in an armchair, and crossed his legs). 'Also, pray give us some luncheon, for we are absolutely ravenous. Also, you might order us a bottle of champagne.'

'You Sybarite!' exclaimed Evdoksia with a smile (a smile always brought her upper gum prominently into view). 'Is he not, Bazarov?'

'No; it is merely that I love the comforts of life,' protested Sitnikov pompously. 'Nor need that in any way prevent me from being a Liberal.'

'But it does, it does,' cried Evdoksia. However, she gave orders to her servant to see both to the luncheon and to the champagne. 'What is *your* opinion on the matter?' she added, turning to Bazarov. 'I feel convinced that you share mine.'

'No, I do not,' he replied. 'On the contrary, I think that, even from the chemical point of view, a piece of meat is better than a piece of bread.'

'Then you study chemistry?' she exclaimed. 'Chemistry is *my* passion also. In fact, I have invented a special liniment.'

'A liniment? You?'

'Yes, I. And please guess its use. It is for making unbreakable dolls and pipe-bowls. You see that, like yourself, I am of a practical turn of mind. But, as yet, I have not completed my course of study. It still remains for me to read up my Liebig. *Apropos*, have you seen an article in the *Viedomosti* on Woman's Work – an article by Kisliakov? If not, you should read it (for I presume that you take an interest in the Feminine Question, and also in the Question of the Schools?). But what is your is friend's line? *Apropos*, what is his name?'

These questions Madame Kukshin, as it were, mouthed, and did so with an affected carelessness which waited for no reply, even as a spoilt child propounds conundrums to its nurse.

'My name is Arkady Nikolaievitch Kirsanov,' Arkady answered for himself. 'And my particular line is doing nothing at all.'

Evdoksia tittered.

'How nice!' she exclaimed. 'Then you do not even smoke? Victor, I am furious with you!'

'Why?' enquired Sitnikov.

'Because I have just heard that you are again standing up for Georges Sand, that played-out woman. How is she even to be compared (that creature, who lacks a single idea on education or physiology or anything else) with Emerson? In fact, I believe that never in her life has she so much as *heard* of embryology – though in these days no one can get on without it.' The speaker flung out her arms in an expressive gesture. 'But what a splendid article was that of Elisievitch's! He is indeed a talented gentleman!' (This was another habit of Evdoksia's – the habit of persistently using the term 'gentleman' for the ordinary word 'man'). 'Bazarov, pray come and sit beside me on the sofa. You may not know it, but I am dreadfully afraid of you.'

'Why are you afraid of me (if you will forgive my curiosity)?'

'Because you are a dangerous gentleman – you are a critic so caustic that in your presence my confusion leads me to begin speaking like a lady-landowner of the Steppes. *Apropos*, I am a lady-landowner myself; for, though I employ a local steward named Erothei (a sort of Cooper's "Pathfinder," but compounded with a blend of independence in his composition), I retain the ultimate reins of management in my own hands. But how unbearable this town is! – yes, even though I have made it my permanent home, seeing that nothing else was to be done!'

'The town is what a town always is,' remarked Bazarov indifferently.

'But its interests are so petty!' continued Evdoksia. '*That* is what troubles me. Once upon a time I used to winter in Moscow, but now good Monsieur Kukshin has to dwell there alone. And Moscow itself is, is – well, not what it used to be. As a matter of fact, I contemplate going abroad. I have spent the whole year in making my preparations for the journey.'

'You will go to Paris, I presume?'

'Yes, and to Heidelberg.'

'Why to Heidelberg?'

'Because there the great Herr Bunsen* has his home.'

Bazarov could not think of a suitable reply.

* Robert Wilhelm Bunsen (1811–99), chemist and physicist; inventor of Bunsen's burner and magnesium light; and originator (with Kirchhov) of spectrum analysis.

'Do you know Pierre Sapozhnikov?' continued she.

'No, I do not.'

'He is always to be found at Lydia Khostatov's.'

'Even with her I am not acquainted.'

'Well, Sapozhnikov is going to escort me on my travels. For at least I am free – I have no children, thank God! Why I should have put in that "Thank God!" I scarcely know.'

She rolled another cigarette between her nicotine-stained fingers, licked it, placed it between her lips, and struck a match. The servant entered with a tray.

'Ah! Here comes luncheon! Will you have some? Victor, pray uncork the bottle. It is your function to do so.'

'Mine, yes, mine,' he hummed; then gave another of his shrill giggles.

'Have you any good-looking ladies in this town?' Bazarov asked after a third glassful of champagne.

'Yes,' replied Evdoksia. 'But uniformly they are futile. For example, a friend of mine, a Madame Odintsov, is not bad-looking, and has nothing against her except a doubtful reputation (a thing of no consequence in itself); but, alas! she combines with it such a complete lack of freedom, or of breadth of view, or, in fact, of anything! The system of bringing up women needs a radical change. I myself have given much thought to the matter, and come to the conclusion that our women are ill-educated.'

'Yes; the only thing to be done with them is to hold them in contempt,' agreed Sitnikov. To him any opportunity of despising, of expressing scornful sentiments, was the most agreeable of sensations. Yet, though he thus chose women for his especial censure, he little suspected that before many months were over he himself would be grovelling at the feet of a wife – and doing so merely for the reason that she had been born a Princess Durdoleosov!

'No, to none of them would our conversation convey anything,' he continued. 'Nor is there a single one of them upon whom the attention of a serious-minded man would be anything but thrown away.'

'Scarcely need they *desire* to have anything conveyed to them by our conversation,' remarked Bazarov.

'Of whom are you speaking?' interposed Evdoksia.

'Of the smart women of the day.'

'What? I suppose you agree with Proudhon's* opinion on the subject?' Bazarov drew himself up.

* Pierre Joseph Proudhon (1809–65), a French doctrinaire who taught that anarchy is the culmination of all social progress.

'I agree with no man's opinions,' he remarked. 'I have some of my own.'

'*A bas les autorités!*' cried Sitnikov, delighted at this unlooked-for opportunity of showing off in the presence of the man whom he worshipped.

'But even Macaulay – ' began Madame Kukshin.

'*A bas* Macaulay!' roared Sitnikov. 'How can you defend those dolls of ours?'

'I am not defending them at all,' said Madame Kukshin. 'I am merely standing up for the rights of women – rights which I have sworn to defend to the last drop of my blood.'

'*A bas* – ' began Sitnikov – then paused. 'I do not reject them,' he added in a lower tone.

'But you *do* reject them, for you are a Slavophil, as I can see very clearly.'

'On the contrary, I am *not* a Slavophil; although, of course, I – '

'But you *are* a Slavophil: you believe in the principles of the *Domostroi*,* and would like always to be holding over women a scourge.'

'A scourge is not a bad thing in its proper place,' observed Bazarov. 'But, seeing that we have reached the last drop of, of – '

'Of what?' said Evdoksia.

'Of champagne, most respected Avdotia Nikitishna – not of your blood.'

'Never when I hear my sex abused can I listen with indifference,' resumed Evdoksia. 'It is all too horrible, too horrible! Instead of attacking us, people ought to read Michel's† *De l'Amour*. What a wonderful work it is! Let us talk of love.'

She posed her arm gracefully upon the tumbled cushions of the sofa. There fell a sudden silence.

'What is there to say concerning love?' at length said Bazarov. 'In passing, you mentioned a certain Madame Odintsov (I think that was the name?). Who is she?'

'A very charming woman,' squeaked Sitnikov, 'as well as clever, rich, and a widow. Unfortunately, she is not sufficiently developed, and a closer acquaintance with our Evdoksia would do her a world of good. Evdoksia, I drink to your health! Let us sing the honours. "Et toc, et

---

* A curious old sixteenth-century work which, usually attributed to the monk Sylvester, purports to be a 'guide to household management,' and, incidentally, gives a terrible picture of the power of the Russian husband over his wife.
† Louise Michel (1830–1906), a French anarchist long resident in London.

toc, et tin, tin, tin! Et toc, et toc, et tin, tin, tin!" '

'You scamp, Victor!'

The luncheon proved a lengthy affair, for to the first bottle of champagne there succeeded a second, and to the latter a third, and to that a fourth. Meanwhile Evdoksia kept up an unceasing flow of chatter, and received effective assistance from Sitnikov. In particular did the pair discuss the nature of marriage ('the outcome of prejudice and vice'), the question whether people are born 'single,' and the consistency of 'individuality.' Then Evdoksia seated herself at the piano, and, red in the face with wine which she had drunk, clattered her flat finger-nails upon the keys, and essayed hoarsely to sing, first of all some gypsy ditties, and then the ballad, 'Dreaming Granada lies asleep'; while, throwing a scarf over his head to represent the dying lover, Sitnikov joined her at the words 'Your lips meet mine in a burning kiss.'

At length Arkady could stand it no longer.

'Gentlemen,' he exclaimed, 'this is sheer Bedlam!'

As for Bazarov, he yawned, for he had done little more than interject a satirical word or two – his attention had been devoted, rather, to the champagne. At length he rose, and, accompanied by Arkady, left the house without so much as a word of farewell to the hostess. Sitnikov pursued the pair.

'Ah, ha!' he exclaimed as he skipped about the roadway. 'Did I not tell you that she would prove a most remarkable personality? Would that more of our women were like her! In her way, she is a moral phenomenon.'

'And your father's establishment?' remarked Bazarov as he pointed to a tavern which they happened to be passing. 'Is that also a moral phenomenon?'

Sitnikov vented another of his shrill giggles. But, being also ashamed of his origin, he felt at a loss whether to plume himself upon, or to take offence at, Bazarov's unexpected pleasantry.

Chapter 14

A FEW DAYS LATER, the ball was held at the Governor's, and Matvei Ilyitch figured thereat as the guest of honour. For his part, the President of the Provincial Council (who was at loggerheads with the Governor) explained at large that only out of respect for Matvei had he deigned to be present, while the Governor continued, even when stationary, his usual process of orders-giving. With Matvei's suavity of demeanour nothing could be compared save his pomposity. Upon every man he smiled – upon some with a hint of superciliousness, upon others with a shade of deference; whilst to the ladies he bowed and scraped *en vrai chevalier français*, and laughed, throughout, the great, resonant, conspicuous laugh which a bigwig ought to do. Again, he clapped Arkady upon the back, addressed him loudly as 'young nephew,' and honoured Bazarov (who had been with difficulty coaxed into an ancient tail-coat) both with a distant, yet faintly condescending, glance which skimmed that individual's cheek, and with a vague, but affable, murmur in which there could be distinguished only the fragments 'I,' 'Yes,' and ' 'xtremely.' Lastly, he accorded Sitnikov a finger and a smile (in the very act, turning his head away), and bestowed upon Madame Kukshin (who had appeared minus a crinoline and in dirty gloves, but with a bird of paradise stuck in her hair) an '*Enchanté!*' The throng present was immense; nor was a sufficiency of cavaliers lacking. True, most of the civilian element crowded against the walls but the military section danced with enthusiasm, especially an officer who, being fresh from six weeks in Paris, where he had become acquainted with daring cries of the type of 'Zut!' 'Ah, fichtrrre!' 'Pst, pst, mon bibi!' and so forth, pronounced these quips to perfection, with true Parisian chic; while also he said '*Si j'aurais*' for '*Si j'avais*,' and '*absolument*' in the sense of 'certainly.' In short, he employed that Franco-Russian jargon which affords the French such intense amusement whenever they do not think it more prudent to assure their Russian friends that the latter speak the tongue of France *comme des anges*.

As we know, Arkady was a poor dancer, and Bazarov did not dance at all; wherefore the pair sought a corner, and were there joined by Sitnikov. Summoning to his visage his accustomed smile of contempt, and emitting remarks mordantly sarcastic in their nature, the great Sitnikov glanced haughtily about him, and appeared to derive some genuine pleasure from thus striking an attitude. But suddenly his face underwent a change. Turning to Arkady, he said in a self-conscious way: 'Here is Madame Odintsov just entering.'

Looking up, Arkady beheld, halted in the doorway, a tall woman in a black gown. In particular was he struck with the dignity of her carriage, and with the manner in which her bare arms hung beside her upright figure. From her gleaming hair to her sloping shoulders trailed sprays of fuchsia flowers, while quietly, intelligently – I say quietly, not dreamily – there gazed, with a barely perceptible smile, from under a white and slightly prominent forehead a pair of brilliant eyes. In general, the countenance suggested latent, but gentle, kindly force.

'Do you know her?' Arkady enquired.

'I do – intimately,' replied Sitnikov. 'Shall I introduce you?'

'If you please; but only when this quadrille has come to an end.'

Bazarov's attention also had been caught by this Madame Odintsov.

'What a face!' he exclaimed. 'No other woman in the room has one anything like it.'

As soon, therefore, as the quadrille was over, Sitnikov conducted Arkady to Madame Odintsov; and though at first – whether through the excessive 'intimacy' of Sitnikov's acquaintance, or whether through the fact that he happened to stumble over his words – she gazed at him with a shade of astonishment, she no sooner heard Arkady's family name than her face brightened, and she enquired whether he was the son of Nikolai Petrovitch.

'I am,' replied Arkady.

'Then I have twice had the pleasure of meeting your father. Also, I have heard much about him, and shall be most glad to know you.'

At this point an aide-de-camp sidled up, and requested the honour of a quadrille: which request she granted.

'Then you dance?' exclaimed Arkady, but with great deference.

'I do. What made you think that I do not? Is it that I look too old?'

'Oh no, pardon me! By no means! Then perhaps I too might ask for a mazurka?'

Smiling indulgently, she replied, 'If you wish,' and then looked at him not so much in a 'superior' manner as in that of a married sister who is regarding a very, very young brother. Though she was not greatly older than Arkady (she had just attained her twenty-ninth year), her presence made him feel the veriest schoolboy, and caused the difference of years to seem infinitely greater than it was. Next, Matvei Ilyitch approached her with a majestic air and a few obsequious words; whereupon Arkady moved away a little, while continuing to observe her. In fact, not until the quadrille was over did he find himself able to withdraw his eyes from her bewitching person. Throughout, her conversation with her partner and the guest of honour was accompanied with small movements of the head and eyes, and twice she uttered a low laugh. True, her nose erred a little on the side of thickness (as do those of most Russian women), nor was the colour of her skin unimpeachable; yet Arkady came to the conclusion that never in his life had he encountered a woman so charming of personality. Continuously the sound of her voice murmured in his ears, and the very folds of her dress looked different from those of other women – they seemed to hang straighter and more symmetrically, and her every movement was smooth and natural.

Nevertheless, when the strains of the mazurka struck up, and, reseating himself beside his partner, he prepared to enter into conversation with her, he felt a distinct touch of diffidence. Nor, though he kept passing his hand over his hair, could he find a word to say. However, this timidity, this state of agitation, did not last long, for soon her calmness infected him, and within a quarter of an hour he was talking to her of his father, his uncle, and life in St Petersburg and the country. For her part, she listened with kindly interest, while gently opening and closing her fan. Thus only at moments when other cavaliers came to ask her for dances (Sitnikov did this twice) did Arkady's chatter become interrupted; and whenever she returned to her place, to reseat herself with her bosom heaving not a whit more rapidly than it had done before, he would plunge into renewed conversation, so delighted was he at the fact that he had found someone to sympathise with him, to whom he could talk, at whose beautiful eyes and forehead and gentle, refined, intellectual features he could gaze at leisure. She herself said little, but her every word showed a knowledge of life which pointed to the fact that already this young woman had thought and felt much.

'Who was the man with you before Sitnikov brought you to me?' she enquired.

'So you noticed my friend?' exclaimed Arkady. 'Has he not a splendid face? His name is Bazarov.'

And, once launched upon the subject, Arkady descanted so fully, and with such enthusiasm, that Madame Odintsov turned to observe his friend more closely. But soon the mazurka began to draw to a close, and Arkady found himself regretting the prospect of losing the companion with whom he had spent such a pleasant hour. True, he had felt, throughout, that he was being treated with condescension, and ought to be grateful; but upon young hearts such an obligation does not press with any great weight.

The music stopped with a jerk.

'*Merci!*' said Madame Odintsov – then rose. 'You have promised to come and see me. Also, bring with you your friend, for I am filled with curiosity to behold a man who has the temerity to believe in nothing.'

Next, the Governor approached Madame with a distraught air and an intimation that supper was ready; whereupon she took his proffered arm, and, as she departed, turned with a last smile and nod to Arkady, who, in answer, bowed and stood following her with his eyes. How straight her figure looked under the sheen of her black gown!

'Already she will have forgotten my existence,' he thought to himself, while an exquisite humility pervaded his soul. Then he rejoined Bazarov in their joint corner.

'Well?' his friend said 'Have you enjoyed yourself? Some man or other has just been telling me that the lady in question is – But in all probability the man was a fool. What do *you* think of her?'

'The allusion escapes me,' replied Arkady.

'Come, come, young innocence!'

'Or at all events your informant's meaning escapes me. Madame is nice, but as cold and formal as – '

'As a stagnant pool,' concluded Bazarov. 'Yes, we all know the sort of thing. You say that she is cold, but that is purely a matter of taste. Perhaps you yourself like ice?'

'Perhaps I do,' the other muttered. 'But of such things I am no judge; and in any case she wishes to make your acquaintance as well as mine, and has asked me to bring you with me to call.'

'The description of me which you gave is easily imagined! On the other hand, you did rightly to offer her us both, for no matter who she may be – whether a provincial lioness or only an "*émancipée*" like the Kukshin woman, she has at least such a pair of shoulders as I have not seen this many a day.'

Arkady recoiled from this cynicism, yet, as often happens in such cases, started to reproach his friend for something wholly unconnected with the utterance which had given umbrage.

'Why do you refuse women freedom of thought?' he asked under his breath.

'For the reason, dear sir, that, according to my observation of life, no woman, unless she be a freak, thinks with freedom.'

And here the conversation terminated, for supper had come to an end, and the friends departed. As they left the room Madame Kukshin followed them with a nervous and wrathful, yet slightly apprehensive, smile in her eyes. The reason of this was that she felt wounded in her conceit at the fact that neither of the young men had taken any notice of her. Nethertheless, she remained at the ball until most of the rest of the company had left; whereafter, it being four o'clock in the morning, she danced a polka-mazurka, *à la Parisienne*, with Sitnikov, and with this edifying spectacle brought the Governor's fête to a close.

Chapter 15

'Now LET US SEE to what category of mortals to assign this young person,' said Bazarov to Arkady as, on the following day, the pair mounted the staircase of the hotel where Madame Odintsov was staying. 'Somehow I seem to scent impropriety in the air.'

'You surprise me!' burst forth Arkady. 'Do *you*, Bazarov, do *you* hold with the narrow-minded morality which – '

'Idiot!' exclaimed Bazarov contemptuously. 'Do you not know that both in our jargon and in the understanding of the ordinary person the term "improper" has now come to mean the same as "proper"? In any case I seem to scent money here. You yourself told me, did you not, that Madame's marriage was a very strange one? – though, for my part, I look upon marrying a rich old man as anything but a strange proceeding – rather, as a measure of prudence. True, I place little reliance upon the gossip of townsfolk, but at least I prefer to suppose that that gossip has, as our cultured Governor would say, "a basis in fact." '

Arkady did not respond, but knocked at the door of Madame's suite; and, the door having been opened, a liveried manservant ushered the visitors into a large hideously furnished room of the type which is always to be found in Russian hotels – the only exception in the present case being that the apartment was adorned with flowers. Presently Madame herself entered, clad in a plain morning gown, and looking even younger in the spring sunlight than she had done in the ballroom. Arkady duly presented Bazarov, and, as he did so, remarked with surprise that his friend seemed confused, while Madame was as imperturbable as ever. This *gaucherie* on his part Bazarov realised, and felt vexed at.

'Phaugh!' he thought to himself. 'The idea that I should be afraid of a woman!'

Yet, like Sitnikov, he could only subside into a chair, and fall to talking with an exaggerated emphasis to the woman who sat with her brilliant eyes riveted with such attention upon him.

Anna Sergievna Odintsov had had for father one Sergei Nikolaievitch Loktev, a well-known gambler, speculator, and beau. After fifteen years of flaunting it in St Petersburg and Moscow, and dissipating his whole substance, he had been forced to retire to the country, where soon afterwards he had died and left to his daughter Anna (aged twenty) and his daughter Katerina (aged twelve) only a small joint competence. As for the girls' mother (who had come of the impoverished house of the Princes X.), she had expired during the heyday of her husband's career in St Petersburg. Anna's position after her father's death was therefore a very difficult one, for the brilliant education which she had received in the capital had in no way fitted her for the care of a household and an estate, nor yet for the endurance of a life in the country. Moreover, she possessed not a single acquaintance in that country neighbourhood, nor anyone to whom to turn for advice, since her father had done his best to avoid associating with his neighbours, in that he had despised them as much as they, in their several ways, had despised him. Howbeit, Anna kept her head, and straightway sent for her mother's sister, the Princess Avdotia Stepanovna X., who, a malicious, presuming old woman, annexed, on the day of her arrival, all the best rooms in the house, raged and stormed from morning till night, and even declined to walk in the garden unless she could be accompanied by her only serf, a sullen-looking lacquey who wore a faded green livery, a blue collar, and a three-cornered hat. Nevertheless Anna put up with these tantrums of her aunt's, superintended the education of her sister, and resigned herself to the idea of living in seclusion for the rest of her life. But fate had ordained otherwise. That is to say, a certain Odintsov – a rich, bloated, unwieldy, soured, semi-imbecile hypochondriac of forty-six who was, nevertheless, neither stupid nor cruel – happened to see her, and became so enamoured that he offered her marriage: and to this proposal she consented. For six years the pair lived together, before the husband died, leaving her all his property. The following year she spent in the country; after which she went abroad with her sister – but only as far as Germany, since she quickly wearied of foreign parts, and was only too thankful to return to her beloved Nikolsköe, which lay some forty versts from the provincial town of – . At Nikolsköe she had at her disposal a splendid, tastefully furnished mansion, a beautiful garden, and a range of orangeries (the late Odintsov having denied himself in nothing); but inasmuch as she made but rare appearances in the town, and then only on flying visits connected with business, the provincial gentry conceived a grudge against her, and took to gossiping of her marriage with Odintsov, and relating such impossible tales as that she had assisted her father in his nefarious schemes, that she had had her reasons for going abroad, and that certain unfortunate results of that tour had had to be concealed. 'I tell you,' the ardent retailer of such fables would say, 'that she has been through the mill right enough.' Eventually these rumours reached her ears, but she ignored them altogether, since her nature was at once bold and independent.

Seating herself at full length in an armchair, and crossing one hand over the other, she set herself to listen to Bazarov's harangue. Contrary to his usual custom, he spoke without restraint, for he was clearly anxious to interest his listener. Arkady again felt surprised at this, though he failed to detect whether or not Bazarov was succeeding in his aim, seeing that Anna Sergievna's face gave no clue to the effect produced, so fixedly did her features retain their faintly polite expression, so unvaryingly did her beautiful eyes reflect unruffled attention. True, at first Bazarov's vehemence gave her an unpleasant impression as of a bad smell or a jarring note; but in time she began to understand that it came of his being ill at ease, and she felt flattered at the fact. Only the paltry repelled her; and no one could well have accused Bazarov of that quality. Indeed wonders were never to cease for Arkady, since, though he had expected Bazarov to talk to Madame Odintsov as to a woman of intellect – to speak to her of his views and convictions (seeing that she had expressed a desire to behold a man who had 'the temerity to believe in nothing'), he discoursed only on medicine, homœopathy, and botany. At the same time, Madame had not wasted her life of solitude, but had read a large number of standard works, and could express herself in the best of Russian; and though at one point she diverted the conversation to music, she no sooner perceived that he declined to recognise the existence of the art than she returned to botany, even though Arkady would gladly have continued the discussion of the importance of national melodies. In passing, her treatment of Arkady as a younger brother remained the same. What she valued in him was, evidently, the good humour and simplicity of youth – nothing more. Thus there was held, for three hours, an animated, but intermittent, discursive conversation.

At length the friends rose to say farewell. With a kindly glance Anna Sergievna offered them her beautiful white hand; then, after a moment's reflection, said irresolutely, but with a pleasant smile:

'If neither of you fear finding the time tedious, will you come and pay me a visit at Nikolsköe?'

'I should deem it the greatest pleasure!' cried Arkady.

'And you, Monsieur Bazarov?'

Bazarov merely bowed: which again surprised Arkady while also he noticed that his friend's face looked flushed.

'Well?' the younger man said as the pair issued into the street. 'Are you still of the opinion that she is, is – ?'

'I cannot say. But what an icicle she has made of herself!' There was a pause. 'At all events, she is an imposing personage, a *grande dame* who lacks but a train to her gown and a coronet to her head.'

'But none of our *grandes dames* speak Russian as she does,' remarked Arkady.

'No; for she has undergone a rebirth, and eaten of our bread.'

'And what a charm is hers!'

'You mean, what a splendid body – the very thing for a dissecting theatre!'

'Stop, stop, for God's sake! Her body differs from all other women's.'

'No need to lose your temper, young innocent. Have I not said that she stands in the front rank of women? Yes, we must pay her that visit.'

'When?'

'The day after tomorrow. Nothing else is to be done here, for we need not stay to drink champagne with the Kukshin woman, and listen to the harangues of your kinsman, the Liberal bigwig. Not we! The day after tomorrow, therefore, let us give the whole thing the go-by. *Apropos*, my father's place lies near Nikolsköe. For Nikolsköe is on the — road, is it not?'

'It is.'

'*Optime*! Then we shall gain nothing by delay: only fools and clever people procrastinate. Her anatomy, I repeat, is splendid.'

Within three days, in bright, but not too warm, weather, the two friends were bowling along the road to Nikolsköe. With a will did the well-fed stage horses trot out, and lightly swish their flanks with their plaited, knotted tails; and as Arkady glanced along the road, he, for some unknown reason, smiled.

'Congratulate me!' cried Bazarov of a sudden. 'Today is the 22nd of June – the feast of my Patron Saint. Certainly he looks after me, does he not?' Then the speaker added in a lower tone: 'But today, also, they are expecting me at home . . . Well, let them expect me.'

Chapter 16

THE MANOR-HOUSE in which Anna Sergievna resided stood on an open hillock, and close to a yellow stone church with a green roof, white columns, and an entrance surmounted by a fresco representative of Our Lord's Resurrection – the latter executed in the 'Italian' style, and having as its most noticeable feature the figure of a swarthy warrior whose rounded contours filled the entire foreground. Behind the church, the village extended into two long wings, and had thatched roofs surmounted by a medley of chimneys; while the manor-house itself was built in a style homogeneous with the design of the church – that is to say, in the style commonly known as 'Alexandrine,' and embracing yellow-painted walls, a green roof, white columns, and a front adorned with a coat-of-arms. In fact, both buildings had been erected by a provincial architect to the order of the late Odintsov, a man impatient (so he himself always expressed it) of 'vain and arbitrary innovations.' Lastly, to right and left of the house there showed the trees of an antique garden, while an avenue of clipped firs led the way to the principal entrance.

The friends having been met in the hall by two strapping lacqueys in livery, one of the latter immediately ran for the butler; who (a stout man in a black tail-coat) proceeded to usher the guests up a carpeted staircase, and into a room which contained a couple of beds and the usual appurtenances of the toilet. Evidently neatness was the order of the day in the establishment, for everything was both spotlessly clean and as fragrant as the chamber wherein a Minister of State holds his receptions.

'Anna Sergievna will be glad to see you in half an hour,' the butler said. 'Meanwhile, have you any orders for me?'

'No, worthy one,' replied Bazarov. 'Except that you might so far condescend as to bring me a small glassful of vodka.'

'It shall be done, sir,' said the butler with a shade of hesitation; whereafter he departed with creaking boots.

'What grandeur!' commented Bazarov. 'In your opinion, how ought our hostess to be addressed? In the style of a duchess?'

'Yes, and of a very great duchess,' replied Arkady. 'The more so, seeing that she has invited such influential aristocrats as ourselves to visit her.'

'I presume that you are referring to your humble servant – a future doctor, the son of a doctor, and the grandson of a sexton? By the way,

are you aware that my grandparent was a sexton, even as was
Speransky's?* A smile curled his lips. 'Thus you see that the lady is
mistaken, woefully mistaken. We haven't such a thing as a tail-coat,
have we?'

Arkady shrugged his shoulders bravely; but he too was feeling a little
awe-stricken.

At the close of the half-hour the pair entered the drawing-room,
which they found to be a large, lofty apartment of rich, but tasteless,
appointments. Against the walls, in the usual affected style, stood
heavy, expensive furniture, the walls themselves were hung with brown
curtains to which were florid gilt borders (all these things the late
Odintsov had ordered through a Muscovite friend who kept a wineshop),
and above a divan in the centre of the room hung a portrait of a
wrinkled, sandy-haired individual who seemed to be regarding the
newcomers with extreme distaste.

'*He*,' whispered Bazarov.

The hostess herself then entered. She was clad in a light dress, and
had her hair dressed behind the ears – a style which communicated to
her pure, fresh countenance an air of almost girlish juvenility.

'Thank you for having kept your promise,' she said. 'And now that
you are come, I think that you will find the time not altogether dull.
For one thing, I intend to introduce you to my sister, who is a skilful
piano-player (of course, Monsieur Bazarov, to you such things are a
matter of indifference, but you, Monsieur Kirsanov, I know, adore the
art of music). Also, an elderly aunt lives with me as my companion, and
at intervals a neighbour looks in for a game of cards. You see our home
circle. Now let us seat ourselves.'

Madame delivered this little speech with the precision of a lesson
which she had learnt by heart, and then turned to converse with
Arkady. On finding that her mother had known his, and that the latter
had made the former her confidant during her love affair with Nikolai
Petrovitch, the lad fell to speaking enthusiastically of his dead parent,
while Bazarov applied himself to the inspection of some albums.

'What a domesticated individual I am!' thought he to himself.

Presently, with much pattering of paws, there burst into the room a
splendid Russian greyhound with a blue collar; and it was followed by a
young girl of eighteen with a dark complexion, dark hair, a round, but
pleasant, face, and small, dark eyes. She was carrying a basket of
flowers.

* A 'Westernist' statesman (1772–1839), who propounded various schemes of
reform in connection with the Russian peasantry.

'My sister Katia,' said Madame Odintsov, indicating the girl with her head.

Katia seated herself beside Madame, and fell to arranging her flowers; while the greyhound (whose name was Fifi) approached each of the guests in turn, laid his cold nose in their hands, and wagged his tail.

'Have you gathered those flowers yourself?' asked Madame Odintsov.

'Yes, Anna Sergievna,' the girl replied.

'And is your aunt going to join us at tea?'

'Yes.'

These replies of Katia's were accompanied with a frank, but gentle and bashful, smile, and an upward glance half grave, half sportive. Everything in her betokened youth and freshness – her voice, the down on her cheeks, her little pink hands with their white, dimpled palms, and the slightly contracted shoulders. Also, she blushed without ceasing, and drew her breath with a fluttering respiration.

Presently Madame Odintsov turned to Bazarov.

'Surely it is only out of politeness that you are looking at those photographs?' she said. 'They cannot possibly interest you. Pray move nearer to us, and let us engage in an argument.'

Bazarov approached her.

'What shall we argue about?' he enquired.

'About anything you like. But first let me warn you that I am a redoubtable opponent.'

'You?'

'Yes, certainly. You look surprised? Why so?'

'Because, so far as I can tell, your temperament is one of the cold and lethargic order, whereas argument needs impulsiveness.'

'How have you contrived so quickly to appraise me? To begin with, I am both impatient and exacting. Ask Katia if I am not. Also, I am easily moved to impulse.'

Bazarov darted a glance at her.

'Possibly,' he said. 'Certainly you ought to know best. But, since you desire to argue, let us argue. While looking at those views of Saxon Switzerland, I heard you remark that they could not interest me. This you said, I presume, because you suppose me to be lacking in the artistic sense. Well, I am so. But might not those pictures be interesting to me solely from the geological point of view – from the standpoint of an observer, say, of the formation of mountains?'

'Pardon me, but, as a geologist, you would prefer to resort to some special work on that science, not to a few pictures.'

'Oh, not necessarily. For a picture may instantly present what a book could set forth only in a hundred pages.'

Anna Sergievna made no reply.

'Well,' she resumed, leaning forward upon the table – a movement which brought her face closer to Bazarov's, 'since you possess not a grain of the artistic instinct, how do you contrive to get on without it?'

'Rather, I would ask you: What is the artistic instinct able to effect?'

'It is able at least to help one to examine and to instruct one's fellow man.'

Bazarov smiled.

'In the first place,' he retorted, 'the prime requisite in that connection is experience of life; and, in the second place, the study of detached personalities is scarcely worth the trouble. For all we human beings are alike, in body as in spirit. In each of us there is an identical brain, an identical spleen, an identical heart, an identical pair of lungs, an identical stock of the so-called moral qualities (trifling variations between which we need not take into account). Therefore from a single specimen of the human race may all the rest be judged. In fact, human beings are like trees in a forest. You never find a botanist studying its individual trunks.'

Katia, who had been arranging her flowers, glanced at Bazarov in amazement, and, in so doing, encountered his keen, contemptuous gaze, and blushed to her ears. Anna Sergievna shook her head.

'Trees in a forest!' she exclaimed. 'Think you, then, that there is no difference between the wise man and the fool, the good and the bad?'

'No, I do not,' replied Bazarov. 'On the contrary, I believe that such differences do exist. The point is that they exist only as between the sound and the ailing. For instance, a consumptive's lungs are not as yours and mine; yet they have been fashioned precisely as our own have been. Also, whereas, to a certain extent, we know whence bodily disorders arise, *moral* disorders come of faulty education, the thousand and one follies with which the human brain is afflicted, in short, any irregular condition of the social body. Rectify that body, and moral sickness will soon cease to be.'

Speaking as though he were saying to himself, 'Believe me or not as you like, it is all one to me,' Bazarov drew his long fingers through his whiskers, while his eyes glowed like coals.

'Then you think,' pursued Anna Sergievna 'that, once the social body has been rectified, stupid and evil people will cease to exist?'

'At all events, once the social body is properly organised, the fact that a man be wise or stupid, good or bad, will cease to be of importance.'

'Ah! I understand! That is because we all possess an identical spleen?'

'Precisely so, madam.'

She turned to Arkady.

'And what is your opinion, Arkady Nikolaievitch?' she enquired.

'I agree with Evgenii,' was his reply as, in his turn, he received a glance of astonishment from Katia.

'I am surprised, gentlemen,' said Madame. 'However, I can hear my aunt approaching, so let us spare her ears, and discuss this later.'

Anna Sergievna's aunt – a small, spare woman with a mallet-shaped face, a pair of narrow, malicious eyes, and a grey false front – bestowed scarcely so much as a bow upon the guests, but at once relapsed into a huge velvet armchair which no one but herself was allowed to use. And even when Katia hastened to place for her a footstool, the old woman did not thank her, nor even look at her, but chafed her hands under the yellow shawl which covered the whole of her frail figure. Beyond all things was she fond of yellow; wherefore she had had her cap trimmed with ribands of the same hue.

'Have you slept well, Auntie?' Madame Odirtsov enquired with a raising of her voice.

'That dog is here again!' the old woman muttered on noticing that Fifi was taking an irresolute step or two in her direction. 'Turn the beast out, I say! Out with it!'

Calling Fifi, Katia opened the door for the animal to leave the room; whereupon, though it bounded out in joyous mood (under the impression that it was about to be taken for a walk), it no sooner found itself marooned outside than it fell to whining and scratching at the panels; which caused the Princess to frown, and necessitated Katia's exit to rectify matters.

'Tea is ready, I believe,' Madame Odintsov continued. 'Gentlemen, pray come. Will you have some tea, Auntie?'

The Princess rose from her chair in silence, and headed a procession to the dining-room, where a Cossack footman pulled a padded armchair from under the table (like the last, it was reserved for the Princess alone), and she subsided into its depths. Katia poured out tea, and handed her aunt the first cup – a cup adorned with a coat-of-arms; whereafter the old woman added some honey to the beverage (she looked upon tea-drinking with sugar as a sin of extravagance, and the more so since never at any time would she consent to spend an unnecessary kopeck), and then asked hoarsely:

'What has Prince Ivan to say in his letter?'

No one answered, and in time Bazarov and Arkady apprised the fact that, though treated, certainly, with respect, the old woman attracted no one's serious attention.

'They keep her here for show,' Bazarov reflected. 'She is kept because she comes of a princely house.'

Tea over, Anna Sergievna proposed a walk; but since at that moment a drop of rain came pattering down, the company (with the exception of the Princess) returned to the drawing-room. Presently the neighbour addicted to a game of cards came in, and proved to be one Porphyri Platonitch – a stout, grey-headed, affable, diverting individual who, in addition, could boast of a pair of legs as shapely as though turned with a lathe. Anna Sergievna then enquired of Bazarov (with whom she had again been in conversation) whether he would care to join them in the old-fashioned game of 'Preferences'; and he consented on the ground that he could not too soon prepare himself for the post of a district physician.

'But take care,' remarked his hostess. 'Porphyri Platonitch and I are not unlikely to beat you. Meanwhile, do you, Katia, go and play something on the piano for the benefit of Arkady Nikolaievitch. I know that he loves music, and we too shall be glad to listen to you.'

Reluctantly Katia approached the piano; nor, in spite of Arkady's fondness for music, did he follow her any more eagerly.

The truth of it was that he felt himself to be being 'got rid of' by Madame Odintsov, and already there was simmering in his heart, as in the heart of any young man of his age, that vague, oppressive feeling which is the harbinger of love.

Raising the lid of the piano, Katia murmured under her breath, and without looking at Arkady:

'What shall I play?'

'Anything you wish,' he replied with indifference.

'But what sort of music do you *prefer*?' she persisted with unchanged attitude.

'Classical music,' was the reply delivered with equal nonchalance.

'Mozart?'

'Certainly – Mozart.'

So Katia produced the Viennese master's Sonata-Fantasia in C minor. She played it well, but coldly, and not with any excess of precision. Likewise, she kept her lips compressed, her eyes upon the keys, and her form erect and motionless. Only towards the close of the piece did her face kindle at all, while at the same moment a tiny curl detached itself from her loosely-bound hair, and fell over her dusky forehead.

Arkady also felt moved by the closing portion of the Sonata – the portion where the charming, careless gaiety of the melody gives place to sudden bursts of mournful, almost tragic lamentation. Yet the

thoughts which Mozart's strains aroused in him bore no relation to
Katia. He merely looked at her now and then, and reflected:

'She plays well; nor is she bad-looking.'

The Sonata over, Katia enquired, without removing her hands from
the keyboard: 'Is that enough?' and Arkady replied that he would not
think of troubling her further. Then he went on to talk of Mozart, and
to ask her whether she herself had selected the Sonata, or whether it
had been selected for her by someone. Katia answered in monosyllables,
and from time to time went into hiding, retired into herself; and on
each occasion of this sort she made her reappearance but reluctantly,
and with a face composed to a stubborn, almost a stupid, air. Yet she
was not timid so much as diffident and a trifle overawed by the
presence of the sister who had brought her up (not that the sister in
question ever suspected it). Finally, she returned to her flowers, and
Arkady found himself reduced to calling Fifi to his side, and stroking
the dog's head with a kindly smile.

As for Bazarov, he had to pay forfeit after forfeit, for Anna Sergievna
was fairly clever at cards, and Porphyri Platonitch was a player fully
able to look after himself. Consequently the young doctor rose a loser,
not by a considerable sum, but by one which, at all events, was
sufficient to be scarcely agreeable. After supper Anna Sergievna started
a discussion on botany.

'I wish you would take me for a walk tomorrow morning,' she said. 'I
want you to teach me the Latin names of our field flowers, and also
their characteristics.'

'But how could the Latin names benefit you?' he enquired.

'System is in all things necessary,' she replied.

'A truly wonderful woman!' Arkady commented the same evening,
on finding himself alone with his friend in the bedroom.

'Yes,' replied Bazarov. 'She certainly possesses brains. Also, she has
dreamed dreams.'

'In what sense?'

'In the best sense, my friend – in the very best sense, O Arkady
Nikolaievitch. Certain also am I that she manages her property well.
But the marvellous phenomenon is not she, but her sister.'

'What? That hoyden?'

'Yes, that hoyden. The hoyden contains an element of freshness and
virginity and timidity and reticence and anything else you like which
makes her really an object worthy of interest. Of the one you could
make whatsoever you might desire, whereas of the other there is
nothing to be said save that she represents a yesterday's loaf.'

Arkady made no reply, and soon the two men were asleep and

dreaming their own dreams.

The same night Anna Sergievna devoted much thought to her two guests. Bazarov she liked both for his total lack of affectation and for the piquancy of his criticisms; so that she seemed to divine in him something new, something which had hitherto remained unknown to her experience. All of which excited her curiosity.

And she too was a strange being. Free from all prejudice, and devoid of all strong beliefs, she rendered obeisance to nothing, and had in view no gaol. Again, though much was open to her sight, and much interested her, nothing really satisfied her, and she had no wish for such satisfaction, since her intellect was at once enquiring and indifferent, and harboured doubts which never merged into insensibility, and aspirations which never swelled into unrest. True, if she had been dowered with less wealth and independence, she might have plunged into the fray, and learnt the nature of passion; but, as things stood, she took life unhastingly, and, though often finding it tedious, spent her days in a deliberate, rarely agitated manner. True, at times rainbow colours gleamed even before her eyes; yet no sooner had they faded than she would draw her breath as before, and in no way regret their disappearance. Again, though, at times, her imagination exceeded the bounds of what is considered permissible by conventional morality, her blood still coursed tranquilly through her lethargic and bewitchingly shaped frame; and only when she was issuing in a warm and tender glow from her comfortable bathroom would she fall to pondering upon the futility of life, its sorrow and toil and cruelty, and feel her soul swell to sudden temerity, and begin to seethe with noble aspirations. Yet even then, let but a draught happen to blow in her direction from an open window, and at once she would shrug her shoulders, commiserate herself, come very near to losing her temper, and become conscious of nothing but the thought that the one thing necessary was to ensure that by hook or by crook that abominable draught should be averted.

Again, like all women who have never known what it is to fall in love, she was sensible of a persistent yearning for something wholly undefined. There was nothing that she actually lacked, yet she seemed to lack everything. The late Odintsov she had merely tolerated (the marriage having been one *de convenance* only – though she would never have consented to become his wife had he not also been kindly of heart), and from the experience she had derived a certain aversion to the male sex in general, which she conceived to be composed exclusively of creatures slovenly, idle, wearisome, and weakly exacting in their habits. In fact, only once had she met (it was somewhere abroad) a man who had in any way attracted her. He had been a young Swede of a knightly countenance, honest blue eyes, and an open brow; but, for all the impression that he had made upon her, the impression in question had not prevented her from shortly afterwards returning to Russia.

'A strange man, that Bazarov,' she thought to herself as she reposed in her magnificent bed with its lace-embroidered pillows and its light silken coverlet. It may be said, that, in addition to having inherited her late father's fastidious and luxurious tastes, she still cherished for that wayward, but kind-hearted, parent a considerable affection, since during his lifetime he had not only adored her and cracked jokes with her on equal terms, but also accorded her his whole confidence, and made it his invariable custom to seek her advice. Of her mother she had but the scantiest of remembrance.

'Yes, a strange man is that Bazarov,' she repeated; after which she stretched her limbs, smiled, clasped her hands behind her head, ran an eye over the pages of two foolish French novels, let fall the second of these volumes from her hands, and relapsed into slumber – a cold, spotless figure in spotless, fragrant white.

When breakfast was over next morning, she set forth upon the botanising expedition with Bazarov; to return home just before luncheon time. Meanwhile Arkady did not leave the house, but spent an hour with Katia, nor found the time wearisome, seeing that of her own accord Katia volunteered to repeat the Sonata. Yet the instant that his eyes beheld Madame Odintsov returning his heart leapt within him. She was crossing the garden with a slightly tired step, but with her cheeks rosy of hue, her eyes shining under her round straw hat with even greater brilliancy than usual, and her fingers twirling between them the stalk of some field flower. Also, her light mantilla had slipped to her shoulders, and the broad ribands of her hat were floating over her bosom. Behind her walked Bazarov with his usual air of supercili-ousness and self-assurance, while on his face there was an expression cheerful, and even good-humoured. Yet somehow, Arkady did not like that expression.

Muttering 'Good-morning,' Bazarov passed towards his room, while Madame Odintsov accorded the young man a negligent handshake – then similarly continued her way.

' "Good-morning!" ' thought Arkady to himself. 'One would think that she and I had made one another's acquaintance only today!'

Chapter 17

As WE KNOW, time either flies like a bird or crawls like a snail. Thus a man is in best case when he fails to notice either the rapidity or the slowness of its flight. Similarly did Bazarov and Arkady spend their fortnight at Madame Odintsov's. Of this another contributory cause was the fact that alike in her household and in her daily life she maintained a *régime* to which she herself strictly adhered, and to which she constrained others to adhere; so that the daily domestic round accomplished itself according to a fixed programme. At eight o'clock the company would assemble for breakfast; whereafter, until luncheon time, individuals could do whatsoever they chose (the hostess herself devoting her attention to her steward – she administered her estate on the *obrok* or tithes system – her household servants, and her head housekeeper). Next, before dinner, the company would reassemble for conversation or for reading aloud; and the rest of the evening would be devoted to a walk, to cards, or to music. Lastly, at half-past ten Anna Sergievna would withdraw to her room, issue her orders for the following day, and retire to bed.

But to Bazarov this measured, slightly formal regularity was not wholly agreeable. 'Somehow it reminds one of running on a pair of rails,' he used to declare; while so much did the sight of liveried lacqueys and graded serfs offend his democratic instincts that once he averred that one might as well dine in the English fashion outright, and wear white ties and black tail-coats. These views he expressed to Anna Sergievna (something in her always led men to lay bare their opinions in her presence); and, after she had heard him out, she said:

'From your point of view, the matter is as you say, and perhaps I play the fine lady too much; but in the country one cannot live anyhow; such a course always leads one to grow slovenly.'

So she continued her *régime* as before. Yet, though Bazarov grumbled, he and Arkady found that to that very formality they owed the fact that everything in the establishment 'ran as on rails.' In passing it may be mentioned that between the two young men there had taken place a change which dated from the day of their arrival at Nikolsköe, and manifested itself, as regards Bazarov (for whom Anna Sergievna evidently entertained a liking, though seldom did she agree with his *dicta*), in the form of an unwonted captiousness which led him easily to lose his temper, to speak always with reluctance, to glare about him, and to be as unable to sit still as though mines had been exploding beneath his seat. As for Arkady (now come finally to the conclusion that he was in love with Madame Odintsov), the change manifested itself, rather, in his falling a prey to a melancholy which in no way prevented him from making friends with Katia, and even helped him to maintain with her kindly and cordial relations.

'Whereas Madame cares nothing for me,' he would reflect, '*this* good-hearted creature does not give me the cold shoulder.'

And these reflections would cause his heart to taste once more the sensuous joy of 'magnanimity.' Dimly Katia herself divined that her society afforded him a sort of comfort; wherefore she saw no reason to deny either him or herself the pleasure of this innocent, half-diffident, half-trustful *camaraderie*. True, in the presence, and under the keen eye, of the elder sister (who always caused Katia to retire precipitately into her shell) the pair never exchanged a single word (indeed, as a man in love, Arkady could not well have paid attention to anyone but the object of his adoration while in the latter's vicinity); but as soon as he found himself alone with Katia he began, to a certain degree, really to enjoy himself. That is to say, whereas he knew himself to be incompetent to interest Madame (seeing that whenever he found himself alone with her he blushed and lost his head, while she, on her side, did not know what to say to him, so jejune was his mind as compared with her own), in Katia's presence he felt perfectly at home, and could treat her with condescension, and let her expound to him the impressions which she derived from music and the reading of tales, poems, and other 'trifles.' Nor did he notice, nor would he have consented to recognise had he noticed, the fact that those same 'trifles' interested him as much as they did Katia. At the same time, the latter in no way acted as a clog upon his melancholy; wherefore, just as Madame was at her ease with Bazarov, so the young man was at his with Katia, and, after a short period of joint converse, the two couples would usually diverge. This happened especially during walks, and the more readily in that, whereas Katia adored nature, and Arkady too loved it (though he would never have admitted the fact), to Madame and Bazarov the charms of the natural world represented more or less a matter of indifference. Hardly need I add that from this constant separation between Arkady and Bazarov there flowed inevitable results which brought about in the relations of the pair a gradual change. That is to say, Bazarov ceased to discourse on Madame Odintsov – he ceased even to censure her for her 'aristocratic manners'; and while, with regard to Katia, he sang her praises as usual (at the same time advising the placing of a check upon her sentimental tendencies), he took to uttering these encomiums only in a half-hearted and a perfunctory way, and, in general, to lecturing his pupil less than he had formerly done. Rather, he seemed to avoid him, to feel in some way uncomfortable in his presence.

These things Arkady duly noted, but kept his observations to himself.

The real cause of the innovation was the feeling which Madame Odintsov inspired in Bazarov's breast, and which he found to be a torture and a madness to him. Yet, had anyone hinted to him, ever so distantly, that what was taking place in his soul could ever have been possible, he would have denied it with a contemptuous laugh and a cynical imprecation, seeing that, though a great devotee of feminine society and feminine beauty, he looked upon love in the ideal, the 'romantic' (to use his own term) aspect as unpardonable folly, and upon the sentiment of chivalry as a sort of aberration or malady which moved him frequently to express his astonishment that Toggenburg and his Minnesingers and troubadours never ended by being clapped in a madhouse.

'Should a woman please you,' he would say, 'strive to attain your goal; but if you cannot attain that goal, waste no further trouble – just turn away. For the world does not rest upon a single keystone.'

In similar fashion Madame Odintsov 'pleased' Bazarov: yet, though the widespread reports in circulation about her might, with the freedom and independence of her views and the undoubted penchant which she entertained for himself, have been reckoned to tell in his favour, he soon discovered that, in her case, the 'goal' was not to be attained. Also, he found to his surprise that he could not 'turn away' – rather, that the mere thought of her made his blood boil. True, that symptom, if it had been the only one, might have been dealt with; but there became implanted in him something else – something which he had hitherto refused to admit, something of which he had hitherto made sport, but something which now aroused his pride. Therefore, although, when conversing with Anna Sergievna, he poured added scorn upon everything 'romantic,' he recognised, during his hours of solitude, that even in his own personality there lurked an element of 'Romanticism.' And at such times there was nothing for it but to rush out of doors into the woods, and to stride along at a pace which snapped off chancemet boughs, and found vent in curses at both them and himself. Or he would seek a hayloft or stable, and, stubbornly closing his eyes, strive to woo sleep, and almost invariably fail. Yet, as he sat there, there would come to him delusions that those proud lips *had* once responded to his kisses, that those chaste arms *had* embraced his neck, that those soulful eyes *had* gazed tenderly – yes, tenderly – into his: and at such times his head would whirl, and for a second or two, and until his discontent returned, he would relapse into a state of trance, and, as though urged by a demon, think thoughts of unavowable import. Again, there were times when he would conceive a change similar to his own to have taken place in *her*, and the expression of her face already to be charged with a special significance. Yet, this point reached, he would end merely by stamping his feet, grinding his teeth, and mentally shaking his fist at himself.

Once, when walking with her in the garden, he announced to her in curt, gruff tones that he intended soon to depart for his father's place; whereupon Anna Sergievna turned pale, as though something had pricked her heart, and pricked it in such a manner as to surprise even herself, and to leave her wondering what it could portend. Yet not for the sake of testing her, nor of seeing what might possibly come of it, had he mentioned his purposed departure (never at any time did he indulge in 'scheming'). Rather, the reason was that, earlier that morning, he had had an interview with his father's steward, Timotheitch, a rough, but quick-witted, old fellow who, in past days, had acted as his nurse, and had now presented himself – with tousled, flaxen hair, red, weather-beaten face, watery, sunken eyes, short, stout jacket of grey-blue cloth, leathern girdle, and tarred boots – at Nikolsköe.

'Good-day to you, ancient!' had been Bazarov's greeting.

'Good-day to *you*, *batiushka*!' had responded the old man with a gleeful smile which had covered his face with wrinkles.

'And how is it that I see you here?' Bazarov had continued. 'Is it that they have sent you to fetch me?'

'By no means, pardon me, *batiushka*!' Timotheitch had stammered out this denial for the reason that he had suddenly recollected certain strict injunctions imposed upon him before starting. 'No, it is merely that I am on my way to the town on affairs connected with the estate, and turned aside a little to pay my respects to your honour. No, not to disturb you at all – oh dear no!'

'Do not lie,' Bazarov had said. 'Is *this* the way to the town?'

Timotheitch, cringing, had returned no reply.

'And how is my father?' Bazarov had continued.

'Quite well, thank God!'

'And my mother?'

'Your mother is the same, thank God!'

'And they are, I suppose, expecting me?'

The old man had cocked his head with a knowing air.

'Evgenii Vasilitch, why should they *not* be expecting you? Yes, as God is my trust, I know that their hearts are simply aching for a sight of you.'

'Well, well! Do not make too long a stay of it, but tell them that I will come presently.'

'I will, *batiushka*.'

Yet it had been with a sigh that Timotheitch had replaced his cap on his head with both hands, left the house, remounted the shabby *drozhki* which he had left waiting at the gates, and disappeared at a trot – though *not* in the direction of the town.

The same evening saw Madame sitting in her boudoir with Bazarov, and Arkady pacing the salon, and listening to Katia's music. As for the Princess, she had gone to bed, for she could not abide the presence of guests – least of all, of 'those upstarts and good-for-nothings' as she termed our friends. In fact, though she confined herself, in the drawing-room or the dining-room, to sulking, she resorted, when alone with her maid in the bedroom, to abuse of Arkady and Bazarov which made her cap and her false front fairly dance on her head. These things, of course, Madame Odintsov knew.

'Why need you depart?' she said to Bazarov. 'Have you forgotten your promise?'

Bazarov started.

'What promise?' he asked.

'Then you *have* forgotten it! I mean the promise to give me a few lessons in chemistry?'

'How can I fulfil it? My father is expecting me at home, and I ought not to stay a day longer. You had better read through *Notions Générales de Chimie*, by Pelouse and Frémy. It is an excellent work, and clearly written – the very thing you want.'

'But you said that no book can adequately replace – I forget the exact phrase you used, but you know what I mean, do you not?'

'I cannot help myself,' he muttered.

'Nevertheless, why go?' She lowered her voice as she spoke. Bazarov glanced at her as she leant back in her chair and crossed her arms (which were bare to the elbow), and saw that by the light of the lamp (softened with a shade of pleated paper) she was looking paler than usual – also that the outlines of her figure were almost buried in a soft white gown, from underneath which there peeped forth the tips of her toes, posed crosswise.

'What reason should I have for remaining?' he replied.

She gave her head the faintest toss.

'What reason should you have?' she re-echoed. 'Well, are you not happy here? Do you think that there will be no one to regret your departure?'

'There will be no one. Of that I am certain.'

'Then you are wrong,' came the reply after a pause. 'But I do not believe you – I have an idea that you are not speaking seriously.'

Bazarov said nothing.

'Why do you not answer me?' she persisted.

'What is there to say? In general, to regret people's absence is not worth while, and, least of all, the absence of people like myself.'

'Why, again?'

'Because I am a prosaic and eminently uninteresting individual. Nor do I know how to talk.'

'But you know how to play the esquire?'

'No, not even that. And, as you know, the softer aspect of life, the aspect which you hold so dear, lies altogether beyond me.'

Madame Odintsov nibbled the corner of her handkerchief.

'Think what you like,' she said, 'but at least *I* shall find things dull when you are gone.'

'Arkady will remain,' he hazarded.

She shrugged her shoulders.

'Nevertheless I shall find the time wearisome,' she repeated.

'Not for long.'

'Why not?'

'Because, as you have very truly said, things never seem dull to you save when your *régime* is infringed. In fact, with such faultless regularity have you ordered your life that there abides in it no room for dullness or depression or any other burdensome feeling.'

'And I too am faultless, I suppose – I have ordered my life too regularly ever to err?'

'I dare say. Take an example of it. In a few minutes it will be ten o'clock; when, as I know by experience, you will request me to leave your presence.'

'Oh no, I shall not. You may remain. By the way, please open that window. The room is simply stifling.'

Bazarov rose and unfastened the casement, which swung backwards with a snap, for the reason that he had not expected it to open so easily, and that his hands were trembling. Into the aperture glanced the soft, warm night with its vista of dark vault of heaven, faintly rustling trees, and pure, free, sweet-scented air.

'Also, please pull down the blind, and then resume your seat. I wish to have a little further talk with you before you go. Tell me something about yourself – a person to whom, by the way, you never refer.'

'I would rather converse with you on more profitable subjects.'

'What modesty! Nevertheless I wish to learn something of you, and of your family, and of the father for whose sake you are soon going to abandon me.'

'Why the word "abandon"?' reflected Bazarov. Then he added aloud: 'Things of that kind interest no one – least of all you. I and my people are obscure folk.'

'Whereas I, you imagine, am an aristocrat?'

Bazarov looked up.

'Yes,' he replied with emphasis.

She smiled.

'Then I can see that your knowledge of me is small,' she remarked. 'But of course – you believe all human beings to be identical, and therefore not worth the trouble of studying. Someday I will tell you my history. But first tell me yours.'

'You say that my knowledge of you is small?' queried Bazarov. 'You may be right. Possibly *every* human being is an enigma. Let us take an example of that. You have withdrawn from society, and find it irksome, and limit your visitors' list to a couple of students. Yet why, with your intellect and your beauty do you live in the country?'

'Why?' came the sharp rejoinder. 'But first be so good as to explain what you mean by my "beauty." '

Bazarov frowned.

'That lies beside the point,' he muttered. 'The point is that I cannot understand why you settle in a rural spot of this kind.'

'You cannot understand it, you cannot explain it?'

'No. There is only one possible explanation: and that is that you remain here because you are a person of self-indulgence who love comfort and the amenities of life and are indifferent to aught else.'

Again Madame Odintsov smiled.

'Then you are still determined to believe that I am incapable of being moved?' she said.

Bazarov glanced at her from under his brows.

'By curiosity, yes,' he said. 'But by nothing else.'

'Indeed? Then I cease to wonder that you and I do not get on together. You are exactly like myself.'

'That you and I do not get on together?' echoed Bazarov vaguely.

'Yes. But I had forgotten – you must be longing to retire?'

Bazarov rose. The lamp was casting a dim light, while into the fragrant, darkened, isolated room there came – wafted at intervals, under the swinging blind, the sensuous freshness of the night, and the sounds of its mysterious whisperings. Madame Odintsov did not stir. Over her was stealing the same strange agitation which had infected Bazarov. Suddenly he realised that he was alone with a young and beautiful woman.

'Need you go?' she asked slowly.

He made no reply – he merely resumed his seat.

'Then you think me a spoilt, pampered, indolent person?' she continued in the same slow tone as she fixed her eyes upon the window. 'Yet this much I know about myself: that I am very unhappy.'

'Unhappy? For what reason? Because you attach too much importance to petty slanders?'

She frowned. Somehow she felt vexed that he should have understood her thus.

'No; things of that kind do not disturb me,' she said. 'Never should I allow them to do so – I am too proud. The reason why I am unhappy is that I have no wish, no enthusiasm, to live. I dare say you will not believe me and will think that a mere "petty aristocrat," a person who is lapped in lace and seated in an armchair, is saying all this (and I will not conceal from you that I love what you call "the comforts of life"): yet all the while I feel as though I had no desire to continue my existence. Pray reconcile that contradiction if you can. But perhaps you consider what I say "Romanticism"?'

Bazarov shook his head.

'You are yet young,' he said. 'Also, you are rich and independent. What more could you have? What more do you desire?'

'What more?' she re-echoed with a sigh. 'I do not know. I only know that I feel tired, antiquated; I feel as though I had been living a long, long time. Yes, I am growing old,' she continued as she drew the ends of her mantilla around her bare shoulders. In doing so, she glanced at Bazarov. Her eyes met his, and the faintest of blushes stole into her face. 'Behind me lie many memories – memories of my life in St Petersburg, of a period of wealth followed by poverty, of my father's death, of my marriage, of my travels abroad – yes, many such memories there are. Yet none of them are worth cherishing. And before me lies only a weary road with no goal to it, along which I have no desire to travel.'

'You are disenchanted,' said Bazarov.

'No,' she replied with a shiver. 'Rather, I am dissatisfied. Oh that I could form a strong attachment of some kind!'

'To fall in love *might* save you,' remarked Bazarov. 'But you are incapable of that. That is where your misfortune lies.'

Madame dropped her eyes upon the sleeve of her mantilla.

'I am incapable of falling in love?' she murmured.

'Not altogether. Moreover, I did wrong to call it a misfortune: for the person most to be pitied is the person who meets with that experience.'

'What experience do you mean?'

'The experience of falling in love.'

'How come you to know that?'

'By hearsay,' he replied irritably, while to himself he added: 'You are a mere coquette whom sheer idleness is leading to weary and madden me.' And his heart swelled within him.

'On the other hand,' he went on, 'it may be that you are too exacting?'

As he spoke he bent forward and fell to playing with the tassels of his chair.

'Possibly I am,' she agreed. 'But, you see, I conceive that it ought to be everything or nothing. "A life for a life." "Take my all, give your all, and put a truce to regrets and any thought of return." That is the best rule.'

'Indeed?' queried Bazarov. 'Well, it is not a bad rule, and I am surprised that you should have failed to attain your desire.'

'Self-surrender, you think, is an easy thing?'

'Not if one considers matters first, and appraises oneself, and sets upon oneself a definite value. It is only surrender *without* consideration that is easy.'

'But how could one not value oneself? If one had value, no one would desire one's surrender.'

'That would not be your concern nor mine: someone else's business would it be to determine our respective values. The one thing that would immediately concern us would be to know *how* to surrender.'

Madame Odintsov sat up sharply.

'I still believe you to be speaking from experience,' she said.

'No; words, idle words – words not meant to be taken personally.'

'Then you yourself might be capable of surrendering?'

'I might. But in any case I should not care to boast.'

Both remained silent for a moment. From the drawing-room came the notes of the piano.

'How late Katia is playing!' remarked Anna Sergievna.

Bazarov raised his head.

'Yes, it *is* late,' he said. 'Time for you to go to rest.'

'Wait a moment, however. Why should you hurry away? I have

something more to say to you.'

'What may it be?'

'Wait,' she repeated. As she did so, her eyes gazed at him as though studying his personality. For a few moments he paced the room – then suddenly approached her, said 'Good-night,' squeezed her hand until she could have shrieked with the pain, and departed.

Raising her fingers to her lips, she blew after him a kiss. Then, rising with an abrupt, convulsive movement, she ran towards the door as though to call him back. But at that moment her maid entered with a decanter on a silver tray, and Madame halted, bid the maid begone, reseated herself, and sank into a reverie. Her hair, like a winding black snake, had broken loose from its fastenings. Dimly illumined by the lamp, she sat motionless, save that at intervals she chafed her hands, for the night air was beginning to grow chilly.

Two hours later Bazarov re-entered his bedroom in a state of dishevelment and despondency, and with his boots soaked with dew. Arkady was seated, fully dressed, at the writing-table, with a book in his hands.

'So you are not in bed yet?' Bazarov remarked irritably.

Arkady's only reply was to ask the counter-question:

'You have been sitting with Anna Sergievna, have you not?'

'I have,' replied Bazarov. 'I was sitting there while you and Katia were playing the piano.'

'Oh, *I* was not playing,' retorted Arkady. Then he stopped, for he felt the tears to be very near his eyes, and had no wish to let them fall in the presence of his satirical mentor.

Chapter 18

WHEN MADAME ODINTSOV entered the breakfast-room next morning, Bazarov had been sitting over his cup for a considerable time. He glanced sharply at her as she opened the door, and she turned in his direction as inevitably as though he had signed to her to do so. Somehow her face looked pale, and it was not long before she returned to her boudoir, whence she issued again only at luncheon time. Since dawn the weather had been too rainy to admit of outdoor expeditions, and therefore the party adjourned to the drawing-room, where Arkady began to read aloud the latest number of some journal, while the Princess manifested her usual surprise at his conduct (as though it had been conduct of an indecent nature!), and fixed upon him a gaze which, though one of lasting malignancy, proved also to be one of which he took not the slightest notice.

'Pray come to my boudoir, Evgenii Vasilitch,' said Anna Sergievna. 'I have something to ask you. I think that last night you mentioned some textbook or another?'

Rising, she moved towards the door, whilst the Princess stared around the room as much as to say: 'Dear, dear! This does surprise me!' Then she brought her eyes back to Arkady, who, raising his voice, and bending towards Katia (by whose side he was sitting), continued his reading as before.

Meanwhile Madame Odintsov walked hurriedly to her boudoir, and Bazarov followed with his eyes fixed upon the floor, and his ears open to no sound but the faint rustling of a silk dress. Arrived at her destination Madame seated herself in the chair which she had occupied overnight, and Bazarov also took a seat where he had sat on the occasion in question.

'What is the title of the book?' she asked after a brief pause.

'*Notions Générales*, by Pelouse and Frémy. I can also recommend Ganot's *Traité Elémentaire de Physique Expérimentale*, which is more detailed in its plates than the other work, and, in general, is – '

But Madame Odintsov held up her hand.

'Pardon me,' she interrupted. 'I have not brought you here to discuss textbooks. I have brought you here to renew our conversation of last night, at the point where you left the room so abruptly. I hope that I shall not weary you?'

'I am entirely at your service. What was it we were discussing?'

She glanced at him.

'Happiness, I think,' she said. 'In fact, I was speaking to you of myself. The reason why I mention happiness is the following. Why is it that when one is enjoying, say, a piece of music, or a beautiful summer evening, or a conversation with a sympathetic companion, the occasion seems rather a hint at an infinite felicity existent elsewhere than a real felicity actually being experienced? Perhaps, however, you have never encountered such a phenomenon?'

' "Where we are not, there do we wish to be," – you know the proverb. Last night you said that you are dissatisfied. Such a thought never enters into my head.'

'Is it that such thoughts seem to you ridiculous?'

'No – rather, that they never occur to me.'

'Indeed? Well, to know what your thoughts are is a thing which I greatly wish to attain.'

'I do not understand you.'

'Then listen. For a long time past I have been wishing to have this out with you. Do not tell me – you yourself know that it is useless to do so – that you are a man apart. As a matter of fact, you are a man still young, with all your life before you. I wish to know for what you are preparing, and what future awaits you, and what is the goal which you are seeking to reach, and whither you are travelling, and what you have in your mind – in short, who and what you are.'

'I am surprised! Already you know that I dabble in natural science; while, as regards my future – '

'Yes? As regards your future? – '

'I have told you that I purpose to become a district physician.'

Anna Sergievna waved her hand impatiently.

'Why tell me that, when you yourself do not believe it? It is for Arkady to return me such answers, not you.'

'And is Arkady in any way – ?'

'Wait. Do you mean to tell me that such a modest rôle will really satisfy you, when you yourself have asserted that the science of medicine does not exist? No, no! You have given me that answer for the reason that you desire to keep me at arm's length, that you have no faith in me. Then let me tell you that I *am* capable of understanding you, that I too have known poverty and ambition, that I too have had my experiences.'

'I dare say: yet pardon me when I intimate that I am not accustomed to bare my soul. Moreover, there is fixed between you and me such a gulf that – '

'A gulf? Do you again say that I am an aristocrat? Come, come,

Evgenii Vasilitch! Have I not already told you that I – ?'

'Can it avail anything to discuss the future when, for the most part, our futures are wholly independent of ourselves? Should the occasion arise to be up and doing, well and good: but, should the occasion not arise, at least let us leave ourselves room for thankfulness that we did not waste time in useless chatter.'

'What? You call a friendly talk "useless chatter"? Then do you deem me, as a woman, unworthy of your confidence, or do you despise all women?'

'You I do not despise: and that you know full well.'

'I know nothing of the kind. Of course I can understand your reluctance to speak of your future career; but as to what is taking place within you at the present moment – '

' "Taking place within me at the present moment"?' Bazarov exclaimed. 'One would think I was a state or a community! Nor is it a process which interests me; while, in addition, a man cannot always put into words "what is taking place within him." '

'I do not see it. Why should you hesitate to express what may be in your soul?'

'Could *you* do as much?' asked Bazarov.

'I could,' came the reply after a brief hesitation.

Bazarov bowed in an ironical manner.

'Then you have the advantage of me,' he said.

Her glance quickened into a note of interrogation.

'Very well,' she said. 'Yet I will venture to say that you and I have not met in vain, and that we shall always remain good friends. Moreover, I feel certain that in time your secretiveness and reserve will disappear.'

'Then have you noticed in me much such "secretiveness and reserve"?'

'I have.'

Bazarov rose, and moved towards the window.

'Do you really want to know the cause of that "secretiveness, and reserve"?' he asked. 'Do you really want to know "what is taking place within" me?'

'I do,' she replied. Yet even as she spoke she felt run through her a tinge of apprehension for which she could not account.

'And you will not be angry with me if I tell you?'

'No.'

'No?'

He approached her and halted behind her.

'Learn, then,' he said, 'that I love you with a blind, insensate passion. You have forced it from me at last!'

She stretched out her arms before her, while Bazarov, turning, pressed his forehead against the window-pane. His breath caught in his throat, and his whole body was quivering. Yet this was not the agitation born of the diffidence of youth, nor was it the awe inspired by a first confession of love. Rather, it was the beating of a strong and terrible emotion which resembled madness and was, perhaps, akin to it. As for Madame Odintsov, a great horror had come over her – also a great feeling of compassion for him.

'Evgenii Vasilitch!' she cried. In the words there rang an involuntary note of tenderness.

Wheeling about, he devoured her with his glance. Then he seized her hands in his, and pressed her to his bosom.

She did not free herself at once. Only after a moment did she withdraw to a corner, and stand looking at him. He rushed towards her again, but she whispered in hurried alarm:

'You have mistaken me!'

Had he taken another step, she would have screamed.

Biting his lips, he left the room.

Half an hour later her maid brought her a note. It consisted of a single line only, and said: 'Must I depart today, or may I remain until tomorrow?'

To it Anna Sergievna replied: 'Why depart? have failed to understand you, and you have failed to understand me – that is all.'

But mentally she added: 'Rather, I have failed to understand myself.'

Until dinner time she remained secluded, and spent the hours in pacing her room with her hands clasped behind her. Occasionally she would halt before the window-panes or a mirror, to draw a handkerchief across a spot on her neck which seemed to be burning like fire. And every time that she did so she asked herself what had led her to force Bazarov's confidence; also, whether or not she had had any suspicion that such a thing might result.

'Yes, I *am* to blame,' she finally decided. 'Yet I could not have foreseen the whole *dénouement*.'

Then she recalled Bazarov's almost animal face as he rushed to seize her in his arms. And at the thought she blushed.

'Or is it that – ' Here she stopped, and shook back her curls. The reason was that she had seen herself in a mirror, and, as in a flash, had learnt from that image of a head thrown back, with a mysterious smile lurking between a pair of half-parted lips and in a pair of half-closed eyes, something which confounded her.

'No, no! Again no!' she cried. 'Only God knows what might come of it. Such things are not to be played with. Freedom from worry is the chief thing in the world.'

Nor had her *sang-froid* really been shattered. Rather, she was a little agitated – so little that, when, for some unknown reason, she shed a tear or two, those tears owed their origin not to any deep emotion, to the fact that she was wounded, but to a sense of having involuntarily been at fault in permitting certain vague yearnings – a certain consciousness of the transience of life, a certain desire for novelty – to urge her towards the boundary line. And over that boundary line she had peeped. And in front of her she had beheld, not an abyss, but a waste, a sheer ugliness.

Chapter 19

IN SPITE OF HER self-command, in spite of her superiority to convention, Madame Odintsov could not but feel a little uncomfortable when she entered the dining-room for the evening meal. Nevertheless the meal passed off without incident, and after it Porphyri Platonitch came in, and related various anecdotes on the strength of a recent visit to the neighbouring town – among other things, a story to the effect that Governor 'Bardeloue' had commanded his whole staff of officials to wear spurs, in order that, if need be, he could dispatch them on their errands on horseback! Meanwhile, Arkady talked in an undertone to Katia, and also paid diplomatic attention to the Princess; while Bazarov maintained such an obstinate, gloomy silence that Madame, glancing at him (as she did twice, and openly, not covertly), thought to herself, as she scanned his stern, forbidding face, downcast eyes, and all-pervading expression of rigid contempt: 'No, no! Again, no!'

Dinner over, she conducted her guests into the garden, and, perceiving that Bazarov desired a word with her, walked aside a little, halted, and waited for him. Approaching with his eyes on the ground, he said in a dull way:

'I must beg your pardon, Anna Sergievna. Surely you must be feeling extremely angry with me?'

'No, not angry so much as grieved,' she replied.

'So much the worse! But I have received sufficient punishment, have I not? My position now (I am sure that you will agree with me) is a very awkward one. True, you wrote in your message: "Why need you depart?" but I cannot and will not remain. By tomorrow, therefore, I shall have departed.'

'But why need you, need you – ?'

'Why need I depart?'

'No, I was going to have said something quite different.'

'We cannot recover the past,' he continued, 'and it was only a question of time before this should happen. I know only of one condition under which I could remain. And that condition is never likely to arise. For (pardon my presumption) I suppose you neither love me now nor could ever do so?'

With the words there came a flash from under his dark brows.

She did not reply. Through her brain there flitted only the one thought: 'I am afraid of this man!'

'Farewell,' he continued, as though he had divined that thought. Then he moved away towards the house.

Entering the house a little later, Anna Sergievna called to Katia, and took the girl by the arm: nor throughout the rest of the evening did she once part from her. Also, instead of joining in a game of cards, she sat uttering laugh after laugh of a nature which ill consorted with her blanched and careworn face. Gazing at her perplexedly, as a young man will do, Arkady kept asking himself the question: 'What can this mean?' As for Bazarov, he locked himself in his room, and only appeared to join the rest at tea. When he did so, Anna Sergievna yearned to say something kind to him, but could think of no words for the purpose. To her dilemma, however, an unexpected incident put an end. This was the entry of the butler to announce Sitnikov!

To describe the craven fashion in which the young Progressive entered the room would be impossible. Although, with characteristic importunity, he had decided to repair to the residence of a lady with whom he was barely acquainted, and who had not accorded him an invitation (his pretext for such presumption being that, according to information received, she happened to be entertaining guests who were both intellectual and 'very intimate' with himself), he had since felt his courage ebb to the marrow of his bones, and now, instead of proffering all the excuses and compliments which he had prepared in advance, blurted out some ridiculous story to the effect that Evdoksia Kukshin had sent him to enquire after the health of Anna Sergievna, and that Arkady Nikolaievitch had always spoken of him in terms of the highest respect. But at this point he began to stammer, and so lost his head as to sit down upon his own hat! No one bade him depart, however, and Anna Sergievna even went so far as to present him to her aunt and sister. Accordingly it was not long before he recovered his equanimity, and shone forth with his accustomed brilliancy. Often the appearance of the paltry represents a convenient phenomenon in life, since it relaxes over-taut strings, and sobers natures prone to conceit and self-assurance by reminding them of their kinship with the newcomer. Thus Sitnikov's arrival caused everything to become duller and a trifle more futile, but also rendered things simpler, and enabled the company to partake of supper with a better appetite, and to part for the night half an hour earlier than usual.

'Let me recall to you some words of your own,' said Arkady when he had got into bed, and Bazarov was still undressing. 'I refer to the words: "Why are you downhearted? Have you just fulfilled a sacred duty?"'

Between the two there had become established those half-quizzical relations which are always a sign of tacit distrust and a smouldering grudge.

'Tomorrow I intend to set out for my father's place,' remarked Bazarov, in disregard of what Arkady had said.

The latter raised himself on his elbow. Though surprised, he also, for some reason, felt glad.

'Ah!' he exclaimed. 'Then *that* is why you are down-hearted?'

Bazarov yawned.

'When you are come to be a little older,' he replied, 'you will know more.'

'And what of Anna Sergievna?' continued Arkady.

'Well? What of her?'

'Is it likely that she will let you go?'

'I am not her hireling.'

Arkady relapsed into thought, and Bazarov sought his bed, and turned his face to the wall.

For a few moments silence reigned.

'Evgenii,' said Arkady suddenly.

'Yes?'

'I too intend to leave tomorrow.'

Bazarov made no reply.

'True, I shall be returning to Marino,' continued Arkady, 'but we might bear one another company as far as Khokhlovskïe Viselki, and there you could hire horses of Thedot. Of course, I should have been delighted to make your family's acquaintance, but, were I to accompany you, I might act as a source of constraint upon them and yourself alike. You must pay us another visit at Marino later.'

'I will. As a matter of fact, I have left some of my things there.'

Bazarov still had his face turned to the wall.

'Why does he not ask *me* the reason of *my* departure – a departure as sudden as his?' reflected Arkady. 'Why is either of us departing, for that matter?'

As he continued to reflect he realised that, while unable to return a satisfactory answer to the question propounded, he seemed to have got a heartache somehow, to be feeling that he would find it hard to part with the life at Nikolsköe to which he was grown so accustomed. Yet he could not remain there alone. That would be worse still.

'Between him and her there is something in the wind,' he reflected. 'That being so, what would my sticking here avail after he had gone? I should weary Anna Sergievna, and lose my last chance of pleasing her.'

Then he began to draw a mental picture of the lady whom he had just named: until there cut across the fair presentment of the young widow another set of features.

'Katia too I shall miss,' he whispered to his pillow (which had already received one of his tears). At length, raising his curly poll, he exclaimed: 'What, in the devil's name, brought that idiot Sitnikov here?'

He heard Bazarov stir under the bedclothes, then remark:

'You yourself are an idiot. We need the Sitnikovs of this world. Such donkeys are absolutely necessary to us, to *me*. The gods ought not to have to bake pots.'

'Ah!' reflected Arkady. For, as in a flash, there had become revealed to him the bottomless profundity of Bazarov's conceit.

'Then you and I are the gods?' he said aloud. 'Or are you a god, and I a donkey?'

'You are,' came the gruff reply. 'As yet, at all events, you are.'

No particular astonishment was evinced by Madame Odintsov when, on the following day, Arkady informed her that it was his intention to accompany Bazarov. Rather, she looked distraught and weary. Katia glanced at him gravely and in silence, and the Princess went so far as to cross herself under her shawl – a precaution against the young men observing the gesture. Sitnikov too was dumbfounded at having just entered the breakfast-room in a new and most elegant suit (this time not of 'Slavophil' cut, not to mention the fact that he had also had the pleasure of amazing his temporary valet with the multitude of his shirts), only to find himself confronted with the prospect of being deserted by his comrades! He shuffled and wriggled like a hare driven to the edge of a covert, and blurted out, almost in panic-stricken fashion, that he too had a great mind to depart. Nor did Madame Odintsov make any great effort to dissuade him.

'I have an exceedingly comfortable *koliaska*,' the unfortunate young man said to Arkady, 'and I could give you a lift in it, and leave Evgenii Vasilitch to use your *tarantass*, which would suit him better than the *koliaska*.'

'But I should not like to take you so far out of your way, for the distance to my home is considerable.'

'That would not matter, that would not matter. I have plenty of time to spare, and also some business to do in that direction.'

'What? Leasehold business again?' enquired Arkady disparagingly. But Sitnikov was so distraught that he forbore to giggle in his usual fashion.

'I can guarantee that the *koliaska* is comfortable,' he repeated. 'Indeed, it could hold all three of us.'

'Do not vex Monsieur Sitnikov by refusing,' put in Madame Odintsov. So, with a meaning glance at her, Arkady nodded assent to Sitnikov.

Breakfast over, the guests departed. Anna Sergievna offered Bazarov her hand.

'I hope we shall meet again?' she said.

'Only if you wish it,' he replied.

'Then we *shall* meet again.'

The first to issue upon the verandah and enter Sitnikov's *koliaska* was Arkady. The butler assisted him obsequiously, although Arkady could with equal readiness have struck the man or burst into tears. As for Bazarov, he took possession of the tarantass.

Khokhlovskïe Viselki reached, Arkady waited until Thedot, the local posting-master, had harnessed fresh horses, and then, approaching the tarantass, said to Bazarov with his old smile:

'Evgenii, take me with you. I should like to come to your place, after all.'

'Get in, then,' muttered Bazarov.

This made Sitnikov, who had been walking up and down beside his conveyance, and whistling, fairly gasp. Nevertheless the heartless Arkady removed his luggage from the *koliaska*, seated himself beside Bazarov, and according his late fellow-traveller a courteous bow shouted: 'Right away!' The *tarantass* started, and soon was lost to view. Much taken aback, Sitnikov gazed at his coachman. But the latter was flicking the flanks of the trace horse with his whip, and therefore Sitnikov had no choice but to leap into the vehicle, to shout to a couple of peasants: 'Off with your caps, you rascals!' and be driven to the town, whither he arrived at a late hour, and where, on the following day, he declared to Madame Kukshin that he had had enough of 'those odious churls and upstarts.'

On Arkady seating himself beside Bazarov in the *tarantass*, he pressed his hand, and Bazarov seemed to divine the meaning of the silent hand-clasp, and to appreciate it. During the previous night the elder man had never once closed his eyes. Also, for several days past he had neither smoked a cigar nor eaten more than the merest scrap of food. Indeed, as he sat in the tarantass, his fine-drawn profile, under the overshadowing cap, looked sharper and grimmer than ever.

'Give me a cigar, will you?' he said. 'Also, pray look at my tongue, and tell me if it has a bilious appearance.'

'Yes, it has,' replied Arkady.

'I thought so, for this cigar seems tasteless. Moreover, the infernal thing has come unrolled.'

'You have changed a good deal of late?' hazarded Arkady.

'I dare say. But I shall be myself again, soon. The only thing now troubling me is the fact that my mother is so good-naturedly fussy.

Should one's paunch not be projecting, or should one not eat at least ten meals a day she relapses into despair. My father, of course, is different, for he has been all over the world, and knows what is what. This cigar is simply unsmokable.' And Bazarov consigned it to the dust of the roadway.

'The distance to your place is twenty-five versts, I suppose?' queried Arkady.

'It is so. But enquire of that sage there.' And Bazarov pointed to the peasant (an *employé* of Thedot's) who was seated on the box.

The 'sage' in question replied that he 'could not say exactly,' since the verst-posts in those parts had not been measured out; after which he went on to swear at the shaft horse for 'kicking' its 'jowl about' – that is to say, jerking its head up and down.

'Aye, aye,' commented Bazarov. 'Take warning from me, my young friend. An instructive example sits before you – an example of the vanity of this world. By a single thread does the destiny of every man hang, and at any moment there may open before him an abyss into which he and his may plunge. For always he is laying up for himself misfortune.'

'At what are you hinting?' asked Arkady.

'At nothing. I am merely saying outright that you and I have behaved very foolishly. However, why talk of it? I have noticed that in surgical operations it is the patient who fights against his hurt who soonest gets well.'

'I do not understand you,' Arkady said. 'So far as I can see, you have nothing whatsoever to complain of.'

'You cannot understand me? Well, mark this: that you had far better go and break stones by the roadside than allow a woman to obtain even the least hold over you. Such a thing is sheer' (he nearly said 'Romanticism,' but changed his mind) 'rubbish.'

'Perhaps you do not believe me?' he went on. 'Nevertheless, I tell you that, though you and I have been cultivating feminine society, and enjoying it, the sense of relief when such society is abandoned is like taking a cold bath on a summer's day. Never ought a man to touch such follies. Always he ought, as the excellent Spanish saying has it, "to remain as the beasts of the field." Look here,' he added to the peasant on the box. 'Do you, my man of wisdom, possess a wife?'

The peasant turned a portion of a flat, near-sighted visage in the friends' direction.

'A wife?' he repeated. 'Yes, I do. Why shouldn't I?'

'Never mind that. Do you ever beat her?'

'My wife? Sometimes. But never without good cause.'

'Excellent! And does she ever beat *you*?'

The peasant gave his reins a jerk.

'What a thing, *barin*!' he exclaimed. 'Surely you must be joking?' Evidently the question had offended him.

'You hear that, Arkady Nikolaievitch?' said Bazarov. 'You and I have been similarly beaten. That is what comes of being gentry.'

Arkady laughed in spite of himself, but Bazarov turned away, and did not speak again until the end of the journey.

To Arkady the twenty-five versts seemed like fifty; but at length there came into view, on the slope of a low hill, the homestead of the manor where Bazarov's parents resided. On one side of it, amid a clump of young birch trees, there could be seen the servants' quarters under their thatched roofs; while at the door of the nearest hut a couple of fur-capped peasants were engaged in a contest of mutual abuse.

'You are an old pig!' one of them said to the other. 'And that is worse than being a young one.'

'Your wife is a witch,' retorted the other.

'From the lack of restraint in their bearing,' commented Bazarov, 'as well as from the playfulness of their terms of speech, you will gather that my father's peasantry are not downtrodden. But here is my father himself. I can see him stepping out on to the verandah. He will have heard the sound of our collar-bells. Yes, it is he! I recognise his figure. But how grey he looks, poor old fellow!'

Chapter 20

BAZAROV LEANT FORWARD from the *tarantass*, and Arkady, peering over his friend's shoulder, beheld, on the entrance steps of the manor-house, a tall, thin man with dishevelled hair and a narrow, aquiline nose. Clad in an old military tunic of which the front was flying open, he was standing with legs apart, a long pipe in his mouth, and eyes blinking in the glare of the sunlight.

The horses pulled up.

'So you have come at last!' exclaimed Bazarov's father, still continuing to smoke (though, as he did so, the stem of the pipe was rattling and shaking between his fingers). 'Now, jump out, jump out!'

Again and again he embraced his son.

'Eniusha, Eniusha!'* the tremulous voice of an old woman also cried as the door of the house opened and there appeared on the threshold a short, rotund old dame in a white cap and a short striped blouse. Gasping and staggering, she would have fallen had not Bazarov hastened to support her. As he did so her fat old arms clasped him around the neck, and her head sank upon his bosom. All then was still for a moment. Only her convulsive sobs broke the silence. Meanwhile Bazarov Senior breathed hard, and blinked more vigorously than ever

'Enough, enough, Arisha!' he said at length with a glance at Arkady, who had remained standing beside the *tarantass* (and even the peasant on the box-seat had turned away his head). 'Pray cease, I tell you. This is not necessary. I beg of you to cease.'

'Ah, Vasili Ivanitch!' whimpered the poor old woman. 'To think of the long while since last I saw my Eniusha, my own, my darling boy!' Still keeping her arms clasped around Bazarov, she withdrew her ruffled, convulsed, tear-stained face from his breast looked at him for a moment with blissful, yet comical eyes, and glued herself again to his bosom.

'Yes, yes,' said Vasili Ivanitch. 'Such is in the nature of things. But had we not better go indoors? See! Evgenii has brought a guest!'

With a slight scrape and a bow, he added to Arkady:

'Pray pardon us, sir, but you will understand the situation. A woman's weakness – ahem! – and a mother's heart.'

His lips, chin, and eyebrows too were working. Evidently he was

* An endearing diminutive of Evgenii.

striving to master himself, and to appear totally indifferent. Arkady responded to his bow with a like salutation.

'Yes, yes, dear mother; let us go indoors,' said Bazarov. Leading the shaking old lady into the house, he seated her in a cosy chair, bestowed upon his father another hurried embrace, and then presented Arkady.

'I am glad indeed to make your acquaintance!' said Vasili Ivanitch. 'I am glad indeed! But do not expect too much of us, my dear sir. My establishment is organised on simple lines; it is placed on what I might call "a war footing." Come, come, Arina! Pray calm yourself, and attend to your duties as a hostess. Oh, fie, to give way in such a manner! What will our guest think of you?'

'My dear, I do not know the gentleman's name,' the old lady sobbed through her tears.

'Arkady Nikolaievitch,' prompted Vasili Ivanitch in an undertone, but with great ceremony.

'Then pray pardon a foolish old woman, sir.' Arina Vlasievna blew her nose, inclined her head to right and left, and wiped each eye in turn as she did so. 'Yes, pray pardon me, but I had thought never again to see my darling boy before I died.'

'But, you see, we *have* seen him again,' said Vasili Ivanitch. 'Here, Taniushka!' – this to a barefooted serf girl of thirteen who, clad in a bright red cotton frock, had been an interested, but timid, observer in the doorway. 'Bring your mistress a glass of water on a salver. Do you hear? And you, gentlemen,' he continued with old-fashioned sprightliness, 'will you be so good as to step into the study of a retired veteran?'

'First another kiss, Eniusha,' gasped Arina Vlasievna. Then, as Bazarov bent over her form, she added: 'How handsome you have grown!'

'Handsome or not, he is human,' said Vasili Ivanitch. 'Wherefore, now that you have satisfied your mother's heart, I look to you to see also to the satisfaction of our honoured guests. For than yourself no one knows better that nightingales cannot be fed on air.'

This caused the old lady to rise from her chair, and to exclaim:

'Yes, yes: in one moment, Vasili Ivanitch. The table shall be laid, and I myself will hurry to the kitchen, and see that the *samovar* be got ready. Everything shall be done. Why, it must be three years since last I gave Eniusha a meal.'

'Yes, three years, dear wife. But now bustle about, and do not let yourself get flurried. Gentlemen, accompany me, I beg of you. But here is Timotheitch coming to pay you his respects. How delighted he looks, the old rascal! Now, pray favour me with your company.'

And he strode fussily ahead with much shuffling and creaking of flat-soled slippers.

The Bazarovian establishment consisted of six small rooms, of which one – the room to which Vasili Ivanitch was now conducting our friends – was looked upon as the study. Between its two windows there stood a fat-legged table, strewn with dusty, fusty papers; on the walls hung a number of Turkish weapons, *nagaiki*,* and swords, a couple of landscapes, a few anatomical plates, a portrait of Hufeland,† a black-framed monogram done in hair, and a diploma protected with a glass front; between two large birchwood cupboards stood a ragged, battered leathern sofa; on shelves lay huddled a miscellany of books, boxes, stuffed birds, jars, and bladders; and, lastly, in a corner reposed a broken electric battery.

'Already I have warned you,' said Vasili Ivanitch to Arkady, 'that we live here, so to speak, *en bivouac.*'

'Make no excuses,' put in Bazarov. 'Kirsanov knows that you and I are not Crœsuses, and that no butler is kept. But where can we find Arkady a bed? That is the question.'

'We have an excellent room in the wing, where he would be most comfortable.'

'You have added a wing, then?'

'Yes, Evgenii Vasilitch,' Timotheitch interposed. 'At least, a bath-room.'

'But it is to a room *next* the bathroom that I am referring,' Vasili Ivanitch hastened to explain. 'However, that will not matter, since it is now summer time. I will run up there at once, and see that it is put in order. Meanwhile, Timotheitch, fetch in the luggage. To you, Evgenii, I will allot the study. *Cuique suum.*'‡

'There!' said Bazarov to Arkady as soon as his father had left the room. 'Is he not just such a jolly, good-hearted, queer old fellow as your own father, though in a different way? He chatters just as he always used to do.'

'Yes; and your mother seems an excellent woman.'

'She is. Moreover, you can see that she does not attempt to hide her feelings. Only wait and see what a dinner she will give us!'

'But as you were not expected today,' put in Timotheitch, who had just re-entered with Bazarov's portmanteau, 'no beef has been got into the house.'

'Never mind. Let us dine *without* beef – or, for that matter, without

* Cossack whips.
† Christoph Wilhelm Hufeland (1762–1836), a well-known German physicist whose treatise *Makrobiotik*, or *The Art of Prolonging Life*, has been translated into almost every European language.
‡ 'To each his own.'

anything at all. "Poverty is no crime." '

'How many souls* are there on your father's property?' asked Arkady.

'It is not his property; it is my mother's. The number of souls on it is, I think, fifteen.'

'No, twenty-two,' corrected Timotheitch with an air of pride. The next moment the sound of shuffling slippers was heard once more, and Vasili Ivanitch re-entered.

'Your room will be ready for you in a few minutes,' he announced grandiloquently to Arkady. 'Meanwhile, here is your servant.' He pointed to a close-cropped urchin who, clad in an out-at-elbows blue *kaftan* and an odd pair of shoes, had also made his appearance. 'His name is Thedika, and, for all my son's injunction, I had better repeat to you not to expect too much of him – though certainly he will be able to fill your pipe for you. I presume that you smoke?'

'I do, but only cigars.'

'A commendable rule! I too prefer cigars, but find them extremely difficult to procure in this isolated part of the country.'

'Have done with bewailing your poverty,' Bazarov good-naturedly interrupted. 'Rather, seat yourself on this sofa, and take a rest.'

Vasili Ivanitch smilingly did as he was bidden. Extremely like his son in features (save that his forehead was lower and narrower, and his mouth a trifle wider), he was for ever on the move – now shrugging his shoulders as though his coat cut him under the armpits, now blinking, now coughing, now twitching his fingers. In this he was sharply differentiated from his son, whose most distinguishing characteristic was his absolute immobility.

'Have done with bewailing my poverty?' repeated the old man. 'Why, you cannot surely think that I would weary our guest with complaints concerning our isolation? As a matter of fact, a man of brains need *never* be isolated, and I myself do everything in my power to avoid becoming moss-grown, and falling behind the times.'

Extracting from his pocket a new yellow handkerchief which he had contrived to lay hands upon while proceeding to Arkady's room, he continued, as he flourished the handkerchief in the air:

'Of the fact that, at some cost to myself, I have organised my peasantry on the *obrok* system, and apportioned them one-half, even more, of my land, I will not speak, since I conceive that to have been my duty, as well as a measure dictated by prudence (though no other landowner in the neighbourhood would have done as much). Rather, I

* i. e. serfs.

am referring to scholarships and to science.'

'I see that you have here *The Friend of Health* for 1855,' remarked Bazarov.

'Yes, a friend sent it me,' Vasili Ivanitch hastened to explain. 'Phrenology too we take into account' (he addressed this last to Arkady rather than to Bazarov, while accompanying it with a nod towards a small plaster bust of which the cranial surface was divided into a series of numbered squares). 'Yes indeed! Nor are we ignorant of Schönlein* and Rademacher.'

'In the province of — you still believe in Rademacher?' queried Bazarov.

Vasili Ivanitch laughed.

'In the province of — we still believe in — ? Ah, gentlemen! Hardly could you expect us to move as fast as you do. You find us in a state of transition. In my day, the humoralist Hoffmann and the vitalist Braun had already come to be looked upon with ridicule (and their fulminations undoubtedly seem absurd); but now you have replaced Rademacher with a new authority, and are making obeisance to that authority exactly as though in twenty years' time he too will not have fallen into contempt.'

'Let me tell you, for your comforting,' said Bazarov, 'that we ridicule all medicine, and render obeisance to no one.'

'What? Do you not wish to become a doctor?'

'Yes; but the one thing does not preclude the other.'

Vasili Ivanitch raked out his pipe until only a glowing morsel of ash remained.

'Perhaps so, perhaps so,' he said. 'That point I will not dispute. For who am I that I should dispute such things – I who am a mere retired army doctor, *et voilà tout* – an army doctor who has taken to agriculture?'

With that he turned to Arkady.

'Do you know, I served under your grandfather,' he said. 'He was then in command of a brigade. Many and many a review have I seen. And the society in which I mixed, the men whom I had as comrades! Yes, this humble individual has felt the pulses of Prince Vitzentschein and Zhukovsky, and also known all the leaders of the Southern Army of '14.' He pursed his lips impressively. 'At the same time, of course, my department was a separate one from theirs. It was the department of the lancet, you understand. Your grandfather stood high in the esteem of everyone, and was a true soldier.'

* Johann Lukas Schönlein (1793–1864), a noted German physician.

'We will agree that he was a decent old curmudgeon,' drawled Bazarov.

'To think of speaking so, Evgenii!' exclaimed the old man. 'General Kirsanov was not one of those who – '

'Never mind him. As we were driving hither I greatly admired your birch plantation. It is doing splendidly.'

Vasili Ivanitch's face brightened instantly.

'Yes, and see what a garden I have made!' he exclaimed. 'Every tree in it has been planted with my own hands – orchard trees, and bush fruit trees, and every sort of medicinal herb. Ah, young sirs, though you may be wise in your generation, many a truth did old Paracelsus* discover *in herbis et verbis et lapidibus*. For myself, I have now retired from practice; yet twice a week am I given a chance to refurbish my ancient store of knowledge, since folk come to me for advice, and I cannot well turn them away. In particular do the poor seek my help, since there is no other doctor hereabouts. Yet stay! A certain retired major dabbles in the art. Once I asked him whether he had ever *studied* medicine, and he replied that he had not, that all that he did he did "out of philanthropy"! "Out of philanthropy"! Ha, ha, ha! What think you of that, eh? Ha, ha, ha!'

'Fill me a pipe, Thedika,' said Bazarov curtly.

'And there was another doctor who came to visit a patient in this neighbourhood,' continued Vasili Ivanitch in a tone of mock despair. 'But by the time he arrived the patient had already joined his forefathers, and the servant of the house would not admit the doctor, saying that the latter's services were no longer required. This the doctor had scarcely expected, and he was rather taken aback. "Did the *barin* gasp before he died?" he enquired. "He did, sir," was the reply. "Very much?" "Yes, very much." "Good!" And the doctor returned home. Ha, ha, ha!'

Yet no one laughed except the old man himself. True, Arkady contrived to summon up a smile, but Bazarov only stretched himself and yawned. The conversation lasted about an hour, and then Arkady managed to get away to his room, which he found to consist of the vestibule to the bathroom, but at the same time to be clean and inviting. Soon afterwards Taniushka arrived to announce dinner.

The meal, though hastily prepared, was excellent, and even sumptuous. Only the wine proved to be rather of the 'gooseberry' order – the

---

* Theophrastus Bombastus von Hohenheim (1493–1541), most commonly known by his self-coined name of Paracelsus, and a German-Swiss traveller and physician.

dark-coloured sherry procured by Timotheitch from a certain wine merchant in the town smacking in equal parts of resin and of honey. Also, in addition, the flies made themselves a nuisance, owing to the fact that the page boy whose duty it was to keep them at bay with a green whisk had, for the nonce, been banished, lest he should excite too much comment on the part of the up-to-date visitors. Lastly, Arina Vlasievna had robed herself in gala attire – that is to say, a high-peaked cap with yellow ribands and a blue, embroidered shawl. She burst into renewed weeping on beholding her beloved Eniusha, but, this time, gave her husband no occasion to chide her, so speedily did her own fear of staining her shawl cause her to wipe away the tears. None but the two young men ate anything, for the host and hostess had long ago dined; while as waiters there officiated Thedika (much burdened with the novelty of wearing shoes) and a woman of a masculine type of face, and with a hump on her back, who was also accustomed to execute the functions of housekeeper, keeper of the poultry, and sempstress. During the meal Vasili Ivanitch paced to and fro, and discussed, in cheerful, and even rapturous, terms, the grave fears which Napoleon's* policy and the intricacy of the Italian question inspired in his breast. Arina Vlasievna, for her part, quite disregarded Arkady, and offered him not a single dish, but, seated with her hand supporting her face (to which a pair of puffy, cherry-coloured lips and a few moles communicated a kindly expression), kept her eyes fixed upon her son, while her breath came in a succession of pants. Her great desire was to ask her son how long he was going to stay, but she dared not do so for fear he should reply: 'Only for two days,' or something of the kind – which was a prospect of a nature to make her heart die within her. On the roast being served, Vasili Ivanitch disappeared, and returned, the next moment, with an uncorked bottle of champagne.

'See here,' he exclaimed. 'Rustic though we may be, we still keep something to make merry with on state occasions.'

That said, he filled three tumblers and a wine-glass, proposed a health to 'our inestimable guests,' heel-tapped his glass in the military fashion, and forced his wife to drain hers to the dregs. Presently the pastry course supervened; during which, though Arkady could not bear anything sweet, he deemed it his duty to partake of no less than four out of the many confections which had been prepared for his benefit. And this obligation he felt to be the more binding in that Bazarov bluntly declined all, and lit a cigar. Lastly there appeared tea, cream,

* Napoleon III.

biscuits, and butter; after which Vasili Ivanitch conducted the party into the garden, in order that the guests might admire the beauty of the evening. As he passed a certain bench he whispered in Arkady's ear:

'This is where I love to sit and meditate as I watch the sun sinking. It is just the spot for a hermit like myself. And, further on, I have planted a few of Horace's favourite trees.'

'What trees?' asked Bazarov, who had partially overheard.

'Acacia trees.'

The other yawned, and, on observing this, Vasili Ivanitch hastened to say:

'I expect that you travellers would like now to seek the arms of Morpheus?'

'We should,' Bazarov assented. 'Yes, that is a true saying.'

Upon which the son said 'Good-night' to his mother, and kissed her on the forehead, while she bestowed upon him a threefold embrace and (covertly) a blessing; while Vasili Ivanitch conducted Arkady to his room, and wished him 'such God-given rest as I myself used to enjoy during the happier years of my life.'

And certainly Arkady slept splendidly in the mint-scented annexe to the bathroom, where the only sound to be heard was that of a cricket chirping lustily against a rival from behind the stove.

Meanwhile, on leaving Arkady, Vasili Ivanitch repaired to the study, where, squatting at the foot of the sofa, he was about to enter into a discursive conversation with his son when the latter dismissed him, on the plea that he desired, rather, to go to sleep. Yet never once did Bazarov close his eyes that night, but lay staring into the darkness, since his memories of childhood had less power to move him than had the remembrance of the bitter experience through which he had recently passed.

For her part, Arina Vlasievna said her prayers with an overflowing heart, and then indulged in a long talk with Anfisushka; who, planted like a block before her mistress, with her solitary eye fixed upon the latter, communicated in a mysterious whisper her opinions and prognostications on the subject of Evgenii Vasilitch. Finally Arina Vlasievna's pleasurable emotion, coupled with the wine and the tobacco smoke, so caused the old lady's head to start whirling that, when her husband came to bed, he found himself obliged to moderate her exuberance with a gesture.

Arina Vlasievna was a true Russian housewife of the old school. That is to say, she ought to have lived a couple of hundred years earlier, during the period when the ancient Muscovite Empire was in being. At once pious and extremely nervous, she believed in every species of portent, divination, proverb, and vision; also in such things as *urodivie*,* household demons, wood spirits, unlucky encounters, spells, popular medicines, Thursday salt, and an ever-imminent end to the world. Again, she placed much faith in such ideas as that, if a lighted candle lasts through the night preceding Easter Day, the buckwheat crops will come up well; that, should a human eye chance to fall upon a mushroom during the process of its growth, such growth will terminate forthwith; that the devil loves to be wheresoever there is water; and that all Jews bear on their breasts a blood-red stain. Again, she stood in great awe of mice, adders, frogs, sparrows, leeches, thunder, cold water, draughts, horses, billy-goats, fair men, and black cats, and also looked upon crickets and dogs as unclean creatures. Again, she never ate veal, pigeons, crabs, cheese, asparagus, arti-chokes, hare, or water melons (the last-named for the reason that, when split open, they reminded her of the head of John the Baptist!). Nor could she ever speak of oysters without a shudder. Again, though she loved eating, she observed every fast; though she slept ten hours out of the twenty-four, she never even went to bed if Vasili Ivanitch had got a headache; she read no books beyond *Alexis* or *Siskins of the Forest*; she wrote, at most, two letters a year; she knew every wrinkle as regards the departments of housekeeping, boiling, and baking (and that even though she herself never laid a finger upon anything, and hated even to have to stir from her place); she was aware that there were certain folk in the world who must command, and others who must serve – wherefore she loved servility and genuflexions; she treated all her subordinates with kindness and consideration; she sent never a beggar away empty; and she condemned no one for a fault although at times she had a tendency to talk scandal. Likewise, in her youth she had been comely, and a player of the clavichord, and able to speak a little French; but owing to long residence with a husband whom she had married purely for love, she had grown rusty in those accomplishments, and forgotten alike her French and her music; she loved and feared her son to a degree almost beyond expression; she deputed the management of her property entirely to Vasili Ivanitch, and never interfered with it, but would fall to gasping, and waving her handkerchief about, and affrightedly raising her eyebrows, whenever her helpmeet happened to broach some new plan or some necessary reform which he had in his mind's eye; and, lastly, she was of so

* *Urodivie*, or 'sacred imbeciles,' were persons who, deficient of intellect in the ordinary sense, were yet believed by ancient Russia to enjoy particularly intimate communication with the divine and the unseen.

apprehensive a temperament that she lived in constant fear of some unknown misfortune, and would burst into tears should anyone mention anything of a mournful character.

Such women are now extinct and only God knows whether we ought to be glad of the fact.

Chapter 21

WHEN, IN THE MORNING, Arkady rose and, opened the window, the first object to greet his eyes was Vasili Ivanitch. Clad in a smock-frock, and belted with a handkerchief, the old man was busily digging in his vegetable garden. As soon as he noticed his young guest, he leaned upon his spade, and cried:

'Good-morning! How have you slept?'

'Splendidly,' replied Arkady.

'And I, as you see, am imitating Cincinnatus, and preparing a bed of late turnips. By the mercy of God do the times compel every man to win his bread with his own hands. At all times, indeed, is it useless to rely upon others: it is best to work oneself. Thus Jean Jacques Rousseau was right. Half an hour ago, however, you would have seen me in a very different rôle – first of all, injecting opium into a woman who had come to me with what the peasants call "the goad," and we dysentery, and then pulling out some teeth for a second woman. And, would you believe it, when I proposed administering ether to the second woman she would have none of it! These things I do gratis, you know, and as an amateur. Yet, let that not surprise you, for, after all, I am but a plebeian, but a *homo novus*. Come downstairs to sit in the shade and enjoy the freshness of the morning until breakfast shall be ready.'

Arkady did as invited.

'You confer a favour upon me,' said Vasili Ivanitch, raising his hand in military fashion to the battered skull-cap which adorned his head. 'You see. I know you to be used to luxury and ease. Yet even the folk of the great world need not disdain to snatch a brief respite under the roof of a cottage.'

'I neither belong to the great world nor am used to luxury,' protested Arkady.

'Come now!' Vasili Ivanitch indulged in an amiable affectation of incredulity. 'I myself, though I am now on the shelf, have rubbed about in my time, and can tell a bird by its flight. Also, I dabble a little in physiognomy and psychology. For that matter, I will not hesitate to say that, had I not enjoyed those advantages, I should long ago have come to rack and ruin, for the reason that, being one of the small fry, I should soon have been jostled out of the way by the crowd. Also, without flattery, I may say that the friendship which I discern to be existing between you and my son affords me the greatest pleasure. Only this moment I was speaking to him; for (as probably you know) he jumps out of bed at a very early hour, and goes careering all over the countryside. M-might I make so bold as to ask you whether you have known him long?'

'Only since last winter.'

'Indeed? Also, might I make so bold as to ask whether – But sit you down, will you not? – might I also, as his father, venture to ask your frank opinion of him?'

'Your son is the most remarkable man that I have ever met,' came the enthusiastic reply.

Vasili Ivanitch's eyes closed suddenly, while his cheeks quivered, and the spade slipped from his hand.

'Then you think – ?' he began.

'I do not *think* – I am certain that there lies before your son a future which will make your name famous. I have felt certain of this since the first moment I met him.'

'Indeed? Indeed?' Vasili Ivanitch could scarcely articulate the words, but on his capacious lips there had dawned, and become fixed, a smile of triumph.

'Would you like to hear how our first meeting came about?'

'Indeed I should! And any other details you like.'

Arkady therefore plunged into a discourse on Bazarov of the same ardour and the same enthusiasm as he had displayed on the night of the mazurka with Madame Odintsov. As Vasili Ivanitch listened, he blew his nose, rolled his handkerchief into a ball, coughed, and ruffled his hair; until, no longer able to contain himself, he reached over in Arkady's direction, and pressed his lips to the young man's shoulder.

'You have indeed cheered my heart!' he exclaimed still smiling. 'I simply idolise my son! But while my dear old wife is able to stand on rather a different footing with Evgenii – she is his mother, you know – I myself dare not express my whole feelings in his presence, for the reason that he dislikes such things, and is opposed to any manifestations of emotion. For the same reason some folk accuse him of hardness of heart and pride and insensibility; but men like Evgenii cannot be measured by ordinary standards, can they? For example anyone but he would have gone on acting as a drag upon his parents; but, would you believe it? never once since his birth has he asked us for a *kopeck* more than he absolutely needed! There, by God!'

'Yes, your son is a sincere, single-minded man,' agreed Arkady.

'Yes, single-minded,' affirmed Vasili Ivanitch. 'And not only do I idolise him – I am proud of him, and have as my one conceit the hope that someday there may stand in his biography the following words:

"He was the son of a plain military doctor who, nevertheless had the wit to divine the merits of the subject of this book, and to spare no pains in his education." '

The old man's voice faltered for a moment, but presently resumed:

'What think you? Will the field of medicine bring him the fame which you have foretold?'

'Not the field of medicine alone – though in it, as elsewhere, he will become a leader.'

'What field, then, Arkady Nikolaievitch?'

'I could not say. But in any case he will rise to fame.'

' "He will rise to fame"!' The old man relapsed into a state of ecstatic contemplation.

Presently Anfisushka arrived with a large plate of raspberries and the message:

'Arina Vlasievna has sent me to say that breakfast is ready.'

Vasili Ivanitch started from his reverie.

'Bring us also some nice cool plums,' he said.

'I will, sir.'

'Yes, mind that they are cool. Arkady Nikolaievitch, do not stand on ceremony, but help yourself. Is Evgenii Vasilitch yet back, Anfisushka?'

'I am,' called Bazarov from Arkady's room.

Vasili Ivanitch wheeled about.

'Aha!' he cried. 'So you have gone to pay your friend a visit? But you are too late, *amice*: he and I have been having a long conversation together, and it is now breakfast time, and your mother is calling us. By the way, Evgenii, a word or two with you.'

'Concerning what?'

'Concerning a peasant who is suffering from jaundice.'

'Jaundice?'

'Yes, of a very chronic and stubborn kind. I have prescribed scurvy grass and St John's wort, and ordered the man to eat carrots, and given him a dose of soda; but such things are mere palliatives – I want something of a more drastic nature. That you laugh at medicine I am, of course, aware; but none the less I feel certain that you could give me some good, practical advice. But that you can do later. At the present moment, let us go in to breakfast.'

And he leapt from the bench on which he had been seated, trolling gaily the couplet:

'Let us take for our rule, for our rule let us take it,
To live but for pleasure, and never forsake it!'

'What high spirits!' Bazarov remarked as he retired from the window.

Later, when the noontide sun was glowing from behind a thin canopy of dense, pale vapour, and all was still save that the chirping of a few birds in the trees lulled the hearer to a curious, drowsy lethargy, and the incessant call of a young hawk on a topmost bough made the air ring with its strident note, Arkady and Bazarov made for themselves pillows of sweet, dry, fragrant, crackling hay, and stretched themselves in the shadow of a rick.

'Do you see that aspen tree?' remarked Bazarov. 'I mean the one growing at the edge of a depression, where a brick kiln used to stand? Well, when I was a boy I used to believe that, together, the depression and the aspen tree constituted a special talisman, in that, when near them, I never found time hang heavy upon my hands. Of course, the explanation is that in those days I failed to understand that that immunity from *ennui* was due to the very fact of my being a boy. But, now that I am grown up, the talisman seems to have lost its power.'

'How long were you here in those days?'

'Only two years. After that we moved elsewhere. In fact, we led a wandering life, and spent it mostly in towns.'

'Is the house an old one?'

'It is. My maternal grandfather built it.'

'Who was he?'

'The devil only knows! I think a major of some sort, a man who had served under Suvorov,* and could tell all manner of tales about crossing the Alps – though I dare say he told plenty of lies too.'

'Ah! I noticed a portrait of Suvorov in the drawing-room. Cheerful-looking old houses like this I simply love. Somehow they seem to have a smell of their own.'

'Yes – a smell of lamp-oil mingled with trefoil,' agreed Bazarov with a yawn. 'But what flies they contain as well!'

There was a pause. Then Arkady resumed:

'Were you strictly kept when you were a boy?'

'You have seen for yourself what my parents are like. Surely they do not seem very severe folk.'

'And do you love them very much?'

'I do.'

'Certainly they seem to love *you*.'

---

* Alexander Vasilievitch Suvorov (1729–1800), the great Russian general who, after defeating Napoleon in Italy, crossed the Alps to join hands with Korsakov, but found the latter to have been routed by Masséna.

Bazarov was silent. Presently, however, clasping his hands behind his head, he asked:

'Do you know what is in my mind?'

'No. What?'

'I am thinking of the pleasant life that my parents must lead. To think that at sixty my father can still fuss about, and talk of "palliatives," and doctor people, and do the bountiful to the peasants, and, in short, enjoy himself, and that my mother has her days so crammed full of occupations (including sighing and groaning! that she does not know which to begin upon first! On the other hand, *I* – '

'Yes, you?'

'Am doing what you see – lying under a rick. The space occupied by my body is small indeed compared with the surrounding immensity in which it has neither part nor lot, and the portion of time allotted to me here on earth is insignificant indeed compared with the eternity which I have never known, and shall never enter! Yet in this same atom, in this same mathematical point which I call my body, the blood circulates, and the brain operates at will. A fine discrepancy for you – a fine futility!'

'I would remark that what you have just said applies to every human being in creation.'

'True. What I mean is that my parents know not a single tedious moment, nor are in the least distressed with the thought of their insignificance – it is a thought which never stinks in their nostrils; whereas *I* – well, I feel nothing but weariness and rancour in my breast.'

'Rancour? Why rancour?'

'How can you ask? Have you forgotten the recent past?'

'No: only, I do not recognise your right to be *angry*: unhappy, perhaps, but not – '

'I perceive you to understand love as it is understood by all our modern young men. That is to say, chirping "Tsip, tsip, tsip!" like pullets, you take to your heels as soon as ever you see love approaching. I, however, am different. – But enough of this. What is past help is best not talked about.' Bazarov rolled over on to his elbow. 'Ah! Here is a young ant towing in its wake a half-dead fly. Pull, brother, pull! Never mind that the fly hangs back, but avail yourself of your animal right to abjure all sympathy, seeing that our friend has only himself to thank for his trouble.'

'Do not speak like that,' expostulated Arkady. 'How are you yourself to thank for your trouble?'

Bazarov raised his head.

'Nay,' he said, 'I was but jesting. Never have I got myself into trouble, and never shall any woman do it for me. Amen! I have spoken. Never will you hear from me another word on the subject.'

For a while the two friends lay without speaking.

'Yes,' continued Bazarov, 'man is a strange being. Contemplating from a distance the dull life led by my parents, one would almost feel inclined to say to oneself: "What could be better than that, seeing that in that existence one merely eats and drinks and knows oneself to be acting in a sane and regular manner?" Yet a man will still become depressed, and yearn for company, even though he may curse it when he has got it.'

'One ought so to order one's life that every moment in it shall be of significance,' said Arkady sententiously.

'Of course; but while the significant, and even the pseudo-significant – yes, the absolutely insignificant as well – may be bearable, it is trifles, trifles that matter.'

'Unless a man recognise their existence, they do not exist.'

'H'm! A contra-platitude.'

'What is that?'

'This – that, should you say that education is useful, you will be uttering a platitude: but, should you say that education is harmful, you will be uttering a contra-platitude. The one is identical with the other, except that they differ a little in elegance of expression.'

'And which has right on its side?'

' "Which has right on its side?" I can only re-echo: Which?" '

'Come! You are out of spirits today.'

'Am I? Then the sun must have touched me a little, or else I must have eaten too many raspberries to be good for me.'

'Then you would do well to have a sleep.'

'I think you are right. Only, do not look at me while I sleep, for a man cuts his very worst figure at such a time.'

'Surely *you* do not care for people's opinion?'

'I do, even though a man in the best sense of the term ought never to trouble his head about such things, seeing that such a man is either above criticism or too feared and hated for critics to wish to tackle him.'

'Curious! For I myself never hate anyone.'

'And I hate a great many people. You, you see, are a tender soul, you are so much pap, and therefore hatred could never come within your purview. People as retiring, as devoid of self-confidence as you are – '

'What about your own self-confidence?' interrupted Arkady. 'What about your own opinion of yourself?'

Bazarov paused – then replied:

'As we were passing the hut of your *starosta* today (what a neat, pretty little place it looked!) you said to me: "Not until every peasant shall have come to own such a place as this, and every one of us shall have contributed his mite to that end, will Russia attain perfection." But, for my part, I abominate the scurvy churl for whom I am supposed to jump out of my skin, even though never a "thank you" should I get from him for doing so. For why should he thank me? His *métier* happens to be living in a white hut, and mine to be – '

'Come, come, Evgenii! One is almost forced to agree with those who accuse us of being unprincipled.'

'You talk like your uncle. No such thing as principle exists. That you seem never to have divined. Instincts only exist, and upon them everything depends.'

'How so?'

'Thus. We will take myself as an example. Owing to the nature of my instincts, I am prone to deny – I am prone to deny because my brain is so constituted. In the same way, if you were to ask me why I am interested in chemistry, and why you like apples, I should reply that the same reason holds good in each case – that our respective instincts are what they are. In other words, there exists between your instincts and mine a certain affinity. Deeper it is not given us to probe.'

'Then is honour an instinct?'

'It is.'

'Oh, Evgenii!' cried Arkady sorrowfully.

'Do you dislike the conversation? Then let us philosophise no more, but "permit nature to waft upon us the silence of sleep," to quote Pushkin.'

'Pushkin never said any such thing,' objected Arkady.

'Then, if he did not, he ought, being a poet, to have done so. Perhaps he had served in the army?'

'Never did he serve in the army.'

'Indeed? Why, in his every line we come across "To battle, to battle, for the honour of Russia!" '

'That is a mere invention on your part. The statement is an absolute calumny.'

'A calumny? What matters a calumny? What is there in the term to be afraid of? Slander a man as much as you like, yet for himself he will hear things twenty times worse.'

'Suppose we sleep,' said Arkady irritably.

'With pleasure,' Bazarov replied.

Nevertheless neither succeeded in the effort, for almost every sleep-destroying sentiment happened to be in the ascendant. So, after five minutes of such ineffectual striving, both opened their eyes, and lay mutely gazing about them.

'Look!' cried Arkady after a pause. 'Do you see that withered maple leaf fluttering to the ground? Are not its movements exactly like those of a butterfly? Strange that an object so joyous and full of life should be able so to counterfeit an object mournful and dead!'

'My friend,' protested Bazarov, 'let me make at least *this* request of you: that you do not talk in "beautiful language." '

'I talk as I am able. I decline to be domineered over. Should a thought chance to enter my head, why should I not express it?'

'Similarly am I at liberty to express the thought that to talk in "beautiful language" is sheerly indecent.'

'Indecent? Then swearing is not indecent?'

'Aha! I perceive you still to be minded to follow in your uncle's footsteps. How the idiot would have rejoiced if he could have heard you!'

'*What* did you call Paul Petrovitch?'

'I called him merely what he is – merely an idiot.'

'Have done!' shouted Arkady.

'Therein I detect the tie of blood,' said Bazarov calmly. 'It is a very stubborn factor, I have noticed, in some people. A man may abjure everything else, and cut himself adrift from every other prejudice, yet still remain powerless to confess that the brother who habitually steals his shirts is a thief. You see, the difficulty lies in the word "my." Is not that so?'

'No. It was from a sense of justice, rather than from a sense of kinship, that I spoke. But since you have no understanding of the former, as an instinct which you simply do not possess, you are not in a position to pass judgement upon such a feeling.'

'In other words, "I, Arkady Kirsanov, am altogether above your comprehension." Well, I make mute obeisance to that.'

'Come, come, Evgenii! We shall end by quarrelling.'

'Oh that you *would* do me the favour to quarrel! We could have a real set-to *à outrance*, and with our coats off.'

'To the end that – ?'

'To the end that we might rend one another in pieces. Why not? Here, amid the hay, in this idyllic setting, far from the madding crowd and every human eye, it would be not at all a bad thing. No, you shall *not* make it up with me! Rather will I seize you by the throat!'

As he extended his long, sharp fingers, Arkady rolled over and prepared jestingly to grapple with his assailant. But the next moment the sight of Bazarov's face, with its expression of malice and the non-jesting menace which lurked in the twisted smile and the flashing eyes, gave him a shock, and filled him with involuntary awe.

'*This*, then, is where you have got to!' cried Vasili Ivanitch from behind them as, vested in a home-made cotton pea-jacket and a home-made straw hat, the old military doctor suddenly confronted the pair. 'I have been searching for you everywhere, and certainly you have chosen a capital spot, and are engaged also in a capital occupation – in the occupation of lying on the earth and gazing at the heavens. For my part, I believe that such an occupation can have its uses.'

'I gaze at the heavens only when I am going to sneeze,' said Bazarov. Then, turning to Arkady, he added in an undertone: 'Forgive me if I hurt you.'

'Do not mention it,' was Arkady's rejoinder in a similar undertone, as covertly he pressed his friend's hand.

Shocks of such a kind, however, were bound, in time, to react upon their friendship.

'As I look at you, young gentlemen,' Vasili Ivanitch continued as, nodding his head, he rested his hands upon a crooked stick, his own manufacture, which had a Turk's head for a handle, 'I cannot suffi-ciently admire you. What strength you embody! How you speak of the flower of youth, of capacity, and of talent! You resemble Castor and Pollux themselves.'

'To think of your flaunting your mythology like that!' said Bazarov. 'At the same time, you must have been a fine Latin scholar in your day. In fact, did not you once receive a silver medal for an essay?'

'The Dioscuri, the Dioscuri themselves!' continued the old man ecstatically.

'Come, come, father! Do not play the fool.'

'Ah, well! No, I have not sought you out to pay you compliments: I have come to inform the pair of you that dinner is nearly ready, and also to give you, Evgenii, a warning. I know that, as a man of sense, as well as a man well versed in the world, you will be charitable. The case is this. This morning your mother took it into her head to organise a thanksgiving ceremony on the occasion of your return. – No, do not think that I am inviting you to the ceremony: on the contrary, it is over. All that I am going to say is that Father Alexis – '

'The priest?'

'Yes, and our private confessor. Well, this Father Alexis is going to dine with us, even though I had not expected it, and it was not my suggestion, but merely an arrangement which has come about some-how – probably through his having failed to understand me aright. Not that we look upon him as anything but a man of rectitude and good sense.'

'Surely you do not mean to imply that he is likely to devour my portion of the food, do you?'

Vasili Ivanitch burst out laughing.

'Ha, ha, ha!' he cried.

'I feel easy, then,' continued Bazarov. 'In fact, never do I mind with whom I sit at table.'

Vasili Ivanitch's face brightened at once.

'I felt sure of that in advance,' he said. 'Yes, I knew that you, a young man, are as superior to prejudice as I am at sixty-two' (Vasili had none the less shrunk from confessing that he had wished for the thanksgiving ceremony as much as his wife had, since his piety was fully equal to hers). 'In any case Father Alexis would like to make your acquaintance; while you, for your part, will very likely take to him, seeing that he not only plays cards, but also (though this is quite between ourselves) smokes a pipe!'

'Indeed? After dinner, then, we will have a game, and I will despoil him utterly.'

'Ha, ha, ha! We shall see, we shall see.'

'Then at times you hark back to old days?' Bazarov asked with a tinge of surprise.

Vasili Ivanitch's bronzed cheeks took on a faint flush.

'For shame, Evgenii!' he muttered. 'Remember that the past is the past. Nevertheless, even in this gentleman's presence I am ready to confess that in my youth I had my addictions, and that, since, I have paid for them. But how hot the weather is! Let me seat myself beside you; though I hope that, in doing so, I shall not interrupt your conversation?'

'By no means,' replied Arkady with alacrity.

Vasili Ivanitch subsided with a grunt and the remark:

'Your *logement* reminds me of my military bivouacking days – this rick being a dressing-station.' There followed a sigh. 'Aye, many and many an experience have I had in my time. For instance, let me tell you a curious story about the black death in Bessarabia.'

'When you received the order of St Vladimir?' said Bazarov. 'Yes, I know the story. But why do you never wear the badge of the order?'

'As I have told you, I care not a jot for appearances,' protested Vasili Ivanitch (though only on the previous day had he had the red riband of the order removed from his coat). He then embarked upon the story.

'Evgenii has gone to sleep,' presently he whispered to Arkady with a good-humoured wink and a pointing finger. 'Come, come, Evgenii!' he added in a louder tone. 'It is time to get up! Time for dinner!'

Father Alexis – a stout, good-looking man with thick, well-combed hair and an embroidered girdle over a lilac cassock – proved a clever, resourceful guest who, taking the initiative as regards shaking hands with Arkady and Bazarov (somehow he seemed to divine that they did not require his blessing), bore himself, in general, with complete absence of restraint, and, while neither demeaning himself nor imposing general constraint, made merry over scholastic Latin, defended his archbishop, quaffed a couple of glasses of wine (refusing a third), and accepted one of Arkady's cigars, though, instead of smoking it, he put it into his pocket to take home with him. The only thing that was at all unpleasant was the fact that every now and then, on raising a stealthy hand to brush from his face a fly, he, in lieu of doing so, crushed the insect flat!

Dinner over, he seated himself with modest zest at the card-table, and ended by despoiling Bazarov of two-and-a-half roubles in paper money (this rural establishment took no account of the system of computing cash in silver). During the game the hostess sat beside her son with her cheek resting on her hand as usual, and only rose from the table when it became necessary to order further relays of refreshment. Yet to caress Bazarov was more than she dared do; nor did he give her the least encouragement in that direction in addition to which Vasili Ivanitch further restrained her ardour by whispering at intervals: 'Do not worry our Evgenii. Young men do not like that sort of thing. Also, hardly need it be said that the dinner of which the company had just partaken had been of the usual sumptuousness, seeing that at break of day Timotheitch had set out for Circassian beef, and that the *starosta* also had galloped in quest of trout, eels, and crabs, while a sum of forty-two kopecks had been paid to peasant women for mushrooms. Arina Vlasievna's eyes, fixed immovably upon Bazarov, had in them something more than tenderness and affection. In them there were also sadness, curiosity, a touch of apprehension, and a kind of painful deference. Yet never did he mark their expression, since never did he turn in her direction, save to put to her the curtest of questions, and, once, to ask her to lay her hand in his, 'for luck.' On the latter occasion she slipped her plump fingers into his hard, capacious palm, waited a little, and then asked him:

'Has that helped you at all in your play?'

'It has not,' he replied with a contemptuous grimace. 'On the contrary, things are even worse than they were before.'

'Yes, the cards seem to be against you,' remarked Father Alexis with an assumed air of sympathy as he stroked his handsome beard.

'But beware of the Code Napoléon, my father,' observed Vasili Ivanitch as he played an ace. 'Beware of the Code Napoléon.'

'Which, in the end, brought Napoleon to St Helena,' retorted the father as he trumped the ace.

'A glass of currant wine, Eniushka dear?' asked Arina Vlasievna.

Bazarov replied with a shrug of his shoulders.

Next day he said to Arkady:

'Tomorrow I must depart. The place wearies me, for I wish to work, and it is impossible to do so here. I will come to your place, I think, for all my chemical preparations are there. Moreover, one can at least lock one's door at your place; whereas here, though my father keeps saying, "My study is entirely at your disposal, and no one shall disturb you," he himself is never absent for a moment. And, for that matter, I should be ashamed to lock him outside, or my mother either. Sometimes I can hear her groaning in the next room. Yet no sooner do I go out to her than I find that I have not a word to say.'

'She will be much distressed at your departure,' said Arkady. 'And so will he.'

'But I intend to return.'

'Exactly when?'

'When I am on my way back to St Petersburg.'

'I am particularly sorry for your mother.'

'Why so? Has she been stuffing you with fruit?'

Arkady lowered his eyes.

'You do not know her,' he said. 'She is not only a good woman, but also a very wise one. This morning I had half an hour's very practical and interesting talk with her.'

'A talk in which she told you all about me?'

'We spoke of other topics besides yourself.'

'Possibly. Possibly, too, you, as an outsider, may see things clearer than I do. Yet when a woman can talk for half an hour it is a good sign, and I will depart as I have said.'

'But you will not find it easy to break the news to her, for her plans for us extend over a couple of weeks.'

'No, it may not prove easy, as you say; and the less so since the devil led me to vex my father this morning. It was like this. A few days ago he had one of his serfs flogged, and therein did rightly. No, you need not look at me with such indignation. I say my father did rightly for the reason that the peasant in question had proved himself to be an arrant thief and drunkard. Unfortunately, my father had not expected me to get to hear of the occurrence; wherefore he was the more put out when he found that I had done so. Well, now his vexation will be twofold! However, no matter. He will get over it before long.'

Yet, though Bazarov had said 'No matter,' he let the whole of the rest of the day elapse before he could make up his mind to acquaint Vasili Ivanitch with his intention. Finally, just as he was saying good-night to his father in the study, he observed with a prolonged yawn:

'By the way, I had almost forgotten to request you to have our horses sent forward to Thedot's.'

Vasili Ivanitch looked thunderstruck.

'Then is Monsieur Kirsanov leaving us?' he enquired.

'Yes, and I am going with him.'

Vasili Ivanitch fidgeted for a moment or two.

'You say that you are going with him?' he murmured.

'Yes. I *must* go. So pray have the horses sent forward as requested.'

'I – I will, I will,' the old man stuttered. 'So they are to go to Thedot's? Yes, yes, very well. Only, only – is there any particular reason for this change of plan?'

'There is. I am engaged to pay Arkady a short visit. That done, I will return to you.'

'Only to be a *short* visit? Good!' And Vasili Ivanitch pulled out his pocket-handkerchief, and blew his nose. In doing so, he bent his head very low – almost to the ground. 'Well, well! Things shall be as you desire. Yet we had hoped that you would have stayed with us a little longer. Three days only! Three days after three years of absence! Ah, that is not much, Evgenii – it is not much!'

'But I tell you I intend to return soon. You see, I *must* go.'

'You have no choice, eh? Very well, very well. Of course, engage-ments must be kept. Yes, yes; of course they must be kept. And I am to send the horses forward? Very good. Naturally, Arina and I had not altogether looked for this. Only today she has been to a neighbour to beg flowers for your room.'

Nor of the fact that, each morning, he had gone downstairs in his slippers to confer with Timotheitch; nor of the fact that, producing, with tremulous fingers, one ragged banknote after another, he had commissioned his henchman to make various purchases with special reference to the question of eatables (in particular, of a certain red wine which he had noticed the young men to like); no, of none of these facts did Vasili Ivanitch make any mention.

'The greatest thing in the world is one's freedom,' he went on. 'I, too, make it my rule. Never should one let oneself be hampered or – '

A sudden break occurred in his voice, and he made for the door.

'I promise you that we will return soon, my father. I give you my word of honour upon that.'

But Vasili Ivanitch did not look round – he just waved his hand and departed. Mounting to the bedroom, he found Arina asleep, so started to say his prayers in an undertone, for fear of awaking her. But at once she opened her eyes.

'In that you, Vasili Ivanitch?' she asked.

'Yes, mother.'

'Have you just left Eniusha? Do you know, I am anxious about him. Does he sleep comfortably on the sofa? Today I told Anfisushka to lay him out your travelling mattress and the new pillows. Also, I would have given him our feather bed had he not disliked soft lying.'

'Do not fret, mother dear. He is quite comfortable. "Lord, pardon us sinners!" ' And Vasili Ivanitch went on with his prayers. Yet his heart was full of an aching compassion for his old companion; nor did he want to tell her overnight of the sorrow which was awaiting her on the morrow.

Next day, therefore, Arkady and Bazarov departed. From earliest morn an air of woe pervaded the household. Anfisushka let fall some crockery, and Thedika's perturbation ended in his taking off his shoes. As for Vasili Ivanitch, he fussed about, and made a brave show – he talked in loud tones, and stamped his feet upon the floor as he walked; but his face had suddenly fallen in, and his glance could not meet that of his son. Meanwhile Arina Vlasievna indulged in quiet weeping. Indeed, but for the fact that her husband had spent two hours that morning in comforting her, she would have broken down completely, and lost all self-control.

But at last, when, after reiterated promises to return within, at most, a month, Bazarov had freed himself from the arms which sought to detain him, and entered the *tarantass*; when the horses had started, and their collar-bow had begun to tinkle, and the wheels to revolve; when to gaze after the vehicle any longer had become useless, and the dust had subsided, and Timotheitch, bent and tottering, had crawled back into his pantry; when the old couple found themselves alone in a house which seemed suddenly to have grown as dishevelled and as decrepit as they – then, ah, then did Vasili Ivanitch desist from his brief show of waving his handkerchief in the verandah, and sink into a chair, and drop his head upon his breast.

'He has gone for ever, he has gone for ever,' he muttered. 'He has gone because he found the life here tedious, and once more I am as lonely as the sand of the desert!'

These words he kept repeating again and again; and, each time that he did so, he raised his hand, and pointed into the distance.

But presently Arina Vlasievna approached him, and, pressing her grey head to his, said:

'Never mind, my Vasia. True, our son has broken away from us; he is like a falcon – he has flown hither, he has flown thither, as he willed: but you and I, like lichen in a hollow tree, are still side by side, we are not parted . . . And ever I shall be the same to you, as you will be the same to me.'

Taking his hands from his face, Vasili Ivanitch embraced his old comrade, his wife, as never – no, not even during the days of his courtship – he had done before. And thus she comforted him.

Chapter 22

IN SILENCE, or merely exchanging a few unimportant words, the travellers made their way to Thedot's posting-house. Arkady felt anything but pleased with Bazarov, and Bazarov felt anything but pleased with himself. Moreover, the younger man's heart was heavy with the sort of unreasoning depression which is known only to youth.

The driver hitched his horses, and then, mounting to the box, enquired whether he was to drive to the right or to the left.

Arkady started. The road to the right led to the town, and thence to his father's house; while the road to the left led to Madame Odintsov's establishment.

He glanced at Bazarov.

'To the left, Evgenii?' he queried.

Bazarov turned away his head.

'Why that folly again?' he muttered.

'Folly, I know,' said Arkady, 'but what does that matter? We need but call in passing.'

Bazarov pulled his cap over his eyes.

'Do as you like,' he said.

'To the left, then,' cried Arkady to the coachman; and the *tarantass* started in the direction of Nikolsköe. Nevertheless, for all that the friends had decided upon this foolish course, they remained as silent and downcast as ever.

Indeed, Madame Odintsov's butler had not even made his appearance upon the verandah before the pair divined that they had done unwisely to yield to such an impulse. The fact that no one in the house had expected them was emphasised by the circumstance that when Madame entered the drawing-room they had already spent a considerable time there in awkward silence. However, she accorded them her usual suave welcome, though she seemed a little surprised at their speedy return, and, at heart, not over-pleased at it. For this reason they hastened to explain that theirs was a mere passing call, and that in about four hours they would be continuing their journey to the town. In reply she said nothing beyond that she requested Arkady to convey her greetings to his father, and then sent for her aunt; and inasmuch as the Princess entered in a state of having just overslept herself, her wrinkled old face betokened even greater malignity than usual. Katia was not well, and did not leave her room at all: and this caused Arkady suddenly to realise that he would have been as glad to see her as Anna Sergievna. The four hours were filled with a desultory conversation which Anna Sergievna carried on without a single smile: nor until the very moment of parting did her usual friendliness seem to stir within her soul.

'I am out of humour today,' she said, 'but that you must not mind. Come again soon. I address the invitation to you both.'

Bazarov and Arkady responded with silent bows, re-entered the *tarantass*, and drove forward to Marino, whither they arrived, without incident, on the following evening. *En route*, neither of the pair mentioned Madame Odintsov, and Bazarov in particular scarcely opened his mouth, but gazed towards the horizon with a hard look in his eyes.

But at Marino everyone was delighted to see them, for Nikolai Petrovitch had begun to feel uneasy at the prolonged absence of his son, and now leapt from the sofa with a cry of joy when Thenichka ran to announce that 'the young gentlemen' were arriving. Yes, even Paul Petrovitch felt conscious of a touch of pleasant excitement, and smiled indulgently as he shook hands with the wanderers. Ensued then much talking and questioning, in which Arkady took the leading part, and more especially during supper, which lasted far into the night, since Nikolai Petrovitch ordered up several bottles of porter which had just arrived from Moscow, and made so merry that his cheeks assumed a raspberry tint, and he fell to venting half-boyish, half-hysterical laughs. Moreover, the general enlivenment extended even to the kitchen, where Duniasha kept breathlessly banging doors, and at three o'clock in the morning Peter essayed to execute on the guitar a Cossack waltz which would have sounded sweet and plaintive amid the stillness of the night had not the performance broken down after the opening cadenza, owing to the fact that nature had denied the cultured underling a talent either for music or for anything else.

Indeed, of late, life at Marino had been far from comfortable. In particular had poor Nikolai Petrovitch been in a bad way, for his troubles in connection with the estate – troubles of an exclusively futile and hopeless order – were growing greater from day to day. The worst of them came of the system of hired labour, which enabled some of the workmen to keep demanding either their discharge or an increase of wages, and others to depart as soon as ever they had received their earnest-money. Also, some of the horses had fallen sick, certain implements had been burnt, all hands were performing their tasks in a slovenly manner, a milling machine ordered from Moscow had turned out to be useless owing to its weight, a second such machine had

broken down on its first being used, half the cattle sheds had disappeared in a conflagration caused by a blind old serf woman 'smoking'
her cow with a firestick during blustery weather (though she herself
asserted that the trouble had come of the *barin's* manufacturing new-
fangled cheeses and lacteal products in general), and, lastly, the steward
had grown so fat and lazy (as do all Russians who fall upon 'easy times'),
and permitted his dislike of Nikolai Petrovitch so to limit his activities,
that he had come to doing no more than bestowing an occasional prod
upon a passing pig, or threatening some half-naked serf boy, while
spending the rest of the time in bed. Again, such of the peasants as had
received allotments under the *obrok* system had failed to pay their dues,
as well as applied themselves to stealing timber to such an extent that,
almost every night, the watchman had to apprehend a culprit or two, as
well as to impound horses which peasants had turned out to graze in
the meadows attached to the manor. For illicit grazing of this sort
Nikolai Petrovitch had decreed forfeiture of the horses; but usually the
matter ended in the animals being kept for a day or two at the *barin's*
expense, and then restored to their owners. Lastly, the peasants had
taken to quarrelling among themselves, through brothers conceiving
the idea of demanding a share of each other's earnings, and through
their wives suddenly finding themselves unable to get on in the same
hut; wherefore feuds had arisen which had caused whole households to
spring to their feet as at a word of command, and to flock to the portico
of the estate office, where, breaking in upon the *barin's* privacy (very
often with bruised faces and drunken gait), they demanded justice and
an immediate settlement, while female sobs and whimperings mingled
with the curses of the male portion of the throng. Whenever this had
happened Nikolai Petrovitch had had to part the hostile factions from
one another, and to shout himself hoarse, even though he had known
in advance that no equitable decision was feasible. Finally, there had
been a deficiency of hands for the harvest, since a neighbouring
*odnovorzty** of benign aspect who had undertaken to provide harvesters
at two roubles per *desiatin* had cheated without compunction, and
supplied women workers who also demanded extortionate wages.
Meanwhile the grain had rotted in the fields, and, later on, the women
had not got through the mowing before the Board of Overseers had
begun to press for immediate payment of percentage dues and arrears.

'I can do nothing,' would be Nikolai Petrovitch's despairing
exclamation. 'My principles forbid me either to contend with these

---

* A freeholder, a member of the class which, in the days of this story, stood
midway between the *pomiestchik*, or landowner, and the *krestianin*, or serf.

people or to send for the *stanovoi*:* yet, without the power to threaten punishment, one can make no headway with such folk.'

'*Du calme, du calme,*' Paul Petrovitch would advise. Then he would growl, frown, and twist his moustache.

From these brawls Bazarov kept entirely aloof: nor, as a guest, was he called upon to interfere in them, but was free, from the day of his arrival, to apply himself solely to his frogs, infusoria, and chemical compositions. On the other hand, Arkady considered himself bound; if not to help his father, at all events to offer to help him; wherefore he listened to Nikolai's complaints with patience, and on one occasion even tendered him advice (though not advice meant to be taken, but advice designed to manifest the interest felt by him, Arkady, in current affairs). As a matter of fact, estate-management was not wholly distasteful to him, and he could find pleasure in thinking out agricultural problems; but his mind was filled with other preoccupations. For one thing, he discovered to his surprise that his thoughts were constantly turning in the direction of Nikolsköe; and though there had been a time when he would have shrugged his shoulders upon being told that he would ever come to find residence under the same roof as Bazarov – least of all, when that roof was his father's – a dull affair, he found time hang heavy on his hands, and his attention easily stray elsewhere. So he tried the expedient of walking until thoroughly worn out, but even this did not help him; until eventually he learnt in conversation with his father, that recently some letters of great interest had been chanced upon – letters which Arkady's mother had indited to the mother of Madame Odintsov. And from that moment onwards he never rested until he had induced Nikolai Petrovitch to re-discover the said letters, and to turn out, during the search, a score of boxes and drawers. Then only, when the half-mouldy documents had been dragged to light, did the young man feel easier in his soul, and bear himself as though now he saw before him the goal of his existence.

' "I address the invitation to both of you," ' he kept whispering to himself. 'Yes, that is what she said. Damn it, I will go.'

But next there would recur to his memory the recent visit and its cold reception; until once more he would be seized with his old timidity and awkwardness. In the end, however, the spirit of adventurous youth, aided by a secret desire to try his luck, to test his strength unaided, and without a protector, contrived to win the day.

Ten days later, therefore, he invented a pretext, in the shape of a desire to study the working of Sunday schools, to drive to the town,

---

* Magistrate.

and thence to Nikolsköe. As he drove, the manner in which he encouraged his postilion communicated to his progress the character, rather, of a young officer's trip to fight his first duel, for diffidence, impatience, and delight were well-nigh choking him.

'Above all things,' he kept reflecting, 'I must not think too much of myself.' And though the postilion who had fallen to his lot was of the type of rascal who pulls up at every tavern door, there hove in sight, before long, the familiar, high-pitched roof of the mansion.

'But what am I doing?' now occurred to him the thought. 'Indeed, would it not be better to go back?'

Unfortunately, to the sound of the postilion's whistlings and tongue-clickings the *troika* of horses trotted bravely forward, and presently the bridge thundered under the combined weight of the hooves and wheels. Ah, *there* was the avenue of clipped firs! Yes, and *there* was a glimpse of a pink dress amid some dark foliage! Yes, and *there* a glimpse of a young face peering from the shade of a silken parasol! Yes, yes – it *was* Katia! He had recognised her in an instant, as she him! Bidding the postilion pull up, Arkady leapt from the carriage, and approached the maiden.

'So it is you?' she exclaimed. And at the same moment a blush overspread her face. 'Let us go and look for my sister. She is in the garden, and will be delighted to see you.'

So she conducted him thither. How lucky that he had met her as he had done! More pleased he could not have felt if she had been his own sister. Yes, things were indeed fortunate! Now there would have to be no butler, and no formal announcement of his arrival.

Of Anna Sergievna he caught sight at a turn in the path. She had her back to him, but presently, on hearing the sound of approaching footsteps, faced about.

Once more confusion seized Arkady in its grip. Yet no sooner had she spoken than he felt his courage return.

'How do you do?' she said in her even, kindly way as she advanced to meet him with a smile that was slightly tempered with the sun and wind. 'Where did you find him, Katia?'

'I have brought with me something which you are unlikely to have been expecting,' he said. 'For I – '

'But you have brought me yourself,' she rejoined. 'And that is the best bringing of all.'

Chapter 23

AFTER SPEEDING ARKADY on his way with satirical expressions of regret (as well as giving him to understand that the satirist laboured under no delusions as to the object of the young man's journey), Bazarov withdrew into complete seclusion, since a perfect fever for work had come upon him. Nor did he quarrel any longer with Paul Petrovitch, and the less so since the latter had now come to adopt an exclusively aristocratic attitude, and to express his sentiments only in monosyllables, not in words. Once, and once only, did he allow himself to engage in a controversy with Bazarov over the then current question of the rights of the *dvoriané*. But suddenly he checked himself, and said with an air of cold politeness:

'It is clear that we shall never understand one another. At all events *I* have not the honour to understand *you*.'

'True,' agreed Bazarov. 'For a man may understand the precipitation of ether, and be *au fait* with what is taking place in the sun, yet, confront him with the fact that another man blows his nose differently from the manner in which he blows his own, and at once that man will become lost in perplexity.'

At the same time, there were occasions when Paul Petrovitch requested permission to attend the other's experiments; and once he went so far as to apply his perfumed, clean-shaven features to the microscope, for the purpose of observing how a transparent infusorium could swallow a greenish-looking particle, and then masticate the same with fang-like protuberances which grew in its throat. Still more frequently was Nikolai Petrovitch present in Bazarov's room. Indeed, but for the counter-distraction of estate-management, he would have spent his whole time in the process of what he called 'self-improvement.' Yet he never hampered the young naturalist: on the contrary, he would seat himself in a remote corner of the room, and, but for a guarded question or two, confine himself solely to silently and absorbedly watching the experiments. Also, at meal times he always endeavoured to turn the conversation in the direction of physics or geology or chemistry, for the reason that he divined in any other direction (that of industry, or, still more, that of politics) there lay a greater danger of collisions, or, at all events of mutual soreness. For rightly did he divine that his brother's enmity towards Bazarov had by no means abated. And to this conclusion an incident which occurred at

a juncture when cholera had just made its appearance in the neighbourhood, and carried off two victims from Marino itself, lent additional
colour. One night Paul Petrovitch happened to be seized with a
fainting fit, yet refused to apply to Bazarov for assistance; and when
Bazarov, on meeting him on the following day, enquired why such a
course had not been adopted, Paul Petrovitch – still pale, but as
carefully brushed and combed as ever – retorted: 'Did not you yourself
tell me that you have no belief in medicine?'

Thus day followed day. Yet, though Bazarov devoted himself
wholly to work, there was one person in the house whom he did not
hold at arm's length, but was always willing to talk to. That person
was Thenichka. Mostly he encountered her in the early mornings,
when she was walking in the garden or the courtyard; but never did he
enter her room, nor did she ever come to his door, save once, for the
purpose of asking him to help her with Mitia's bath. And she not only
trusted Bazarov; she also held him in no awe, and allowed herself
more freedom in his presence than she did in that of Nikolai
Petrovitch himself. The reason is difficult to determine. Perhaps it
was the fact that unconsciously she detected in Bazarov none of the
dvorianin element, none of that superiority which at once attracts and
repels; the young Nihilist, to her, was just a clever doctor, and no
more. At all events, she was so free from shyness in his presence that
she would dandle her child unabashed, and, on one occasion, when
seized with a headache, went so far as to accept at his hands a spoonful
of medicine. True, in Nikolai Petrovitch's presence she seemed to
shun Bazarov; but this was done more out of a sense of decorum than
through subtlety. As for Paul Petrovitch, she feared him as much as
ever, for he had taken to watching her with a keen, steady eye, and to
making his appearance behind her as though his figure, clad in its
inevitable English suit, and posed in its usual attitude of hands in
trousers pockets, had suddenly sprung from the floor. 'Whenever I
see him I feel cold all over,' once she complained to Duniasha;
whereupon that maiden's thoughts reverted longingly to another
'unfeeling' individual who had, all unwittingly, come to be 'the cruel
tyrant' of her heart.

Thenichka, therefore, liked Bazarov, and Bazarov liked Thenichka.
Indeed, no sooner did he speak to her than his face would undergo a
change, and, assuming a bright, almost a good-humoured, expression,
exchange its habitual superciliousness for something like playful solicitude. Meanwhile she grew more beautiful daily. In the lives of young
women there is a season when they begin to unfold and bloom like the
roses in summer: and to that period Thenichka had just come.

Everything, even the July heat then prevalent, contributed to it. Dressed in a gown of some light white material, she looked even lighter and whiter than it; and though she escaped actual sunburn, the heated air imparted to her cheeks and ears a faint tan, and, permeating her frame with gentle indolence, imbued her exquisite eyes with dreamy languor. No longer could she do any work; she could only let her hands sink upon her lap, and there remain. Seldom going even for a stroll, she spent the most of her time in a state of gently querulous and panting, but not distasteful, inertia.

'You should go and bathe as often as you can,' Nikolai Petrovitch said to her one day (he had had a large, canopied bathing-place constructed in one of the last few ponds on the estate).

'Ah!' she gasped. 'Even to walk to the pond half-kills me: and to walk back from it half-kills me again. There is no shade in the garden you see.'

'True,' he agreed, wiping his forehead.

At seven o'clock one morning, when Bazarov was returning from a walk, he encountered Thenichka in the midst of a lilac clump which, though past the season of flowering, was still green and leafy. As usual, she had a white scarf thrown over her head, and beside the bench on which she was sitting there was a bunch of red and white roses with the dew yet glistening on their petals. He bade her good-morning.

'It is you, then, Evgenii Vasilitch!' she exclaimed as she put aside a corner of her scarf to look at him – a movement which bared her arm to the elbow.

'What are you doing?' he asked as he seated himself beside her. 'Is it a nosegay you are making?'

'Yes, for the breakfast table. Nikolai Petrovitch is so fond of such things.'

'But breakfast is not yet. What a waste of flowers!'

'I know, but I gather them now because later the weather becomes too hot for walking. This is the only time when it is possible even to breathe. The heat makes me faint, and I am afraid of falling ill with it.'

'Mere fancy. Let me feel your pulse.'

He took her hand in his, and found the pulse to be beating with such regularity that he did not trouble even to count its throbs.

'You will live to be a hundred,' he said as he relinquished her wrist.

'God preserve me from that!' exclaimed she.

'Why so? Surely you would like to live a long time?'

'Yes – I should; but not for a hundred years. You see, my grandmother lived to be eighty-five, but suffered terribly. Long before she died she had a constant cough, and was also blind and deaf and crooked, and had become a burden to herself. What would be the use of a life like that?'

'You think that it is better to be young?'

'I do. And why not?'

'How is it better? Tell me that.'

'How is it better? Oh, as long as one is young one can do what one wants to do – one can walk about, and carry things, and not be dependent upon other folk. Is not that the best way?'

'I do not know. At all events *I* care not whether I be young or old.'

'What makes you say that? Surely you cannot mean it?'

'No? Well, think of what my youth means to me. I am a lonely man, a man without home or – '

'But all depends upon yourself.'

'No, it does not. I only wish that someone would take pity upon my loneliness!'

She glanced at him, but said nothing. After a pause she resumed:

'What is that book of yours?'

'This? It is a learned, scholarly work.'

'How you study! Do you never grow tired of it? By this time, I should think, you must know everything.'

'Indeed I do not . . . But try reading a few lines of the book.'

'I should never understand them. Is it a Russian book?' (She took the heavily bound volume into her hands.)

'What a large book!' she continued.

'Yes. Also, it is a Russian book.'

'Nevertheless I should not be able to understand it.'

'I do not want you to understand it. I merely want to be able to watch you as you read. For when you read you twitch your little nose most charmingly!'

She began to read aloud a page 'on Creosote,' but soon burst out laughing, and replaced the book upon the bench, whence it slipped to the ground.

'I love to see you laugh,' said Bazarov.

'Say no more,' she interrupted.

'Also, I love to hear you speak. Your voice is like the bubbling of a brook.'

She turned away her head, and fell to sorting her flowers. Presently she resumed:

'Why do you love to hear me speak? You must have talked to many much finer and cleverer ladies?'

'I assure you, nevertheless, that all the "fine and clever ladies" in the world are worth less than your little finger.'

'Oh, come!' And she crossed her hands.

Bazarov picked up the book.

'It is a work on medicine,' he observed. 'Why did you throw it away?'

'It is a work on medicine?' she re-echoed, and turned to him again. 'Do you know, ever since you gave me those capsules – you remember them, do you not? – Mitia has slept splendidly! I can never sufficiently thank you. You are indeed good!'

'But the physician ought to be paid his fee,' remarked he with a smile. 'Doctors never do their work for nothing.'

Upon this she raised her eyes. They looked all the darker for the brilliant glare which was beating upon the upper portion of her face. As a matter of fact, she was trying to divine whether he was speaking in earnest or in jest.

'Of course I should be delighted to pay you!' she said. 'But first I must mention the matter to Nikolai Petrovitch.'

'What?' he exclaimed. 'You really think it is *money* I want? No, I do not require of you money.'

'What, then?' she queried.

'What? Well, guess.'

'How can I guess?'

'Then I must tell you. I want, I want – I want one of those roses.'

She burst into a peal of laughter, and clapped her hands with delight at the request. Yet the laughter was accompanied with a certain sense of relief. Bazarov eyed her.

'Ah, you must excuse my laughing, Egenii Vasilitch,' she said (bending over the seat of the bench, she fumbled among the roses). 'Which sort should you prefer? A red rose or a white one?'

'A red one, and not too large.'

'Then take this one,' she said, sitting up again. Yet even as she spoke she drew back her outstretched hand, and, biting her lips, glanced in the direction of the entrance to the arbour, and listened intently.

'What is it?' asked Bazarov. 'Do you hear Nikolai Petrovitch coming?'

'No. Besides, everyone has gone out to the fields. Nor do I fear anyone except Paul Petrovitch. I merely thought that, that – '

'You thought what?'

'That someone *might* be coming this way. It seems I was wrong. Take this rose.'

She handed Bazarov the gift.

'*Why* do you fear Paul Petrovitch?' he asked.

'I do so because he frightens me – when I speak to him he returns me no answer; he just stares at me in a meaning sort of way. You, too, do not like him, I believe? It was with him that you had such a quarrel, was it not? What it was all about I do not know, but at least I know that you worsted him like, like – '

With a gesture she signified the manner in which she considered Bazarov to have routed Paul Petrovitch.

'And, had *he* worsted *me*,' he enquired, 'would you have taken my part?'

'How could I? We should have agreed no better than you and he.'

'You think so? Then let me tell you that a certain little hand could twist me around its little finger.'

'Whose hand is that?'

'I expect you can guess. But smell this rose which you have just given me.'

She bent forward in the direction of the flower, and as she did so her scarf slipped from her head to her shoulders, and revealed a mass of dark, soft, fluffy, glossy hair.

'Wait,' said Bazarov. 'I, too, will smell the rose.'

And, reaching forward, he kissed her full on her parted lips.

She started back, and pressed her hands against his breast as though to repel him; but so weak was the act of repulsion that he found it possible to renew and to prolong his kiss.

Suddenly there sounded from among the lilac bushes a dry cough, and just as Thenichka darted to the other end of the bench Paul Petrovitch appeared, bowed slightly to the pair, said with a sort of melancholy acidity in his tone: 'It is you, then?' and turned on his heel and departed. The next moment Thenichka picked up her roses and rushed from the arbour. As she passed Bazarov she whispered in his ear: 'That was indeed wrong of you, Evgenii Vasilitch!' And the words voiced a note of reproach that was palpably genuine and unfeigned.

Instantly Bazarov's thoughts recurred to another scene in which he had recently taken part, and he became conscience-stricken, as also contemptuous of himself, and vexed. He shook his head, congratulated himself ironically on his folly, and departed to his room.

As for Paul Petrovitch, he left the garden and walked slowly into the forest. He remained there a considerable time; and, on returning to breakfast, looked so dark of mien that Nikolai Petrovitch enquired anxiously whether he were not ill.

'As you know,' replied the other quietly, 'I suffer habitually from biliousness.'

Chapter 24

Two hours later he knocked at Bazarov's door.

'I feel that I must apologise for disturbing you in your pursuits,' he said as he seated himself near the window and rested both hands upon a fine ivory-headed cane which he had brought with him (as a rule he did not carry one). 'But the fact is that circumstances compel me to request five minutes of your time.'

'The *whole* of my time is at your disposal,' replied Bazarov, across whose features, as Paul Petrovitch had crossed the threshold, there had flitted a curious expression.

'No; five minutes will be sufficient. I have come to ask you a simple question.'

'And what might that question be?'

'Listen. When first you came to stay in my brother's house, and I had not yet been forced to deny myself the pleasure of conversing with you, it fell to my lot to hear you hold forth on many different subjects. But, unless my memory deceives me, never once did the conversation between you and myself, or in my presence, happen to fall upon the subject of the duel or single combat. Would you, therefore, mind putting yourself out to the extent of giving me the benefit of your views on the subject mentioned?'

Bazarov, who had risen to receive his visitor, now reseated himself upon the edge of the table, and folded his arms upon his breast.

'My views are as follows,' he replied. 'From the theoretical standpoint, the duel is a sheer absurdity. From the practical standpoint, it is another matter altogether.'

'You intend to convey (if I have understood you aright?) that, apart from your theoretical views on the duel, you would not, in practice, allow yourself to be insulted without subsequently demanding satisfaction?'

'You have guessed my meaning precisely.'

'Good! It is a view which I am indeed glad to hear you express, in that it delivers me from a dilemma.'

'You mean, from a state of indecision?'

'They are one and the same thing. I express myself in this manner to the end that you may understand me. I am not one of your college rats. Consequently I repeat that through your words I am relieved of the necessity of resorting to what would have been a painful expedient. To speak plainly, I have made up my mind to fight you.'

Bazarov raised his eyebrows a little.

'To fight me?' he said.

'Yes, to fight you.'

'And for what reason – if you do not mind telling me?'

'For a reason which I might explain, but concerning which I prefer to remain silent. Suffice it for me to intimate that your presence offends me, that I detest and despise your person, and (should the foregoing be insufficient) that I – '

'Enough!' interrupted Bazarov. His eyes had flashed even as Paul's had done. 'Further explanations would be superfluous. You have presumed to whet upon me your chivalrous spirit; wherefore, though I might have refused it, I will afford you satisfaction to the top of your bent.'

'I have to express to you my sincere obligation. From the first did I feel encouraged to hope that you would accept my challenge without constraining me to resort to more forcible measures.'

'In other words, and speaking without metaphor, to that cane?' said Bazarov in a tone of supreme indifference. 'Well, that is fair enough. Further insults are not needed – nor would you have found the offering of them altogether free from danger. Pray, therefore, remain a gentleman. It is as one that I accept your challenge.'

'Good!' replied Paul Petrovitch; and he laid aside his cane. 'Next, a few words on the subject of the conditions of our duel. First, pray be so good as to inform me whether or not you deem it necessary to resort to the formality of some such small difference of opinion as might serve as an ostensible excuse for my challenge?'

'I think that unnecessary. Such things are best done without formalities of any kind.'

'I agree – that is to say, I, like you, consider that to go into the true reasons for our antagonism would be inexpedient. Let us therefore allege to the world that we could not abide one another. What need would there be to say more?'

'What indeed?' echoed Bazarov in a tone decidedly ironical.

'Also, with regard to the actual conditions of the duel. Inasmuch as we have no seconds – for where could we find them? – '

'Quite so. Where indeed?'

'I have the honour to propose to you the following. Let us fight tomorrow morning – say, at six o'clock: the rendezvous to be behind the copse, the weapons to be pistols, and the distance ten paces.'

'Ten paces. Quite so! You and I abhor each other even at ten paces.'

'Eight, then, if you wish?'

'The same applies to eight.'

'And the number of shots to be two apiece. Also, in case either of us should fall, let each of us previously place in his pocket a letter laying upon himself the entire blame for his demise.'

'To that condition I wholly demur,' said Bazarov. 'I think that you are straying into the pages of a French novel, and away from reality.'

'Possibly I am. But, also, you will agree that to incur an unmerited suspicion of murder is a prospect not pleasant to contemplate?'

'I do. Yet still there remains another method of avoiding such an awkward imputation. That is to say, though we shall have no seconds, we can have a witness.'

'Whom precisely, if I might ask?'

'Peter.'

'Peter? What Peter?'

'Peter the valet, a man who stands at the apex of contemporary culture, and could therefore play the rôle and perform the functions, proper to such an occasion pre-eminently *comme il faut*.'

'I think that you are jesting, my good sir?'

'No, I am not. If you will deign to give my proposal consideration you will speedily arrive at the conviction that it is as simple as it is charged with good sense. Schiller it would be impossible to hide in a bag, but I will undertake to prepare Peter for the part, and to bring him to the rendezvous.'

'Still you are pleased to jest,' said Paul Petrovitch as he rose. 'But as you have so kindly met me, I have not the right to make further claims upon your time. All is arranged, then? In passing, have you any pistols?'

'How should I have any pistols? I am not a man of war.'

'Then perhaps you will allow me to offer you some of mine? Rest assured that they have not been fired by me for five years.'

'A very comforting assurance!'

'Lastly,' said Paul Petrovitch as he reached for his cane, 'it only remains for me to thank you, and to leave you to your pursuits. I have the honour to bid you good-day.'

'And I to say farewell until our pleasant meeting.'

With which Bazarov escorted his visitor to the door.

Paul Petrovitch gone, Bazarov stood awhile in thought. Then he exclaimed:

'Splendid indeed! Yet also unutterably stupid! What a comedy to play! Talk of educated dogs dancing on their hind legs! . . . However, I could not have refused him, for, otherwise, he would have struck me and *then*' – Bazarov turned pale, for his pride had been aroused – 'well, *then*, I should have strangled him like a kitten!'

He returned to his microscope, but found his heart to be still beating, and the coolness necessary to scientific observation to have disappeared.

'I suppose he saw us this morning,' he continued to himself. 'Yet surely he is not doing this on his brother's behalf? For what is there in a kiss? No; something else is in the background. Bah! What if it should be that he himself is in love with her? Yes, that is it. It is as clear as day. What a mess! Truly a horrible mess, however it be viewed! For first of all I am to have my brains blown out, and then I am to be made to leave this place! And there is Arkady to consider, and that old heifer Nikolai Petrovitch. Awkward! Awkward indeed!'

However, the day dragged its slow length along. Thenichka remained practically non-existent (in other words, she kept to her room as closely as a mouse to its hole), Nikolai Petrovitch walked about with a careworn air (it had been reported to him that mildew had begun to attack the wheat), and Paul Petrovitch's mien of icy urbanity succeeded in damping the spirits of Prokofitch himself.

Presently Bazarov sat down to write a letter to his father, but tore it up, and threw the pieces under the table.

'Should I be killed,' he reflected, 'my parents will hear of it soon enough. But I shall not be killed – I have yet far to wander about the world.'

Next he ordered Peter to call him at dawn; and inasmuch as the order was accompanied with a mention of important business, Peter jumped to the conclusion that it was Bazarov's intention to take him to St Petersburg. Bazarov then retired to rest. Yet, late though he had done so, he was troubled with fantastic visions. Ever before him there flitted Madame Odintsov, who was also his mother. And ever behind her there walked a black cat, which was also Thenichka. For his part, Paul Petrovitch figured as a forest which the dreamer was engaged to fight.

At length, when four o'clock arrived, Peter came to rouse him. Hastily dressing himself, he left the house with the valet. The morning was fine and fresh, and though a few wisps of cloud were trailing across the pale-blue transparency of the zenith, a light dew had coated the grass and foliage with drops, and was shining like silver on spiders' webs. The steaming earth seemed still to be seeking to detain the roseate traces of dawn in her embrace; but presently every quarter of the sky became lit up, and resounded again to the songs of larks.

Bazarov walked straight ahead until he reached the copse – then seated himself at the shadowy edge of the trees, and explained to Peter the services which he looked to the latter to perform; upon which the 'cultured' menial came near to fainting, and was calmed only with an assurance that he would but have to stand at a distance, as a looker-on, and that in no case would responsibility attach to his person.

'And think,' Bazarov concluded, 'in what an important rôle you are about to figure!'

But Peter, extending his hands deprecatingly, only turned up his eyes, became green in the face, and went and leant against a birch tree.

The copse was skirted by the road from Marino, and the light coating of dust bore no mark of having been disturbed since the previous evening, whether by wheel or by foot. Involuntarily Bazarov kept glancing along this road as, plucking and chewing stems of grass, he repeated again and again to himself: 'What a piece of folly!' More than once, too, the morning air made him shiver, and Peter gaze plaintively in his direction; but Bazarov only laughed, for *he* at least was no coward.

At length hoofs sounded along the road, and there came into sight from behind the trees a peasant driving two horses with traces attached. As the man passed Bazarov he looked at him inquisitively, but failed to doff his cap; and this circumstance impressed Peter unfavourably, since the valet considered it a bad omen.

'Like ourselves, that peasant has risen early,' thought Bazarov 'But whereas *he* has risen to work, *we* – !'

'Someone else is coming, I believe,' whispered Peter.

Bazarov raised his head, and saw Paul Petrovitch, in a light check jacket and a pair of snow-white trousers, walking briskly along the road. Under his arm was a green, baize-covered box.

'Pardon me for having kept you waiting,' he said with a bow to Bazarov, and then one to Peter (for even to the latter he, for the nonce, seemed to accord something of the respect due to a second). 'As a matter of fact, I was loth to arouse my valet.'

'I beg that you will not mention it,' replied Bazarov. 'We ourselves have only just arrived.'

'So much the better!' And Paul Petrovitch glanced about him. 'There will be no one to see us or disturb us. Are you agreeable to proceeding?'

'Quite.'

'And I presume that you require no further explanations?'

'None whatsoever.'

'Then kindly load these.' Paul Petrovitch took from the box a brace of pistols.

'No. Do you load, while I measure the distance – my legs are longer than yours.' This last Bazarov added with a dry smile. 'Now, one, two, three – '

'I beg your pardon, sir,' gasped Peter, who was trembling as with ague. 'I beg your pardon, but might I move further away?'

'Four, five – Certainly, my good fellow! Pray do so. You can go and stand behind that tree there, and stop your ears – provided that you do not also stop your eyes. Lastly, should either Monsieur Kirsanov or myself fall, you are to run and pick up the fallen. Six, seven, eight – ' Bazarov halted. 'That will do, I suppose?' he added to Paul Petrovitch. 'Or would you prefer me to add another couple of paces?'

'Do as you please,' the other replied as he rammed home the second of the two bullets.

'Then I will add those two paces.' And Bazarov scratched a line in the soil with his toe. 'Here is the mark. *Apropos*, how many paces is each of us to retire from our respective marks?'

'Ten, I presume,' said Paul Petrovitch as he proffered Bazarov a brace of pistols. 'Will you kindly make choice of these?'

'I will. Nevertheless you will agree that our duel is singular, even to the point of absurdity? For pray observe the countenance of our second!'

'It is still your pleasure to jest,' Paul Petrovitch responded coldly. 'Of the singularity of our contest I make no denial. I merely consider it my duty to warn you that I intend to fight you in grim earnest. So, *à bon entendeur, salut!*'

'Yet, even though we intend to exterminate one another, why should we not enjoy our jest, and thus combine *utile* with *dulce*? You have spoken to me in French. I reply in Latin.'

'I repeat that I intend to fight you in grim earnest,' said Paul Petrovitch; with which he moved to his place, and Bazarov, after counting ten paces from his mark, turned, and halted.

'Are you ready?' enquired Paul Petrovitch.

'I am.'

'Then engage.'

Bazarov started to advance, and Paul Petrovitch did the same, with his left hand thrust into his coat pocket, and his right gradually elevating the muzzle of his pistol.

'The fellow is aiming straight for my nose,' thought Bazarov to himself. 'And how the rascal is screwing up his eyes as he marches! This is not a wholly pleasing sensation. I had better keep my eyes fixed upon his watch-chain.'

Past Bazarov's ear something suddenly whistled, while almost at the same moment there came the sound of a report.

'I seemed to hear something, but no matter,' was the thought which flashed through Bazarov's brain. Then he advanced another step, and, without aiming, pulled the trigger.

As he did so Paul Petrovitch gave a faint start, and clapped his hand to his thigh, down the white trouser-leg of which there began to trickle a thin stream of blood.

Bazarov threw aside his pistol and approached his antagonist.

'Are you wounded?' he enquired.

'Pray recall me to the mark,' said Paul Petrovitch. 'You have the right so to do, and we are merely wasting time. The conditions of the contest allow of a second shot apiece.'

'Pardon me, that can be deferred,' said Bazarov, catching hold of Paul Petrovitch, who was beginning to turn pale in the face. 'I am no longer a duellist, but a doctor, and must examine your wound. Peter! Here! Where the devil has the man got to?'

'This is sheer folly,' gasped Paul Petrovitch. 'I need no help. Let us – ' Yet, even as he tried to twirl his moustache, his arm fell to his side, his eyes closed, and he collapsed in a swoon

'Something new!' involuntarily cried Bazarov as he laid his antagonist upon the grass. 'A swoon! Let us see what is the matter with him.'

Taking out his pocket-handkerchief, he wiped away the blood, and probed the neighbourhood of the wound.

'The bone is intact,' he muttered. 'Yes, and the bullet has merely pierced the flesh a little below the surface. Nothing but the *musculus vastus externus* is so much as touched. In three weeks' time we shall have him trotting about again. A swoon! Oh these men of nerves! What thin skins, to be sure!'

'Is – is he dead?' came in Peter's tremulous voice from behind.

Bazarov looked up.

'No,' he said. 'Run for a little water, and he will outlive us both.'

Unfortunately the 'perfect servant' did not understand what was said to him, but remained stock still. In fact, even when, the next moment, Paul Petrovitch opened his eyes Peter went on crossing himself and repeating: 'He is dying!'

'Monsieur Bazarov,' the wounded man said with a twisted smile, 'you were perfectly in the right when you said that the face of that man was the face of a fool.'

'It is so,' agreed Bazarov. 'Damn you, will you fetch some water!' (The latter to the valet.)

'There is no need,' put in Paul Petrovitch. 'It was, only a passing vertigo. Kindly assist me to sit up. That is it. A scratch like this will require only to be bandaged for me to walk home again. There will be no necessity to have the *drozhki* sent. For that matter, the duel need not be renewed unless you wish it. At least today you have acted like a gentleman. Kindly note that I have said so.'

'To the past we have no need to refer,' said Bazarov. 'And, as regards the future, it calls for equally little remark, seeing that I intend to leave here at once. Allow me to bind your leg. The wound is not dangerous, but one of a nature which will make it as well to have the blood staunched. But first I must restore that stuck pig to life.'

Shaking Peter vigorously by the collar, he dispatched him in search of the *drozhki*.

'But see that you do not alarm my brother,' was Paul Petrovitch's injunction also to the man. 'You are not to breathe a word of what has happened.'

Peter set off at full speed. During the time that he was hastening for the *drozhki*, the two antagonists sat silently side by side on the ground, while Paul Petrovitch tried his best not to look at Bazarov, for the reason that he did not feel inclined to become reconciled with him, while at the same time he felt ashamed alike of his impulsiveness, his failure, and the scheme which had had this ending, though he realised that it might have been worse.

'At least will the fellow swagger here no more,' he thought to himself by way of consolation. 'And, for that, much thanks!'

The silence was a heavy, awkward silence, for neither of the pair felt comfortable – each of them recognised that the other had taken his measure. To friends, such a recognition may be very agreeable, but to foes it is far from welcome – least of all, when neither explanations nor a parting are feasible.

'I hope that I have not bound your leg too tightly?' said Bazarov at last.

'Oh no,' replied Paul Petrovitch. 'As a matter of fact, it is doing splendidly.' After a pause he added: 'But we cannot deceive my brother. How would it be if we were to tell him that we fell out over politics?'

'Capital!' agreed Bazarov. 'Tell him, for instance, that I started cursing Anglomaniacs.'

'A good idea! But what can that man be thinking of us? I cannot imagine.' The speaker pointed to the same peasant who, shortly before the duel, had driven a pair of loose horses past Bazarov, and was now shuffling homewards, while doffing his cap at the sight of the gentlemen.

'Who can say?' replied Bazarov. 'Probably he is thinking of nothing at all. As Madame Radcliffe* frequently reminds us, the Russian *muzhik* is an unknown quantity. Does *any*one understand him? He does not even understand himself.'

---

* Ann Radcliffe, *née* Ward (1764–1823), an English novelist who wrote *The Mysteries of Udolpho* and other tales, and travelled extensively.

'There you go again!' began Paul Petrovitch, but suddenly broke off to say in a still louder tone: 'See what that fool Peter has done! Here comes my brother himself!'

Sure enough, on turning his head, Bazarov saw Nikolai Petrovitch's pale face peering from the *drozhki*. Nor had the vehicle come to a halt before Nikolai had sprung from the step, and rushed towards his brother.

'What is this?' he cried in agitated accents. 'Evgenii Vasilitch, I beg of you to tell me what has happened.'

'Nothing has happened,' replied Paul Petrovitch in Bazarov's stead. 'You are disturbing yourself to no purpose. I had a small quarrel with Monsieur Bazarov, and have paid a penalty as small.'

'But whence did it arise? For God's sake tell me!'

'What is there to say? It arose from the fact that Monsieur Bazarov spoke in disrespectful terms of Sir Robert Peel. I would hasten to add that, throughout, I alone was at fault, and that Monsieur Bazarov bore himself admirably – I being the challenger.'

'But look at the blood!'

'Pshaw! Did you suppose my veins to run with water? As a matter of fact, the blood-letting will do me good. Is not that so, doctor? Help me to mount the *drozhki*, and away with melancholy! By tomorrow I shall be recovered. Splendid! That is the way to do it. Right away, coachman!'

When on the point of starting homewards in the wake of the *drozhki*, Nikolai Petrovitch perceived Bazarov to be for remaining behind.

'Evgenii Vasilitch,' he said, 'I would beg of you to attend my brother until a doctor can be procured from the town.'

Bazarov nodded in silence.

An hour later Paul Petrovitch was reposing in bed with his leg neatly and artistically bandaged. The whole house was in a turmoil, Thenichka greatly upset, and Nikolai able to do nothing but wring his hands. The sick man, on the contrary, laughed and jested, especially with Bazarov, and, to meet the occasion, had donned a fine linen shirt, an elegant morning jacket, and a Turkish fez. Lastly, he forbade anyone to close the shutters, and kept venting humorous protests against the necessity of abstaining from food.

Towards nightfall, however, fever supervened, and his head began to ache; with the result that when the doctor arrived from the town (Nikolai Petrovitch had disobeyed his brother in this respect, and Bazarov also had consented to his doing so, in that, after paying the patient a single visit, and that a very brief one, and being put to the mortification of having to avoid Thenichka on two occasions when he met her, he had felt that he preferred to spend the rest of the day in loneliness, bitterness, and rancour) – when the doctor arrived from the town he advised a cooling draught, but at the same time confirmed Bazarov's opinion that no danger was to be apprehended. In passing, it may also be mentioned that, on being informed by Nikolai Petrovitch that Paul Petrovitch's wound had been self-inflicted through an accident, the said doctor replied 'H'm!'; to which, on receiving into his hand a fee of twenty-five roubles, he added that of course things of the kind often occurred.

No one in the house, that night, retired to bed, or even undressed, but at intervals Nikolai Petrovitch would tiptoe into his brother's room, and as silently withdraw. At intervals, too, Paul Petrovitch would awake from a doze, sigh faintly, and say to Nikolai either *'Couchez-vous'* or 'Please give me a drink.' But once it happened that Nikolai sent the invalid a glass of lemonade by the hand of Thenichka; and this time Paul Petrovitch scanned her long and searchingly before draining the tumbler to the dregs. Towards morning the fever increased a little, and a trace of light-headedness made its appearance which for a while caused the patient only to utter disconnected words. But suddenly he opened his eyes, and, on seeing his brother bending solicitously over the bed, murmured:

'Nikolai, do not you think that Thenichka slightly resembles Nelly?'

'What Nelly, Paul? Who is Nelly?'

'How can you ask? The Princess R., of course. In the upper portion of the face especially Thenichka resembles her. *C'est de la même famille.'*

Nikolai Petrovitch made no reply. He could only remain lost in wonder that bygone fancies could so survive in the human consciousness.

'That *this* should have cropped up again!' he reflected.

On another occasion Paul Petrovitch muttered as he clasped his hands behind his head: 'How I love this idle existence!' And again, a few minutes later, he whispered: 'I will not allow a single rascal to touch me!'

Nikolai Petrovitch sighed. To whom the words referred he had not a notion.

At eight o'clock next morning Bazarov entered Nikolai's room. His stock of insects, birds, and frogs had either been packed up or liberated.

Rising to meet him, Nikolai said:

'So you have come to say goodbye?'

'I have.'

'I understand your feelings, and I commend them. I know that my poor brother alone was to blame, and is now paying the penalty. Also, I gather from what he says that your position was such that you could not possibly have acted otherwise than as you did – that for you to have avoided this duel would have been impossible. That being so, we must attribute the mischance to the – er – standing antagonism of your views (here Nikolai Petrovitch tripped over his words a little). 'My brother is one of the old school, a man of hot temper and great persistency. Consequently we have God to thank that things have turned out no worse. Finally I may say that every possible precaution against publicity has been taken.'

'Quite so,' said Bazarov carelessly. 'But I will leave my address with you, in case of anything occurring.'

'I hope that nothing *will* occur. Indeed, my one regret is that your stay in my house should have – should have terminated in such a fashion. And I am the more grieved in that Arkady – '

'I expect to be seeing him very soon,' interrupted Bazarov, whom 'explanations' or 'speeches' of any kind always roused to fever pitch. 'On the other hand, should I *not* do so, pray convey to him my greetings and my regrets.'

'I will,' said Nikolai Petrovitch with a bow; but even before he had finished Bazarov had left the room.

Paul Petrovitch, too, as soon as he heard that Bazarov was on the point of departing, expressed a desire to see him, and to shake hands with him. Yet Bazarov remained as cold as ice, for well he knew that Paul Petrovitch's only aim was to make a show of 'magnanimity,' while to Thenichka he did not say goodbye at all – he merely exchanged with her a glance as she peeped from one of the windows. Her face looked to him careworn.

'Before long she will either trip or elope,' he reflected.

On the other hand, Peter was so moved at the prospect of parting with his patron that he wept on the latter's shoulder until his transports were cooled with the question: 'Surely your eyes are not made of water?' while Duniasha's emotion was such that she had to take refuge in a thicket. Meanwhile the cause of all this grief mounted the travelling-cart, and lit a cigar; and even when he had travelled four versts, and reached a spot where a turn in the road brought the Kirsanov farm into line with the new manor-house, he merely expectorated some tobacco juice, and muttered, as he wrapped himself closer in his cloak: 'The cursed tomnoddies!'

Thenceforth Paul Petrovitch began to mend, but still was ordered to keep his bed for another week. What he called his 'imprisonment' he bore with very fair patience, although he remained fussy in the matter of his toilet, and constantly had himself sprinkled with eau-de-Cologne. Meanwhile Nikolai Petrovitch read aloud to him the newspapers, and Thenichka served him with soup, lemonade, scrambled eggs, and tea. Yet she never entered the room without feeling a mysterious nervousness come over her. Paul Petrovitch's unexpected behaviour had frightened everyone in the house, but her it had frightened most of all. Only old Prokofitch seemed undismayed at the occurrence, and kept asserting that, in his day, 'the gentry used to bore holes in one another right enough, but only the gentry. Jackanapes like that Bazarov would have been ducked in the gutter for their pains.'

Thenichka felt little pricking of conscience, but there were times when the thought of the true cause of the quarrel rendered her at least uneasy, and the more so because Paul Petrovitch's way of looking at her was now so strange that, even when she turned her back to him, she could still feel his eyes upon her. In combination, therefore, her worries led to her growing thinner, and also (as often happens in such circumstances) to her adding to her beauty.

At length, one morning, Paul Petrovitch felt so much better that he left his bed, and removed to the sofa; while Nikolai Petrovitch, after seeing that he had all he wanted, betook himself to the farm. Also, it fell to Thenichka's lot to take the invalid a cup of tea; and when she had placed it on the table, she was about to withdraw, when Paul Petrovitch requested her to remain.

'Why should you hurry away?' he said. 'Is it that you have other things to do?'

'No – yes. That is to say, I have to go and pour out tea for the servants.'

'Duniasha can do that. Surely you will stay awhile with a sick man who has something of great importance to say to you?'

Silently she seated herself on the edge of a chair.

'Listen,' he continued, as he tugged at his moustache. 'For some time past I have been wanting to ask you why you are so afraid of me?'

'Afraid of you?'

'Yes; for you never look at me. In fact, one would think that your conscience was uneasy.'

Her face reddened, but she looked Paul Petrovitch straight in the eyes. Somehow his aspect struck her as peculiar, and her heart began to throb.

'Is your conscience clear?' he asked.

'Yes, Why should it not be?' she responded in a whisper.

'I do not know. Certainly I can recall no one against whom you can have committed a fault. Against me? It is scarcely probable. Against others in this house? That is as improbable. Against my brother? But him you love, do you not?'

'I do.'

'With your whole heart and soul?'

'With my whole heart and soul.'

'Really and truly, Thenichka?' (never before had he addressed her thus). 'Look me in the eyes. To lie is a terrible sin. You know that, of course?'

'But I am *not* lying, Paul Petrovitch. Did I not love Nikolai Petrovitch, I should not want to live.'

'And you would exchange him for no one else?'

'*Whom* should I exchange him for?'

'I do not know. Surely not for the gentlemen who has just left us?'

Thenichka rose to her feet.

'Why should you torment me in this way?' she cried. 'What have I done that you should speak to me so?'

'Thenichka,' came the mournful reply, 'I speak to you in this manner for the reason that I saw – '

'You saw what?'

'I saw *you* – in the lilac arbour.'

She blushed to her ears, to the very roots of her hair.

'But how was I to blame?' at length she contrived to say.

Paul Petrovitch raised himself on the sofa.

'You swear, do you, that you were *not* to blame?' he said. 'That you were not in the slightest degree to blame? Not at all?'

'I love Nikolai Petrovitch,' came the reply, delivered with sudden energy and a rising sob, 'and never shall I love any other man. As for what you saw, before the Throne of Judgement I swear that I am innocent, that I have always been so, and that I would rather die than be suspected of having deceived Nikolai Petrovitch, my benefactor.'

Her voice failed her. Then, behold! she felt Paul seize and press her hand! Turning her head, she looked down at him – and stood almost petrified. For his face was even paler than usual, his eyes were glistening, and – most surprising thing of all! – a great tear was trickling down his cheek!

'Thenichka,' he whispered in a voice which hardly seemed his own, 'I beg of you always to love, and never to cease loving, my brother. He is such a good, kind fellow as has not his equal in the world. Never desert him for another; never listen to any tales which you may hear of him, but reflect how terrible it would be for him to love and not to be loved! Yes, think well, Thenichka, before ever you forsake him.'

Thenichka's amazement caused her eyes almost to start from her head, and her nervousness completely to vanish. Judge, also, of her surprise when, though he did not draw her to himself, nor kiss her,

Paul Petrovitch raised her hand to his lips, and then burst into a convulsive fit of sobbing!

'God in Heaven!' she thought to herself. 'What if this should make him have another fainting fit?'

Meanwhile, in that one moment Paul Petrovitch was living over again a past phase of his ruined life.

Presently hurried footsteps were heard causing the staircase to creak; and just as Paul pushed Thenichka away from him and replaced his head upon the pillow, the door opened, and Nikolai Petrovitch – fresh, ruddy, and smiling – entered with little Mitia. The latter, equally fresh and ruddy, was leaping in Nikolai's arms, and pressing his tiny, naked feet against the buttons of his father's rural smock.

Running to father and child, Thenichka threw her arms around both alike, and sank her head upon the former's shoulder. This caused him to halt in amazement for never before had the bashful, reserved Thenichka shown him any endearment in the presence of a third person.

'What is the matter?' he exclaimed. Then he glanced at Paul, handed Mitia to Thenichka, and, approaching the bedside, enquired if his brother were worse.

Paul's face was buried in his handkerchief, but he replied:

'Oh dear no. Not at all. If anything, I am better – yes, very much better.'

'Nevertheless you have been over-hasty in removing to the sofa,' said Nikolai Petrovitch; after which he turned to ask Thenichka why she was leaving the room, but she departed abruptly, and closed the door behind her.

'I had come to show you my little rascal,' Nikolai continued. 'He had been pining for a sight of his uncle. But she has carried him away for some reason. What is the matter? Has something occurred?'

'My brother,' replied Paul Petrovitch – and as he uttered the words Nikolai Petrovitch gave a start, and felt ill at ease, he knew not why. 'My brother, pray give me your word of honour that you will fulfil the request which I am going to make.'

'What request, Paul? I beg of you to continue.'

'A request of the first importance. Upon it, I believe, your entire happiness depends. Also, what I am going to say represents the fruit of much thought. My brother, the request is that you will do your duty, the duty of a good and honourable man. In other words, I beseech you to put an end to this scandal and bad example, which is unworthy of you, unworthy of a man who is the best of souls.'

'To what do you refer, Paul?'

'To this. You ought to *marry* Thenichka. She loves you, and is the mother of your child.'

Stepping back, Nikolai Petrovitch clasped his hands together.

'Do *you* say this?' he exclaimed. 'Do *you* say this – *you* whom I have always understood to be opposed to such unions? Do *you* say this? Surely you know that solely out of respect for yourself have I hitherto refrained from doing what rightfully you call my duty?'

'Wrongfully, then, have you respected me,' said Paul Petrovitch with a sad smile. 'In fact, almost I am beginning to think that Bazarov was right when he accused me of only feigning the aristocratic instinct. For it is not enough for you and me to trouble ourselves about worldly matters alone. We are old men past our prime, who ought to lay aside all pettinesses, and to fulfil strictly our obligations. Nor forget that, should we thus act, we shall receive an added measure of happiness as our reward.'

Nikolai Petrovitch flung himself upon his brother, and embraced him again and again.

'You have opened my eyes,' he cried. 'When I described you as the best man in the world I was not wrong: and now I perceive your wisdom to be equal to your magnanimity.'

'Quieter, quieter!' advised Paul. 'Do not further inflame the leg of an old fool who, at fifty, has fought a duel like a young ensign. Then the matter is settled, and Thenichka is to become my *belle-sœur*?'

'Yes, my dearest Paul. But what will Arkady say?'

'Arkady? He will be delighted. True, marriage does not come within his purview or principles, but at least his sense of social equality will be tickled. And, in the nineteenth century, what does caste matter?'

'Paul, Paul, let me embrace you once more. You need not be afraid. I will do it very carefully.' And the two brothers flung their arms around one another.

'Well?' continued Paul Petrovitch. 'What think you? Shall we tell her at once?'

'No, we need not be in too much of a hurry,' replied Nikolai Petrovitch. 'As a matter of fact, you have been having a talk with her, have you not?'

'I have been having a talk with her? *Quelle idée!*'

'However, your first business is to recover. Thenichka will not run away, and in the meanwhile the affair must be carefully considered.'

'Then you have decided upon it?'

'Certainly I have! And I thank you with all my heart. But I must leave you for a while now, for you ought to have some rest, and any excitement is bad for you. Matters can be discussed later. Go to sleep, dearest of brothers, and may God restore you to health!'

'Why did he thank *me*?' thought Paul Petrovitch to himself after Nikolai had gone. 'Does not the affair depend upon him alone, seeing that, after the marriage, I myself shall have to depart elsewhere – to Dresden or to Florence, and to abide there until I die?'

He bathed his forehead with eau-de-Cologne, and then closed his eyes. As he lay with his handsome, refined head resting on the pillow, he looked, in the clear light of the sun, like a corpse.

Chapter 25

IN THE SHADE of a tall ash tree in the garden at Nikolsköe Katia and Arkady were seated on a bench. Beside them, on the ground, lay Fifi – his lengthy body twisted into the curve known to sporting folk as 'the hare's crouch.' Neither from Arkady nor from Katia was a word proceeding. Arkady was holding in his hands a half-opened book, and she was picking a few crumbs from a basket, and throwing them to a small family of sparrows which, with the timid temerity of their tribe, were chirping and hopping at her very feet. A faint breeze was stirring the leaves of the ash tree, and dappling Fifi's tawny back and the dark line of the pathway with a number of wavering circles of pale golden light; but Arkady and Katia were wholly in shade, save that an occasional streak glanced upon, and gleamed in, her hair. Just for the reason that the pair were silent and side by side was there present to their consciousness a *camaraderie* which, while causing neither to have the other definitely in mind, pleased each with the sense of the other's propinquity. The expression of both is changed since last we saw them. Arkady's face wears a staider air, and Katia looks more animated and less retiring.

At length, however, Arkady spoke.

'Do you not think,' he said, 'that our Russian term *yasen* is particularly suitable to the ash tree? For no other tree cleaves the air with such airy brightness.'*

Katia looked up.

'I agree,' she replied, while Arkady proudly reflected: 'At all events *she* does not reprove me for talking in "beautiful language." '

'By the way,' Katia continued with a glance at the book in his hands, 'I cannot say that I always approve of Heine. I like him neither when he is laughing nor when he is in tears – I like him only when he is meditative and languid.'

'Well, *I* like him when he is laughing,' Arkady remarked.

'Then still there survives in you a trace of your old satirical tendency. Still your reformation needs to be completed.'

'Indeed?' thought Arkady. 'My satirical tendency? Oh, that Bazarov could have heard that!'

While aloud he said:

* *Yasen* is derived from the adjective *yasni*, meaning clear or bright.

'Who is "we"? Yourself?'

'Oh dear no! My sister, and Porfiri Platonitch, with whom you no longer quarrel, and my aunt, whom, three days ago, you escorted to church.'

'I did so only because I could not refuse. And as regards Anna Sergievna, kindly remember that, in many things, she agrees with Bazarov.'

'Yes, she used to be greatly under his influence, and so did you.'

'And so did I? Then am I now emancipated from that influence?'

Katia returned no reply.

'I know that you never liked him,' Arkady continued.

'Did I not? It was not for me to judge him.'

'Never do I hear that reply without declining to believe it. There is not a person living whom *all* of us have not the right to judge. A disclaimer of that kin always represents an excuse.'

'To tell the truth, I disliked him less than I felt him to be a stranger to me – as complete a one as I to him – or you either, for that matter.'

'What do you mean?'

'I mean that – well how can I express it? That whereas he was a wild bird, you and I are tame ones.'

'*I* am a tame one?'

Katia nodded assent. Arkady scratched his ear.

'Look here,' he said. 'I may tell you that that constitutes, in essence, an insult.'

'Why so? Do you *want* to be a wild bird?'

'Not necessarily a wild one, but at least one strong and energetic.'

'You need wish no such thing. Your friend was both, yet he would rather have been otherwise.'

'H'm! You believe that he used to exercise a considerable influence over Anna Sergievna?'

'Yes. But no one can hold a rein over her for long.' Katia added this last *sotto voce*.

'What makes you think that?'

'The fact that she is very proud – rather, that she values her independence.'

'Who does not?' queried Arkady, while there flashed through his mind the thought: 'Why this mention of her?' Curiously enough, the same thought occurred to Katia too. But this was not so curious as might have been supposed, seeing that when young people meet in frequent and amicable converse, identical thoughts are apt to enter their brains.

Arkady smiled, edged nearer to Katia, and said in a whisper: 'Confess that you are a little afraid of her.'

'Of whom?'

'Of *her*,' repeated Arkady meaningly.

'Are *you* afraid of her?' countered Katia.

'I am. Please note that I believe you to be the same.'

Katia raised a menacing finger.

'I am surprised at you!' she exclaimed. 'Never at any time has my sister been better disposed towards you than she is now. She likes you considerably more than when you first came.'

'Really?'

'Yes. And have you not noticed it? You ought to be pleased at the notion.'

Arkady reflected.

'How I have contrived to win Anna Sergievna's good graces I do not know,' at length he said. 'Surely it cannot be because I brought her those letters which were written by your mother?'

'It is, though, and because of other reasons as well – reasons which I will forbear to mention.'

'Why will you?'

'Because I will.'

'Oh, I know your faculty for obstinacy.'

'It is one which I possess.'

'Also, your faculty for observing things.'

Katia glanced at him. Then she enquired:

'Why lose your temper? What are you thinking of?'

'This: that I cannot understand how you come to possess those powers of observation which undoubtedly are yours. I understand it the less because you are so nervous and distrustful and shy of everybody and – '

'It is because I have lived such a lonely life. A life of that kind leads one to reflect in spite of oneself. Am I shy of *everyone*, though?'

Arkady bestowed upon her an appreciative glance.

'Never mind,' he said. 'At all events it is not often that people in your position – I mean, people of your wealth – possess such a gift. To them, as to the Tsars, truth penetrates hardly.'

'But I am *not* wealthy.'

Arkady failed at first to follow her meaning, but reflected: 'Certainly the property belongs to her sister, not to her.' Nor was the thought wholly unpleasing – so little so that presently he added:

'You said that very prettily.'

'I said what?'

'That you are not wealthy. You said it so simply, so without any false shame, so without the least *arrière pensée*. *Apropos*, the consciousness of the ordinary person who both knows and confesses that he or she is poor always seems to me to contain more than the mere words imply – it harbours also a touch of vanity.'

'I have, thanks to my sister, had no experience of poverty. And as for my possessions, I mentioned them only because the words came of themselves to my lips.'

'Quite so. Yet confess that you too harbour a grain of the vanity to which I have alluded.'

'Give me an example of my doing so.'

'An example? Well, may I ask why you have not married a rich man?'

'Were I to love such a one very much, I – But no man of that sort has come my way: wherefore I have made no such marriage.'

'There, now!' cried Arkady. 'But why should you not do so in the future?'

'Because even the poets deprecate *mésalliances*.'

'You mean that you wish either to rule or – ?'

'Oh no! What good would that be? On the contrary, I am prepared to be ruled, even though I believe that inequality in any form works badly. A union of self-respect with submission – that is what I best understand, that is what spells true happiness. A mere subordinate existence is – well, something which I do not fancy.'

' "Something which I do not fancy," ' commented Arkady. 'Yes, you are of the same blood as Anna Sergievna: you are as independent as she, and you are even more secretive. In fact, however deep-rooted and sacred a stock of sentiments you might hold, you would never, of your own accord, give them utterance.'

'Of course! How could you suppose anything else?'

'Also, you are clever, and have a measure of character equal to, if not greater than, hers.'

'I dislike being compared with my sister. You seem to have forgotten that she is both "beautiful" and "intellectual" and – Moreover, you, above all people, ought not to say anything to her disparagement, and still less to say it seriously.'

'Why "*you*, above all people"? Do you think that I am jesting?'

'I am certain of it.'

'Indeed? But what if I were to say that I really mean my words? What if I were to say that, if anything, I have under-expressed what is in my mind?'

'I fail to follow you.'

'Do you? Your quickness of perception has been overrated.'

'Why has it?'

Averting his head, Arkady returned no reply, while Katia fell to searching for the last crumbs in her basket, and throwing them to the sparrows. Unfortunately, the throw of her arm proved too strong, and the birds flew away without even touching the food offered them.

'Katia,' said Arkady, 'it may be that you look upon these things as matters of no moment. Kindly note, therefore, that neither for your sister nor for any other person would I exchange Mademoiselle Katerina Sergievna.'

Rising, he walked away as though in sudden alarm at having allowed the words to escape his lips. Meanwhile Katia, with her hands resting upon the basket and her head bent, gazed after him. Gradually there crept into her cheeks a rosy tint; and though her lips were not smiling, and her dark eyes contained a hint of perplexity, there lurked also in her expression another unexpressed feeling.

'Are you alone?' said Anna Sergievna's voice from behind her. 'I thought that Arkady came with you into the garden?'

Katia slowly raised her eyes to her sister (tastefully and even showily, dressed, the latter was standing on the path, and engaged in stirring Fifi's ears with the point of an open parasol), and as slowly replied:

'Yes – I am alone.'

'So I see,' commented Madame with a smile. 'He has gone indoors, I suppose?'

'Probably.'

'And you have been reading with him?'

'I have.'

Anna Sergievna took Katia under the chin, and raised her face towards her own.

'You have not quarrelled, I hope?' she said.

'Oh no,' said Katia, and quietly put away her sister's hand.

'What solemn replies! Well, I came here to propose a walk, since he is always asking me to go one. But, to pass to another subject, some shoes have arrived for you from the town, so you had better go and try them on. Only yesterday I was noticing how shabby your old ones are. In general, you do not take sufficient pains in such matters, for you have charming feet, and also not ugly hands, even though a trifle too large. You ought to take care of your feet. When you are here you do not do so sufficiently.'

Madame passed onwards with a light rustle of her handsome gown, while Katia rose from the bench, and taking the volume of Heine, departed in another direction – though *not* to try on the boots.

' "You have charming feet," ' she repeated to herself as she tripped up the sun-baked steps of the terrace. ' "You have charming feet." Well, before long someone shall be at them.'

Confusion then overcame her, and she took the remaining steps at a bound.

Meanwhile Arkady made for his room. As he was passing through the hall he was overtaken by the butler and informed that Monsieur Bazarov was awaiting him above.

'Evgenii Vasilitch?' exclaimed Arkady in a tone very much as of alarm. 'Has he been here long?'

'A few minutes only. He instructed me not to announce him to Madame but to take him straight to your room.'

'I hope that nothing unfortunate has occurred at home,' reflected Arkady as he ran up the stairs and opened the door of the bedroom. But the first sight of Bazarov's face reassured him, even though a more experienced eye might have detected in the features of the unlooked-for guest certain signs that inward turmoil underlay their usual rigidity. Clad in a dust cloak and a travelling cap, he was seated on the window-sill, and did not rise even when, rushing towards him with exclamations of astonishment, and fussing to and fro like a man who believes himself to be overjoyed, as well as desires other people to believe it, Arkady cried:

'What a surprise! What has brought you here? Surely everything at home is well, and all are in good health?'

'Everything at your home is well,' said Bazarov; 'but all are not in good health. However, if your brains are not hopelessly wandering, first tell them to bring me some *kvass*, and then sit down and listen to my few but, I hope, well-chosen words.'

This quieted Arkady, and upon that Bazarov told him of the duel with Paul Petrovitch. The recital finished, Arkady stood amazed, as well as distressed. But this he did not think it necessary to state – he merely enquired whether his uncle's wound were really a harmless one, and, on receiving the reply that it was of a nature uninteresting from every but the medical point of view, forced a smile. Yet all the while he felt secretly hurt, and also secretly ashamed. This Bazarov seemed to divine.

'See,' he said, 'what comes of consorting with feudal folk! Should one's lot be cast among them, inevitably one gets drawn into their knightly tourneys. Being on my way to my parents' place, I have turned aside to – But no; I will not be guilty of a foolish and useless lie. The real reason why I have turned aside is that – oh, the devil only knows why! Times there are when a man ought to take himself by the scruff of the neck, and uproot himself like a radish from a garden border. That is what *I* did when I was last here. But, since, a longing has come upon me to take just another peep at all that I then forsook – to view once more the border where I used to grow.'

'By the words "all that I then forsook" I hope that you do not mean myself as well?' cried Arkady anxiously. 'Do not say that you intend to sever me also from your friendship?'

Bazarov looked at him. He did so fixedly, almost sharply.

'Would the eventuality distress you?' he enquired. 'Rather, it is you who have forsaken me, O verdant and transparent soul. *Inter alia*, I hope that your affair with Anna Sergievna is progressing?'

'My "affair with Anna Sergievna"?'

'For her sake, was it not, you came hither from the town? Ah, tender young chicken of mine, what about those Sunday Schools? Come, come! Do not tell me that you are not in love with her. Or have you at last learnt to be secretive?'

'Always I have been frank with you, as you know; wherefore pray believe me when I say – I call God to witness that it is true – that your surmises are mistaken.'

'Truly a new song!' remarked Bazarov *sotto voce*. 'But do not disturb yourself: it is all one to me. Certainly, a Romanticist would have said: "Our roads are beginning to diverge"; but *I* say no more than that clearly we have no further use for one another.'

'Oh, Evgenii!'

'Dear lad, it is no misfortune. At all times is something in the world finding out that it has no use for something else. So we must say goodbye. Ever since I arrived in this place I have been feeling as uncomfortable as a Governor's lady when she hears a work of Gogol's read aloud. In fact, I did not order my horses to be unharnessed.'

'But you cannot act like this!'

'Why not?'

'Because, apart from my own feelings, such a speedy departure would be the height of rudeness to Anna Sergievna. I know that she would like to see you.'

'No, she would not.'

'I am positive that she would. Why pretend like this? Are you going to say that it is not for her sake alone that you are here?'

'You have grounds for that surmise, yet I say that you are wrong.'

But Arkady proved to be right, for Anna Sergievna really desired to see Bazarov, and, through the butler, sent him word to that effect. After tidying his costume, therefore, and tucking his new great-coat under his arm (in readiness to depart as soon as the interview should be concluded), he went downstairs, and was received, not in the room where he had unexpectedly disclosed his passion, but in the drawing-room. Anna Sergievna's manner, as she offered him the tips of her fingers, was pleasant enough, yet her face betrayed involuntary tension.

'To begin with,' Bazarov hastened to say, 'allow me to reassure you. You see before you a corpse which has long returned to its senses, and is also not destitute of hope that others have forgotten its folly. I am unlikely to see you again for an extended period, but, though (as you know) I am not given to sentiment, I feel that I should like to bear away with me the thought that my image still fills your mind with aversion.'

She caught at her breath like a person who has just arrived at the summit of a lofty mountain. Then her face lightened into a smile, and, offering Bazarov her hand a second time, she allowed it to respond to the pressure of his.

'When sorrow is asleep, do not wake it,' she said. 'And the less so since my conscience convicts me, if not of coquetry on that occasion, at all events of something else. One word more. Let us be friends again. For it was all a dream, was it not? And who remembers dreams?'

'Who indeed? And love – well, love is a mere empirical sentiment.'

'I am glad to hear you say so.'

Thus Anna Sergievna, and thus Bazarov. And both conceived themselves to be speaking the truth. But was it the truth? – at all events, the whole truth? The speakers themselves did not know, and therefore the author does not. Nevertheless both the man and the woman framed their words to create an atmosphere of mutual confidence.

Next Anna Sergievna asked Bazarov how he had spent his time at the Kirsanovs'; and though he came within an ace of telling her of the duel with Paul Petrovitch, he checked himself in time, and replied that he had been engaged in work.

'And I,' she said, 'have been, for some unknown reason, out of humour, and meditating going abroad; but the fit is passing now (thanks to the arrival of your friend Arkady Nikolaievitch), and already I find myself relapsing into my old rut, and resuming my true rôle.'

'And what is your true rôle?'

'The rôle of acting as aunt or preceptress or mother – call it what you like – to my sister. In passing, I wonder if you are aware that once upon a time I did not altogether understand your close friendship with Arkady Nikolaievitch? Somehow he seemed too insignificant for you. But now, I know him better, and have convinced myself that in his head there is a brain. Above all things, he is young, young – not like you and myself, Evgenii Vasilitch.'

'But he is still shy in your presence?' queried Bazarov.

'He – ' began Anna Sergievna; then, checking herself, continued: 'No; he is gaining confidence, and has taken to talking to me quite freely; whereas once upon a time, though I did not seek his company, he used to flee whenever I came near him. By the way, he is great friends with Katia.'

Somehow this irritated Bazarov.

'Never can a woman forbear dissembling,' was his reflection. Aloud he said with a frigid smile: 'Then you say that he used to flee from you? But surely it cannot be a secret that formerly he cherished for you *une grande passion*?'

'What? He too?'

'Yes, he too,' affirmed Bazarov with a nod. 'But I think that you knew that? It was not a piece of news that I have just told you?'

Her eyes became fixed upon the floor.

'I believe you to be wrong,' she observed.

'So do not I. But perhaps I ought not to have mentioned it?' To himself he added: 'And perhaps you will not, in future, play the hypocrite with me.'

'Why should you not have mentioned it?' she queried. 'As a matter of fact, I believe you to be attaching importance to a mere passing impression and shall soon think that you have a tendency to exaggerate.'

'Suppose we talk of something else?' he suggested.

'For what reason?'

However, of her own accord she diverted the conversation into another channel. True, she had assured him, and she herself believed, that everything was buried in the past; yet she felt ill at ease, and conscious that, even while jesting or exchanging the merest of baga-telles, she had weighing upon her a nervous oppression. In fact, it was akin to the case of passengers afloat. Though such folk will laugh and talk with the same apparent indifference as on land, let but the machinery stop, or the least sign of anything unusual appear, and at once every face will display that peculiar expression of anxiety which comes only of constant knowledge of ever-present danger.

Of similar sort was Anna Sergievna's interview with Bazarov; nor was it prolonged, in that soon she began to feel so absent-minded, and to answer with such vagueness, that she proposed a move to the hall, where there were found Katia and the Princess.

'And where is Arkady Nikolaievitch?' enquired the hostess; and, on being told that he had not been seen for over an hour, she sent messengers to summon him. But this proved a lengthy task, seeing that he had withdrawn to the remotest corner of the garden, and, sitting with chin upon hands, was plunged in thought. Those thoughts were important and profound, but not sad; and though he knew that Anna Sergievna was alone with Bazarov, he felt none of his old jealousy, but, rather, gazed before him with quiet I cheerfulness – with an air as though something had pleased and surprised him, and led him to arrive at a certain decision.

Chapter 26

ALTHOUGH THE LATE Monsieur Odintsov had disliked 'innovations,' he had not been opposed to the indulgence of 'a certain play of refined taste,' and had erected, in a space between the hothouses and the lake, a building modelled in the style of a Greek temple, but consisting of undeniable Russian bricks. Also, he had caused to be inserted in the massive rear wall of this temple or gallery six niches for six statues which were designed to represent Solitude, Silence, Thought, Melancholy, Modesty, and Sensibility, and which he had purposed to import from abroad; but only one of these, the statue of the Goddess of Silence, with a finger to her lips, had actually been delivered and erected; and even of that the household underlings had knocked off the nose on the very day of the statue's arrival. True, a neighbouring sculptor had offered to furnish the goddess with a nose 'twice as good as the last one,' but Odintsov had none the less ordered her removal to a corner of the millhouse, where for several years past she had acted as a source of superstitious awe to the peasant women of the district. Likewise, the front wall of the temple had become so overgrown with bushes that only the capitals of the supporting columns remained visible above the mass of verdure, and even at midday the interior of the building was cool and pleasant; and though Anna Sergievna had never really liked the place since the day when she had discovered an adder there, Katia paid it frequent visits, and, seating herself on a great stone bench which was fixed under one of the niches, would read or work, or surrender herself to the influence of that perfect restfulness which, known, probably, to everyone, comes of a silent, half-unconscious contemplation of the great waves of life as they break for ever around and against us.

On the morning after Bazarov's arrival Katia was in her usual position on the bench, and beside her was Arkady – he having specially asked her to accompany him thither.

Though an hour was still wanting to luncheon time, the dew and the freshness of the morning had already given place to the sultriness and the aridity of noontide. Arkady's face yet bore the expression of yesterday, but Katia's features were stamped with one, rather, of depression. This was because after breakfast her sister had called her into the boudoir, and to some of those blandishments which always alarmed the girl had added a word of advice that Katia should observe more caution in her converse with Arkady, and, above all things, avoid such solitary *tête-à-têtes* with him as appeared to have aroused the attention of the household in general, and of the Princess in particular. Since the previous evening Anna Sergievna had been out of humour; and inasmuch as Katia's conscience was not wholly clear of responsibility in the matter, she had intimated, when yielding to Arkady's request, that it must be for the last time.

'Katia,' he began with a sort of easy uneasiness, 'since the day when I had the good fortune to reside under the same roof as yourself I have talked to you on many different subjects. But one particular question has for me a paramount importance: nor upon that question have I yet touched. Yesterday you said that during my stay here I have undergone a process of reformation' – he neither sought nor avoided Katia's eye – 'and, to be frank, such a reformation has, in part at least, come about. Better than anyone else do you know that this is so – you to whom, above all others, that remaking is due.'

'To me?' she re-echoed.

'Yes, to you,' Arkady repeated. 'No longer am I the presumptuous lad who came here a short while ago: not for nothing have I attained my twenty-third year. And though I still wish to be of use in life, though I still wish to consecrate the whole of my faculties to the service of Truth, I no longer seek my ideals where I was wont to do – they appear to me to stand much nearer home. Hitherto I have been in ignorance of myself, hitherto I have set myself tasks beyond my powers; but now, through a certain feeling which is within me, my eyes have become opened. By the way, the manner in which I express myself may be lacking in clarity, yet I venture to hope that I have made myself understood?'

Katia said nothing; but she ceased to look at the speaker.

'In my opinion,' he went on in a tone of rising emotion, while in a birch tree overhead a chaffinch started pouring forth a flood of unstudied song, 'in my opinion, it is the duty of an honourable man to be frank with those who, with those who – in short, with those who stand nearest to him in life. Consequently I, I am minded to – to – '

Here Arkady's eloquence failed him. He stumbled and stuttered and had to pause for a moment. Meanwhile Katia's eyes remained lowered. One would have thought that she did not in the least understand this preamble, but was expecting to hear something quite of a different nature.

'That I shall surprise you I know in advance,' continued Arkady, once more spurring his faculties. 'And that surprise will be the greater when I tell you that the feeling to which I have alluded concerns, to a certain extent – yes, to a certain extent, yourself. For yesterday, you will remember, you imputed to me a lack of gravity' – he was speaking much like a man who, having blundered into a bog, feels that at each step he sinks deeper and deeper, yet struggles on in the hope of eventually extricating himself – 'and such a reproach is all too often levelled against, all too often falls upon, young people who have ceased to deserve it. Were I but possessed of more self-confidence' ('God help me! God help me!' he thought despairingly, but Katia did not even turn her head) – 'had I but the right to hope that – '

'Did I but feel sure that you really mean what you say,' broke in, at this moment, the clear accents of Anna Sergievna.

Arkady became dumb, and Katia turned pale; for along a little path which skirted the bushes screening the temple there were advancing Bazarov and Madame! Katia and Arkady could not actually see the pair, yet they could hear every word uttered, and even catch the sound of their breathing, and the rustle of Anna Sergievna's dress. Advancing a few more steps, the couple halted, and remained standing in front of the building.

'It is like this,' Anna Sergievna continued. 'You and I have blundered into an error. That is to say, while neither of us is in the heyday of youth – I so least of the two – and both of us have lived our lives and are weary, we are also (for I need not stand on ceremony) individuals of intellect. Consequently, though, at first, we interested one another, and felt our mutual curiosity aroused, it happened that subsequently – '

'That subsequently I grew stale in your eyes,' hazarded Bazarov.

'Oh no! That that was not the cause of the situation you are well aware. But, whatever the cause, you and I have not a *compelling need* of one another. Therein lies the point. In other words, both of us have in us – how shall I express it? – both of us are too mutually *akin*. We were slow to grasp that fact. Now, Arkady – '

'Have you a "compelling need" of him?' put in Bazarov.

'For shame, Evgenii Vasilitch! You yourself have averred that he is not wholly indifferent to me; and I too have long suspected that he cherishes for me at least a measure of admiration. As we are on the subject, I will not attempt to conceal from you that of late the fact that I am old enough to be his aunt has not prevented me from devoting to him more of my thoughts than I used to do. In his fresh young sentimentality there is a certain charm.'

'The term "fascination" comes handier in such cases,' said Bazarov in the deep, quiet tone which, with him, always signified sarcasm. 'As a matter of fact, I found Arkady secretive yesterday – he made but the scantiest of references either to you or your sister. That constitutes an important symptom.'

'Katia and he are brother and sister to one another,' said Madame. 'Indeed I am pleased to see it – though perhaps I ought not to connive at so much familiarity.'

'I presume that the element speaking in you is the sister?' drawled Bazarov.

'Of course! But need we stand here? Let us move on. We hold curious conversations, do we not? Indeed, to think of all the things which I now say to you! Yet I still fear you a little, even though I trust you as being, at heart, a good man.'

'I am far from good; and you only call me so because I have lost all significance in your eyes. Ill boots it to weave chaplets for the head of a corpse.'

'Evgenii Vasilitch, we cannot always command ourselves,' came the sound of Anna Sergievna's next words; but the next moment the wind soughed, the leaves rustled, and the rest of what she was saying was carried away into the distance. Nothing beyond it save (after a pause) 'You are free, are you not?' on the part of Bazarov could be distinguished. Then the sound of their footsteps died away, and once more complete silence reigned.

Turning to Katia, Arkady saw that she was sitting as before, but with her head more bent.

'Katerina Sergievna,' he said tremulously, and with his hands clasped, 'I shall love you always, and beyond recall; nor shall I ever love another woman. This is what I have been trying to say to you this morning, in the hope that I might ascertain your views, and then beg for your hand. I am not a rich man, but I would make any sacrifice for your sake. Come, then! Will you answer me? Will you trust me? Surely you do not think that I am speaking out of frivolity? Recall the past few days: may you not rest assured now that my remaining self (you know what I mean) is gone for ever? Come, look at me – look at me and speak but a word, a single word. I love you, I love you! Do not refuse to believe that I mean what I say.'

Gravely, yet with a radiant look in her eyes, Katia raised her head, and, after a moment's thought, said with the trace of a smile: 'Yes.'

Arkady leapt up.

' "Yes"? You have said "Yes," Katia! But what do mean by that word? Do you mean that you believe in my love, or do you mean that – ? No, no; I dare not finish the sentence.'

Katia repeated only the word 'Yes,' but this time she left no room for misunderstanding. Arkady seized her large, but not unshapely, hands in his, and, panting with rapture, strained her to his breast. He could scarcely stand upon his feet – he could only keep repeating again and again: 'Katia! Katia!' Meanwhile she shed a few innocent tears at which she smiled as they fell. The man who has not seen such tears in the eyes of his beloved does not know the height of happiness to which, with mingled joy and gratitude and modesty, a woman can attain.

Next morning Anna Sergievna sent for Bazarov to her boudoir; and when he arrived she, with a forced smile, handed him a folded sheet of notepaper. That sheet represented a letter from Arkady, a letter in which he begged for her sister's hand.

Bazarov skimmed the epistle – then scarcely could forbear venting the rancour which blazed for a moment in his breast.

'It is as I said, you see,' he commented. 'Only yesterday you were telling me that his feeling for Katerina Sergievna was that of a brother for a sister! And what are you going to do?'

'What would you advise me to do?' she said, still smiling.

'I presume' – he also was smiling, although he was feeling as wholly out of spirits, as little inclined towards gaiety, as she was 'I presume that we have no choice but to bestow our blessing upon the young couple. In every respect it would be a good match, for his father has a nice little property, Arkady is the only son, and the father is too easy-going to be likely to raise any difficulty.'

Madame Odintsov rose and paced the room for a moment or two – her face alternately flushing and turning pale.

'So that is what you think,' she said. 'Well, I too see no impediment. Indeed, the affair rejoices me both for Katia's sake and for – yes, for his. But first I must await his father's consent; and for that purpose I will send Arkady himself to interview Nickolai Petrovitch . . . So I was right yesterday, was I not? I was right when I said that you and I are become, elderly. How did I fail to foresee this? I am indeed surprised at it!'

Again she smiled, but, in the very act of smiling turned away.

'Our young folk are indeed cunning,' remarked Bazarov. After a pause he added:

'Goodbye now. I hope that the affair may develop well. From a distance I, too, shall rejoice.'

She turned and faced him.

'Need you really go?' she asked. 'Why not stay a little longer? Pray stay, for I find talking to you a stimulant – it is like walking on the edge of a precipice: at first one is afraid, then one gathers courage. Do not go.'

'I thank you for the proposal, as also for your flattering estimate of my conversational powers,' said Bazarov. 'Nevertheless, I have tarried overlong in a sphere which is alien to my personality. Only for a while can flying fish support themselves in the air. Then they relapse into their natural element. Allow me to flop back into mine.'

Yet a bitter laugh was twisting his pale features. She saw it, and felt sorry for him.

'The man still loves me,' was her thought, and she extended a sympathetic hand.

He understood her, however.

'No, no!' he exclaimed as he withdrew a step or two. 'Though poor, I have never yet accepted alms. Goodbye, and may your lot always be happy.'

'Yet we shall meet again,' she replied with an involuntary gesture. 'Of that I am certain.'

'Anything may occur in this world,' he remarked – then bowed and was gone.

That afternoon he said to Arkady as he knelt down to pack his trunk:

'I hear that you are going to make a nest for yourself? And why should you not? It is an excellent course to take. But for you to dissemble is useless, and I had scarcely expected that you would do so. Has the preoccupation of it all deprived you of your tongue?'

'When I left you at Marino I had no thought of this,' said Arkady. 'You are the dissembler, though, are you not? For when you say, "It is an excellent course to take," you dissemble, as well as waste your time, seeing that I am well aware of your views on marriage.'

'Merely my way of expressing myself. You see what I am doing at this moment. In my trunk is a vacant space. I am packing it with straw. And the same with life's trunk. To avoid leaving empty spaces therein we pad the interstices. You need not be offended. You cannot fail to remember what I really think of Katerina Sergievna. While some maidens earn cheap reputations by merely smiling at right moments, your *inamorata* can show more – indeed, so much more that soon you will be (and very properly) under her thumb.'

Slapping down the lid of the trunk, Bazarov rose from the floor.

'Now, farewell,' he said. 'No, I will not deceive you: we are parting for ever, and you know it. In my opinion you have acted wisely, for you were not meant to live the hard, bitter, reckless life of Nihilism – you lack at once the necessary coolness and the necessary venom. But this is not to say that in you there is not a due measure of youthful spirit. What I mean is that that asset alone is not sufficient for the work. The *dvorianin* is powerless to progress beyond either well-bred effervescence or well-bred humility: and both sentiments are futile. For example, you have not yet been blooded, yet already you think yourself a man: whereas the two chief conditions of our existence are battle and bloodshed. Yes, the dust from our heels hurts your eyes, and the grime on our bodies makes you feel dirty. In other words, although you derive a certain gratification from indulging in self-criticism, and think no small beer of yourself, you have failed to grow to our stature. To us such things are vanities. Tools of an altogether different kind are what we need for the task. Consequently I repeat that, though a fine young fellow enough, you are also just a little-minded, so-called "liberal-minded" *baritch** – what my father calls a "product of evolution." '

'Evgenii,' was Arkady's sad reply, 'we are parting for ever, yet this is all that you have to say to me!'

Bazarov scratched his head.

'Something else I could say, Arkady,' he replied. 'But I will not say that something – it would savour too much of Romanticism. Get married as soon as you can, line your nest, and beget plenty of offspring. Nor will those offspring be altogether fools, seeing that they will be born in due season, and not when you and I were . . . My horses are ready and I must depart. Of the rest of the household I have taken leave already. Shall we embrace once more, eh?'

The tears gushed in torrents from Arkady's eyes as he flung himself upon his old friend and mentor.

'Ah, youth, youth!' commented Bazarov. 'See what comes of being young! But before long, I know, Katerina Sergievna will have set things right. Yes, she will console you.'

With a last goodbye he mounted the travelling cart, and, in the act of doing so, pointed to a pair of jackdaws which were sitting perched upon the stable roof.

'See!' he cried. '*There's* an instructive lesson for you!'

'What do you mean?' queried Arkady.

'What?' was Bazarov's ejaculation. 'Are you so ignorant of, or so forgetful of, natural history as not to know that the jackdaw is the most respected of family birds? Mark the good example before you. Farewell, señor!'

And with a clatter the cart started on its way.

Nor was Bazarov mistaken, for, even before nightfall, Arkady, deep in conversation with Katia, had completely forgotten his vanished instructor. Moreover, already the young fellow was beginning to play second fiddle to his *fiancée*: which circumstance the girl, on realising, in no way felt surprised at. So it was arranged that on the following day he should depart for Marino to interview his father; and in the meanwhile, Anna Sergievna, having no desire to hamper the young couple, merely

* A small squire.

observed such a show of propriety as involved her not leaving them together for long, but at the same time keeping at a distance the Princess, who, since the tidings of the impending union, had been in a state of lachrymose rancour. For herself, Anna Sergievna had at first feared that the spectacle of the young people's happiness would prove too much for her; but now the contrary proved to be the case, and she not only failed to feel hurt at the spectacle, but even found that it interested her and eventually softened her – a consummation which brought both relief and regret.

'Bazarov was right,' she reflected. 'It was mere curiosity, mere love of ease, mere egoism, mere – '

'Children, is love an empirical sentiment?' once she asked of Arkady and Katia: but neither of the pair understood her meaning. Moreover, they were fighting a little shy of her, since they could not altogether forget the conversation which they had involuntarily overheard; but in time Anna Sergievna succeeded in overcoming also this timidity, and found the task the more easy to perform in that she had succeeded also in overcoming her disappointment.

Chapter 27

THE OLD BAZAROVS' DELIGHT at their son's return was the greater in that the event was so unexpected. To such an extent did Anna Vlasievna fuss and flounce about the house that Vasili Ivanitch likened her to a hen partridge (no doubt the short tail of her blouse did impart to her rather a bird-like aspect); while, as regards Vasili himself, he grunted, and sucked the amber mouthpiece of his pipe, and, grasping the shank, inverted the bowl as though to make sure that it was secure, and, finally, parted his capacious lips, and gave vent to a noiseless chuckle.

'I am going to spend with you six whole weeks,' said Bazarov. 'But I desire to work, and therefore must not be disturbed.'

'Before we will disturb you, you shall forget what my face looks like,' replied Vasili Ivanitch.

And he kept his word; for, after allotting his son the study, he not only remained completely out of sight, but even prevented his wife from manifesting the least sign of tenderness.

'When Evgenii last visited us,' he said to her, 'you and I proved a little wearisome; so this time we must be more discreet.'

Anna Vlasievna agreed, much as she lost by the arrangement, seeing that now she beheld her son only at meal times, and feared, even then, to speak to him.

'Eniushenka,' she would begin – then, before he had had time to raise his eyes, pluck nervously at the strings of her cap, and whisper: 'Oh no; it was nothing,' and address herself, instead, to Vasili Ivanitch; saying, for instance (with cheek on hand as usual): 'My dear, which would our darling Eniusha prefer for dinner – cabbage soup or beef with horse-radish?' And when Vasili Ivanitch would reply: 'Why should you not ask him yourself?' she would exclaim: 'Oh no, for that might vex him.'

But eventually Bazarov ceased to closet himself, in that there came an abatement of the work fever, and to it succeeded fits of depression, *ennui*, and an inordinate restlessness. In his every movement there began to loom a strange discontent, from his gait there disappeared its old firm, active self-confidence, and, ceasing to indulge in solitary rambles, he took to cultivating society, to attending tea in the drawing-room, to pacing the kitchen garden, and to joining Vasili Ivanitch in a silent smoking of pipes. Nay, on one occasion he even paid Father Alexis a visit!

At first the new order of things rejoiced Vasili Ivanitch's heart: but that joy proved short-lived.

'Though I could not say why, Eniusha makes me anxious,' he confided to his spouse. 'Not that he is discontented or ill-tempered – such things would not have mattered: rather, it is that he is sad and brooding, and never opens his lips. Would that he would curse you and me, for instance! Also, he is thinner; nor do I like the colour of his face.'

'O God!' whispered the old woman. 'Yet I may not even put my arms around his neck!'

From that time onwards Vasili Ivanitch began to make cautious attempts to question Bazarov concerning his work, his health, and his friend Arkady; but always Bazarov returned reluctant, indifferent replies, and once, when his father was for introducing the foregoing topics, said irritably:

'Why are you for ever tiptoeing around me? Your present manner is even worse than your former one.'

'There, there – I did not mean anything,' was poor Vasili Ivanitch's reply.

Political allusions proved equally fruitless. For instance, when Vasili Ivanitch was seeking to engage his son's interest on the score of the impending emancipation of the serfs and progress in general, the other muttered carelessly:

'Yesterday, when passing through the courtyard, I heard some peasant lads singing, not one of the good old songs, but "The age of truth is coming in, when hearts shall glow with love." There's progress for you!'

Occasionally Bazarov would repair to the village, and, in his usual bantering fashion, enter into conversation with some peasant.

'Well,' he said to a *muzhik*, 'pray expound to me your views on life. For they tell me that in you lie the whole strength and the whole future of Russia – that you are going to begin a new epoch in our history, and to give us both a real language and new laws.'

The peasant made no reply at the moment. Then he said:

'We might do all that if first we had a new chapel here.'

'Tell me something, though, about the world in general,' Bazarov interrupted. 'The world stands on three fishes, does it not?'

'It does that, *batiushka*,' the peasant replied with the quiet, good-humoured sweetness of the patriarchal age. 'But above it stands the will of the masters. The *baré* are our fathers, and the harder the *barin* drives, the better for the *muzhik*.'

Shrugging his shoulders contemptuously at this statement, Bazarov turned away, while the peasant slunk off homewards.

'What did he say?' asked a sullen-looking, middle-aged peasant who had been standing at the door of his hut during the course of the foregoing colloquy. 'Was he talking of arrears of taxes?'

'Of arrears of taxes!' retorted the first peasant, his tone now containing not a trace of its late patriarchal sweetness, but, rather, a note of purely dry contempt. 'He was chattering just for chattering's sake – he likes to hear his own tongue wag. Do not all of us know what a *barin* and the likes of him are good for?'

'Aye,' agreed the second peasant; whereafter, with much nodding of caps and gesticulating of fists, they fell to discussing their own affairs and requirements. So alas for Bazarov's scornful shrug of the shoulders! And alas for that knowledge of the ways in which the peasant should be talked to whereof the young Nihilist had made such boast when disputing with Paul Petrovitch! In fact, never had it dawned upon the mind of the self-confident Bazarov that, in the eyes of the *muzhik*, he was no better than a pease-pudding.

However, he succeeded in discovering for himself an occupation. This was when, in bandaging a peasant's leg, Vasili Ivanitch's hands shook a little through senility, and his son hastened to his assistance: and from that time forth Bazarov acted as Vasili Ivanitch's partner, even though he maintained unabated his ridicule both of the remedies which he himself advised and of the father who hastened to put them into practice. Yet in no way did his son's raillery annoy Vasili Ivanitch: rather, it heartened the old man. Smoking his pipe, and drawing his dirty overall in to his waist with both thumbs, he would listen delightedly to the scoffer, and chuckle, and show his blackened teeth the more in proportion as the sallies contained a greater measure of venom. Nay, stupid or simply senseless as many of these witticisms were, he would frequently catch them up, and repeat them. To take one instance, he, for several days in succession, kept assuring everyone in the village and in the town that 'we call this the nine o'clock office' – the sole basis being the fact that once, on learning of his (Vasili Ivanitch's) habit of attending Matins, Bazarov had made use of the phrase in question.

'Thank God, Evgenii has ceased to mope,' he confided in a whisper to his wife. 'In fact, you should have heard him rating me today!'

Also, the thought that he had such an assistant in his labours filled the old man with pride.

'Yes, yes,' he would say as he handed some peasant woman in a man's jacket a phial of medicinal water or a pot of cold cream, 'you ought daily to thank God that my son happens to be staying with me, since otherwise you could not possibly have been treated according to the latest and most scientific methods. Do you understand? I say that even Napoleon, the Emperor of the French, has not at his disposal a better physician than my son.'

And the peasant woman (who had come, it may be, to complain of 'a lifting with the gripes' – an expression which probably she herself could not have explained) would bow, then proffer the three or four eggs which would be tied up in a corner of her neckcloth.

Also, when Bazarov extracted a tooth from the jaw of a travelling pedlar, Vasili Ivanitch could not allow even the very ordinary character of the tooth to prevent him from preserving it as a rarity, and showing it to Father Alexis.

'See what a fang!' he said. 'And to think of the strength which Evgenii must possess! He lifted the pedlar clean from the ground! It was like uprooting an oak tree!'

'Splendid!' was Father Alexis' comment – he knew not what else to say, nor, for that matter, how else to get rid of the enthusiastic veteran.

Lastly, there was an occasion when a peasant from a neighbouring village brought his brother to be treated. Suffering from typhus, the patient was lying face downwards on the straw in the cart, and had reached the last stage, since already his body was covered with spots of a hectic nature, and he had long lost consciousness. To an expression of regret that resort had not sooner been had to medical aid, Vasili Ivanitch could add no more than an intimation that no hope was left: nor was he wrong, seeing that even before the peasant succeeded in conveying his brother back to the village, the sick man had breathed his last.

Three days later Bazarov entered his father's room with an enquiry for some hell-stone.

'I have some,' said Vasili Ivanitch; 'but what do you want it for?'

'For the cauterisation of a wound.'

'A wound on whom?'

'A wound on myself.'

'On yourself? Let me see the place. Where is it?'

'There – on that finger. Today I went to the village whence they brought the typhus patient the other day; and though they tried to conceal the body, I succeeded in discovering it. Not for a long time had I had a chance of doing that sort of work.'

'Yes?'

'And the sequel was that I cut myself, and, on repairing to the district physician, found that he did not possess what I wanted.'

Vasili Ivanitch went white to the lips. Hurrying, without a word, into his study, he returned thence with some hell-stone. Bazarov was for carrying it away forthwith.

'No, no!' cried Vasili Ivanitch. 'For God's sake allow me to see to this in person.'

Bazarov smiled.

'You are indeed a keen practitioner,' he commented.

'Do not jest, I beg of you. Show me the finger. No, it is not a large wound. Am I hurting it at all?'

'Not in the least. Have no fear. You can press it harder still if you like.'

Vasili Ivanitch paused.

'Do you not think,' he said, 'that it would be better to cauterise the finger with an iron?'

'No, I do not. Moreover, that ought, in any case, to have been done sooner; whereas by now even the hell-stone is unlikely to prove effectual, seeing that, as you know, once absorbed into the system, the germ renders all remedies too late.'

'How "too late"?' gasped Vasili Ivanitch.

'What I say. Four hours have elapsed since the injury.'

Vasili Ivanitch gave the wound a further cauterisation.

'So the district physician had no hell-stone?' he queried.

'None.'

'God in heaven! To think of that man calling himself a doctor, yet being without such an indispensable remedy!'

'You should have seen his lancets!' remarked Bazarov. Then he left the room.

Throughout that evening and the next few days Vasili Ivanitch kept making every possible excuse to enter his son's room; and though he never actually referred to the wound – he even strove to confine his conversation to purely extraneous subjects – his observation of his son remained so persistent, his solicitude so marked, that at length Bazarov, losing patience, bade him begone. Of course Vasili Ivanitch promised not to repeat the intrusion, and as a matter of fact he kept this promise the more religiously in that Arina Vlasievna (who had had the matter carefully concealed from her) was beginning to scent something in the wind, and to press for reasons why, during the previous night, her husband had never once closed his eyes. Accordingly, for the next two days Vasili Ivanitch faithfully observed the undertaking he had given; and that although the covert observation of his son's looks which he maintained showed them to be growing by no means to his liking: but on the third day, during dinner, Vasili Ivanitch could bear it no more, for Bazarov was sitting with his eyes lowered and his plate empty.

'You are eating nothing, Evgenii?' he said with his face composed to express absolute indifference. 'In my opinion, the dinner is well cooked.'

'The only reason why I am eating nothing,' replied Bazarov, 'is that I am not hungry.'

'You have no appetite?' the old man queried timidly. 'Also, is – is your head aching at all?'

'Yes. Why should it not ache?'

Arina Vlasievna began to prick up her ears.

'Do not be angry, Evgenii,' Vasili Ivanitch continued, 'b – but might I feel your pulse and examine you?'

Bazarov looked at him.

'You need not feel my pulse,' he said. 'Without that, I can tell that I have a touch of fever.'

'You feel shivery, eh?'

'Yes. I think I will go and lie down. Pray make me a little lime-juice tea, for I seem to have caught a chill.'

'Yes,' Arina Vlasievna put in, 'I heard you coughing last night.'

'But it is only a chill,' added Bazarov, and left the room.

So Arina Vlasievna set to work to make the lime-juice tea, and Vasili Ivanitch went into an adjoining room and tore his hair.

Bazarov did not get up again that day, but passed the night in a state of heavy coma. At one o'clock he opened his eyes with an effort, and, on seeing his father's pale face in the lamp-light, bade him depart. At once the other excused himself for the intrusion, but nevertheless returned on tiptoe, and, concealing himself behind the open doors of a cupboard, remained there to watch his son. Nor did Arina Vlasievna go to bed, but at intervals set the study door ajar, in order that she might 'see how our Eniusha was sleeping' and look at Vasili Ivanitch: for though nothing of the latter was to be discerned except a bowed, motionless back, even that much afforded her a little comfort.

In the morning Bazarov attempted to rise, but his head swam, and blood gushed from his nose, so he desisted from the attempt. In silence Vasili Ivanitch tended him, and Arina Vlasievna came to ask him how he felt. He replied, 'Better,' then turned his face to the wall. Instantly Vasili Ivanitch fell to gesticulating violently at his wife with both hands: which proceeding proved so far successful that, by dint of biting her lips, Arina Vlasievna contrived to force back the tears, and leave the room. Of a sudden everything in the house had seemed to turn dark. Everywhere faces looked drawn, and everywhere there was to be observed a curious stillness of which one cause, among others, was the fact that there had hastily been removed from the courtyard of the village a vociferous cock which no reasoning had been able to convince of the necessity of silence.

So Bazarov continued lying with his face to the wall. Once or twice Vasili Ivanitch essayed a tentative question or two, but the attempt only wearied Bazarov, and the old man at length subsided into an armchair, and sat nervously twitching his fingers. Next, Vasili repaired to the garden for a few minutes, and looked, as he stood there, like a statue which has been stuck with immeasurable astonishment (never at any time was the expression of surprise absent from his features); where-after he returned to his son's room, in the hope of evading questions on the part of his wife, but she took him by the hand, and grimly, almost threateningly asked: 'What is the matter with our Eniusha?' and when Vasili strove to pull himself together, and to force a smile, there issued, to his horror, not a smile at all, but a sort of irresponsible laugh.

Earlier in the morning he had sent for a doctor to assist him; wherefore he now considered that it would be well to advise his son of the fact, lest Bazarov should lose his temper on discovering the fact in question for himself.

Vasili Ivanitch explained the situation, and then Bazarov turned himself about on the sofa, gazed at his father for a moment or two, and asked to be given something to drink. Vasili Ivanitch handed him some water, and seized the opportunity also to feel his son's forehead. It seemed to be on fire.

'My father,' said Bazarov in a hoarse, dragging voice, 'I fear that my course is run. The infection has caught me, and in a few days you will be laying me in my grave.'

Someone might have thrust Vasili Ivanitch violently backwards, so sharply did he stagger.

'Evgenii,' he gasped, 'why say that? God have you in his keeping! It is merely that you have caught a chill.'

'Come, come!' interrupted Bazarov, but in the same dragging tone as before. 'It is useless to talk like that to a doctor. All the signs of infection are present. That you know for yourself.'

'But – but where are the signs of – of infection?'

'Look at these. What do they mean?'

And Bazarov pulled up the sleeve of his shirt. What he showed his father was a number of red, angry-looking patches that were coming into view.

Vasili Ivanitch started and turned cold with fear. At length he contrived to stammer out:

'Yet – even supposing that, that there should be anything in the nature of infection – '

'Of pyæmia, you mean,' the son prompted.

'Anything in the nature of epidemic infec –'

'Of pyæmia, I repeat,' grimly, insistently corrected Bazarov. 'Have you forgotten your textbooks?'

'Yes – well, have it your own way. But we will cure you, all the same.'

'Fiddlesticks! But, apart from that question, I had scarcely looked to die so soon. To be frank, I think it hard upon me. And now you and my mother must fall back upon the fund of religious strength which lies within you. The hour to put it to the test has arrived.' He drank some more water. 'One particular request I desire to make while my brain is yet clear, for, by tomorrow, or the day after, it will, as you know, have failed, and even now I am not sure whether I am expressing myself sensibly, seeing that, as I was lying here just now, I seemed to see a pack of red dogs leaping around me, and yourself making a point at me as a dog does at a partridge. Yes, it was like being drunk. Can you understand what I say?'

'Yes, yes, Evgenii; you are talking quite sensibly.'

'Very well. Now, I believe that you have sent for a doctor; and if the fact will give you any comfort, I too shall be pleased. But also I beg that you will send word to, to –'

'To Arkady Nikolaievitch?' the old man suggested.

'To whom? To Arkady Nikolaievitch?' re-echoed Bazarov bewilderedly. 'Oh, you mean that young cockerel of ours? No, no – do not disturb him, for he has just joined the company of the jackdaws. You need not be surprised at these words – they do not mean that delirium is setting in; they are merely a metaphor. Well, it is to Madame Odintsov, the lady landowner of this neighbourhood, that I desire a messenger to be sent. I suppose you have heard of her?' (Vasili Ivanitch nodded assent.) 'All that the messenger need say is that Evgenii Vasilitch sends his compliments, and is dying. Will you do this?'

'Of course I will, Evgenii! But why think that you are going to die? Come, come! Were such a thing to happen, where would be the justice of the world?'

'I could not say. I only know that I desire the messenger to be sent.'

'He shall start at once, and I myself will write the letter.'

'No, no: that will not be necessary. Merely let the messenger deliver my greeting. That, and nothing more. Now I will return to my red dogs. How curious it is that, though I strive to concentrate my thoughts upon death, there results from them nothing – I see before me only a great blur!'

And he turned his face wearily to the wall, while Vasili Ivanitch left the room, ascended to the bedroom above, and fell upon his knees before the sacred *ikons*.

'Pray, Arina, pray!' he moaned. 'Our son is dying!'

On the doctor arriving, the latter proved to be the district physician who had failed to produce hell-stone when required. After an examination of the patient he prescribed a watching course, and also added a few words as to a possible recovery.

'Have you ever known people in my condition *not* set out for the Elysian Fields?' asked Bazarov sharply as he caught hold of the leg of a table which stood beside his sofa, and shook it until the table actually altered its position. 'See my strength!' he continued. 'All of it is still there, yet I must go hence! To think that, whereas an old man has lost touch with life, I should – ! Ah, however much you may deny death, it never will deny you . . . I hear someone weeping. Who is it?' There was a pause. 'Is it my mother? Poor soul! No one will be left for her to stuff with her marvellous *borstchi*.* And you, Vasili Ivanitch – are you too whimpering? Come, come! If Christianity cannot help you, try to become a Stoic philosopher. You have often enough boasted of being one.'

'Aye, a fine philosopher I, to be sure!' sobbed poor old Vasili with the tears hopping down his cheeks.

Thereafter Bazarov grew hourly worse, for the disease was taking the rapid course inevitable under the circumstances. Yet his powers of memory were unimpaired, and he understood everything that was said to him, for as yet he was making a brave fight to retain his faculties.

'No, I must not let my senses fail,' he kept whispering to himself as he clenched his fists. 'But oh, the folly of it all!' And then he would repeat to himself, over and over again, some such formula as 'Eight and ten – what do they make?'

Meanwhile Vasili Ivanitch wandered about in a state bordering upon distraction – proposing first one remedy, and then another, and constantly covering up his son's feet.

'Suppose we wrap him in an ice-sheet?' he suggested once in a tone of agony. 'How, too, about an emetic, or a mustard plaster on his stomach, or a little blood-letting?'

But to each and all of these remedies the doctor (whom Vasili Ivanitch had begged to remain in the house) demurred. Likewise the doctor drank the patient's lemonade, and then requested to be given a pipe and 'something warm and strengthening' – to wit, a glassful of vodka. Meanwhile Arina Vlasievna sat on a chair by the door, and only

* Roast beef with horseradish

at intervals retired to pray. It seemed that a few days earlier she had let fall, and broken, a toilet mirror, and that all her life long she had looked upon such an occurrence as an evil omen. With her, in silence, sat Anfisushka; while, as for Timotheitch, he had departed with the message to Madame Odintsov.

That night Bazarov did not improve, for he was racked with high fever; but as morning approached, the fever grew a little easier, and after he had asked Arina Vlasievna to perform his toilet, and had kissed her hand, he managed to swallow a little tea: which circumstance caused Vasili Ivanitch to pluck up courage, and to exclaim:

'Thank God, the crisis has both come and gone!'

'Do not be too sure of that,' rejoined Bazarov 'For what does the term "crisis" signify? Someone once invented it, shouted "Crisis!" and congratulated himself ever after. Extraordinary how the human race continues to attach credence to mere words! For example, tell a man that he is a fool, yet refrain from assaulting him, and he will be downcast; but tell him that he is a man of wisdom, yet give him no money, and he will be overjoyed.'

So reminiscent of Bazarov's former sallies was this little speech that Vasili Ivanitch's heart fairly overflowed.

'Bravo!' he cried, clapping his hands in dumb show. 'Well said!'

Bazarov smiled a sad smile.

'Then you think,' said he, 'that the "crisis" is either approaching or retiring?'

'I know that you are better. That I can see for myself. And the fact rejoices me.'

'Well, it is not always a bad thing to rejoice. But have you sent word to, to – to *her*? You know whom I mean?'

'Of course I have, Evgenii.'

The improvement did not long continue, for to it there succeeded attacks of pain. Vasili Ivanitch sat by the bed: and as he did so it seemed as though something in particular were worrying the old man. Several times he tried to speak, and each time he failed. But at length he contrived to gasp out:

'Egenii! Son! My dearest son! My own beloved son!'

Even Bazarov could not remain wholly indifferent to such an unwonted appeal. Turning his head a little, and making an evident effort to shake off the unconsciousness that was weighing him down, he murmured:

'What is it, my father?'

'This, Evgenii.' And all of a sudden the old man fell upon his knees beside the bed. 'Evgenii, you are better now, and with God's help will recover; but do, in any case, seize this hour to comfort me and your mother by fulfilling all the duties of a Christian. Yes, though to say this is painful for me, how much more terribly would it hurt me if – if this chance were to pass for ever, Evgenii! Think, oh think of what – '

The old man could say no more, while over the son's face and closed eyes there passed a curious expression. A pause followed. Then Bazarov said:

'To comfort you, I will not altogether refuse your request; but, since you yourself have said that I am better, surely there can be no need for hurry?'

'Yes, you *are* better, Evgenii – you are better; but who can say what may lie in the dispensation of God? Whereas, once this duty shall have been fulfilled – '

'Yet I will wait a little,' interrupted Bazarov. 'This much, however, I will concede: that, should you prove to be wrong in your surmise as to my recovery, I will allow the Last Sacrament to be administered.'

'And, Evgenii, I beg of you to – '

'I will wait a little, I repeat. And now let me go to sleep. Do not disturb me.'

And he replaced his head in its former position, while the old man rose from his knees, reseated himself in the chair, rested his chin upon his hands, and fell to biting his fingers.

Presently Vasili's ear caught the rumble of a light carriage – the sound which is always so distinguishable in a quiet country spot. Nearer and nearer came the sound of the wheels; nearer and nearer came the hard breathing of horses. Springing from his chair, he rushed to the window. Into the courtyard of the mansion there was turning a two-seated, four-horsed buggy! Without stopping to think what this could mean, he darted forward to the front door, where, transported with joy, he was just in time to see a liveried footman open the door of the vehicle, and assist thence a lady in a black cloak, with a veil of the same hue.

'I am Madame Odintsoy,' she said. 'Is Evgenii Vasilitch still alive? I presume you are his father? I have brought with me a doctor.'

Even as she spoke the doctor in question – a German-looking little individual in spectacles – descended in a slow and dignified manner from the buggy.

'O angel of mercy!' cried Vasili Ivanitch as, seizing her hand, he pressed it convulsively to his lips. 'Yes, our Evgenii is still alive! And now he will be saved! Wife! Wife! There is an angel come to us from Heaven!'

'What?' responded the old woman with a gasp as she came running out of the hall. So lost in bewilderment was she that, falling at Anna Sergievna's feet, she actually began madly to kiss the hem of the visitor's cloak.

'Come, come!' Madame exclaimed. 'What does all this mean?'

But Arina Vlasievna was deaf to everything, and Vasili Ivanitch too could only continue repeating:

'There is an angel come to us from Heaven! There is an angel come to us from Heaven! There is an angel come to us from Heaven!'

'*Wo ist der Kranke?* (Where is the patient)?' asked the doctor with a touch of impatience.

This restored Vasili Ivanitch to his senses.

'Come this way, come this way,' he said. 'Yes, pray follow me, *Werthester Herr Kollega*' (titles based upon the strength of bygone memories).

For answer the German exclaimed 'Eh?', and pulled a not very gracious smirk.

Vasili Ivanitch led the way to the study.

'Here is the doctor brought by Madame Anna Sergievna Odintsov,' he said as he bent over his son. 'She herself too is here.'

Bazarov opened his eyes with a start.

'What do you say?' he asked.

'I say that Madame Anna Sergievna Odintsov is here, and that she has brought with her this good doctor.'

Bazarov peered around.

'Where is Anna Sergievna?' he murmured. 'Do you say that she is here? Then I wish to see her.'

'You shall see her, Evgenii; but first of all I must have a chat with this gentleman, and tell him the story of your illness: for Sidor Sidorovitch' (that was the name of the district physician) 'has gone home, and a short consultation must be held.'

Bazarov eyed the German.

'All right,' he said. 'Hold your consultation as soon as you like. Only, do not speak in Latin, for I know the meaning of the words *Jam moritur.*'

'*Der Herr scheint des Deutschen mächtig zu sein,*' the newly-arrived disciple of Æsculapius remarked to Vasili Ivanitch.

'*Ich habe –* ' the old man began; then added: 'But perhaps we had better speak in Russian, my dear sir?'

And the consultation followed.

Half an hour later Vasili Ivanitch conducted Anna Sergievna into the study. As the doctor passed out he whispered to her that recovery was hopeless.

She glanced at Bazarov, and halted as though petrified, so striking was the bloodshot, deathlike face, with the dim eyes turned so yearningly in her direction. Nevertheless her feeling was one merely of chill, oppressive terror, while at the same moment there flashed through her brain the thought that, if she had loved him, no such feeling could now have been present.

'I thank you,' he said with an effort. 'I had not expected this, and you have done a kind act in coming. So we meet once more, even as you foretold!'

'Has not Madame Anna Sergievna indeed been kind?' put in Vasili Ivanitch.

'Father, pray leave us,' said Bazarov. 'I know, Anna Sergievna, that you will excuse him. For at such a time as this – ' And he nodded towards his weak, prostrate form.

Vasili Ivanitch left the room.

'A second time I thank you,' continued Bazarov. 'To have acted so is worthy of the Tsars. For they say that even the Sovereign visits a deathbed when requested.'

'Evgenii Vasilitch, I hope that – '

'Let us speak plainly. My course is run. I am under the wheel, and we need not think of the future. Yet how curious it is that to each individual human being death, old though it is as an institution, comes as a novelty! . . . Nevertheless, it shall not make me quail: and then there will fall the curtain, and then – well, then they will write *Fuit*.' There followed a feeble gesture. 'But what did I want to say to you? That I have loved you? There was a time when the phrase "I love" had for me no meaning; and now it will have less than ever, seeing that love is a form, and that my particular embodiment of it is fast lapsing towards dissolution. It – Ah, how perfect you are! You stand there as beautiful as – '

There passed over Anna Sergievna an involuntary shudder.

'Nay,' he said. 'You need not be afraid. But will you not sit down? Seat yourself near me, but not too near, for my malady is infectious.'

She crossed the room with a rapid step, and seated herself beside the sofa on which he was lying.

'O woman of kind heart!' he whispered. 'And to think that you are beside me once more! To think that you, so pure and fresh and young, are in this sorry room! Well, goodbye, and may you live long, and enjoy your time while you may. Of all things in this world long life is the most desirable: yet you can see for yourself what an ugly spectacle I, a half-crushed, but still wriggling, worm, am now become. There was a time when I used to say: "I will do many things in life, and refuse to die before I have completed those tasks, for I am a giant": but now I have indeed a giant's task in hand – the task of dying as though death were nothing to me . . . No matter. I am not going to put my tail between my legs.

He broke off, and groped for his tumbler. She handed it him without drawing off her glove. Her breath was coming in jerks.

'It will not be long before you will have forgotten me,' he went on. 'For a dead mortal is no companion for a living one. I dare say that my father will tell you what a man is being lost to Russia; but that is all rubbish. Nevertheless, do not undeceive him, for he is old, old. Rather, comfort him as you would comfort a child, and also be kind to my mother. Two such mortals as them you will not find in all *your* great world – no, not though you search for them with a candle by daylight . . . Russia needs me, indeed! Evidently she does *not* need me. Whom, then, does she need? She needs shoemakers, tailors, butchers . . . What does a butcher sell? He sells meat, does he not? . . . I think that I am wandering – I seem to see before me a forest . . . '

He pressed his hand to his forehead, and Anna Sergievna bent over him.

'Evgenii Vasilitch,' she said, 'I am here.'

With a combined movement he took her hand and raised himself a little.

'Goodbye,' he said with a sudden spasm of energy and a last flash of his eyes. 'Goodbye . . . I kissed you that time, did I not, when, when? . . . Ah, breathe now upon the expiring lamp, that it may go out in peace.'

She pressed her lips gently to his forehead.

'Enough,' he murmured as he sank back upon the pillow. 'Now let there come – darkness.'

She left the room quietly.

'Well?' whispered Vasili Ivanitch.

'He has gone to sleep,' she replied in a voice that was scarcely audible.

But Bazarov was not fated to go to sleep. Rather, as night approached he sank into a state of coma, and, on the following day, expired. Father Alexis performed over him the last rites of religion, and at the moment when Extreme Unction was being administered, and the holy oil touched his breast, one of the dying man's eyelids raised itself, and over the face there seemed to flit something like an expression of distaste at the sight of the priest in his vestments, the smoking censer, and the candles before the *ikon*.

Finally, when Bazarov's last breath had been drawn, and there had arisen in the house the sound of 'the general lamentation,' something akin to frenzy came upon Vasili Ivanitch.

'I declare that I protest!' he cried with his face blazing and quivering with fury, and his fist beating the air as in menace of someone. 'I declare that I protest, that I protest, that I protest!'

Upon that old Arina Vlasievna, suffused in tears, laid her arms around his neck, and the two sank forward upon the floor. Said Anfisushka later, when relating the story in the servants' quarters: 'There they knelt together – side by side, their heads drooping like those of two sheep at midday.'

Ah, but in time the heat of noontide passes, and to it there succeed nightfall and dusk, with a return to the quiet fold where for the weary and the heavy-laden there waits sleep, sweet sleep.

Chapter 28

SINCE THAT TIME six months have passed, and there has fallen upon the country a 'white' winter – a winter of clear, keen, motionless frosts, of deep, crackling snow, of pink-rimed trees, of pale-emerald heavens, of smoke-capped chimneys, of puffs of vapour from momentarily opened doors, of faces fresh and hard-bitten, of horses galloping headlong to thaw their frozen limbs. It is now the close of a January day, and the increasing chill of evening is nipping the still air in an ever-tightening vice as the sun sinks downward into a sea of red.

But in the windows of Marino there are lights burning, and Prokofitch, vested in a black tail-coat, a pair of white gloves, and a peculiar atmosphere of solemnity, is laying the table with seven covers. This is because a week ago there were solemnised in the tiny church of the parish – solemnised quietly, almost without a witness – two sets of nuptials: the nuptials of Arkady and Katia and those of Nikolai Petrovitch and Thenichka. And today Nikolai Petrovitch is offering his brother a farewell dinner, for the reason that Paul is on the point of departing for Moscow, whither Anna Sergievna has already removed after bestowing upon the younger of the two couples a handsome dowry.

At three o'clock precisely the company gathers around the board. Mitia too is present with his *niania* (in nurse's cap), while Paul Petrovitch is seated between Katia and Thenichka, and the bridegrooms are ranged one on either side of their newly-wedded spouses. A change has taken place in our old acquaintances since last we saw them – they have improved, as regards the younger ones, both in appearance and in sedateness of demeanour. Only Paul Petrovitch looks thinner; though the circumstance imparts, if anything, an added touch of refinement and 'grand-seignorishness' to his always expressive features. Thenichka, in particular, is a different person from what she was. Clad in a brand-new silken gown, and wearing a broad velvet band over her hair and a necklace around her throat, she holds herself with an immovable dignity, yet also with an immovable deference towards her surroundings. And meanwhile she smiles, as much as to say: 'Pardon me, but *I* am not responsible for this'; while the others respond with similar smiles, as though they too would be glad to excuse themselves for their share in the proceedings. Yet the fact that on everyone present sits a touch of gravity and embarrassment becomes the company no less than do their other characteristics. Everywhere, too, there is to be seen such an anxious solicitude for mutual wants that the company could seem unanimously to be playing some simple-minded comedy; and though, of the guests, the quietest is Katia, it is plain, from her confidence of bearing, that, as a daughter-in-law, she has found favour in the eyes of Nikaiai Petrovitch.

At length the meal comes to an end, and Nikolai, rising and grasping a wine-glass, addresses Paul Petrovitch:

'Dearest brother, you are about to leave us. Yes, you are about to leave us. But not for long must you be absent, since I, for one, could never express to you how much I, how much I – that is to say, how much we – But, to tell you the truth, I am not good at making a speech. Arkady, to you I depute the task.'

'But I am not ready, Papa.'

'Neither am I. However, Paul, I embrace you, and wish you every joy, and beg of you to return to us soon.'

Whereupon Paul Petrovitch exchanges greetings all round (not excluding little Mitia), and, in particular, kisses Thenichka's hand (which she has not learnt to offer in the right way), drinks a twice-filled glass to the company at large, and says with a profound sigh: 'May you all be happy, my friends! Farewell!'* And though the English terminal flourish passes unnoticed, everyone is touched with the benediction which has preceded it.

'Yes, and I drink to the memory of Bazarov,' whispers Katia to her husband as she clinks glasses with him: but though, in response, he squeezes her hand, he decides not to propose the toast in public.

And here, apparently, there ought to follow the word *Finis*; but since some of my readers may care to know how each of the characters in the book is faring at the present day, I will satisfy that curiosity.

To take Anna Sergievna first, she has married – not for love, nor yet out of a sense of duty – a rising young statesman who is an intelligent legislator, a severely practical thinker, a man of strong will and elo-quence, and a lover with a temperament as cold as ice. Nevertheless the pair reside on amicable terms, and may, in time, attain to happiness – nay, even to love.

As for the Princess, she is dead, and her memory perished with her.

The Kirsanovs, father and son, are settled at Marino, and appear to be righting their industrial affairs, in that Arkady has developed into a capable manager, and the estate now brings in a fair income. Nikolai

---

* In the text this word is given in English.

Petrovitch, too, is constant in his endeavours to make peace on the property, and, riding systematically round it, delivers long speeches in the belief that only need the peasantry be 'reasoned with' – that is to say, plied with the same words over and over again – for the *muzhik* gradually to become a tractable animal. Yet Nikolai earns the approval neither of the educated gentry, who speak with affected jauntiness of the coming ' 'mancipation'* (they invariably give the syllable 'an' a nasal inflection), nor of those uneducated landowners who roundly curse what they term 'that — 'mun'cipation.' In other words, for both classes Nikolai Petrovitch is too 'mild.'

Katerina Sergievna has had a son born to her, and named him Kolia; Mitia is now a big, active, volubly lisping boy; and Thenichka (rather, Theodosia Nikolaievna) adores her daughter-in-law only less than her husband and Mitia. In fact, that adoration reaches the point that, should Katia sit down to the piano, Thenichka cannot leave her though the playing continue all day.

Then a word concerning Peter the valet. As much a lump of mingled stupidity and conceit as ever, he still pronounces his e's as u's, but has taken unto himself a wife, and, with her, a respectable dowry. The daughter of a market gardener of the neighbouring town, she had already refused two eligible *partis* solely on the ground that they did not possess watches! But Peter possesses not only a watch, but also a pair of patent leather pumps.

Again, any day on the Brühl Terrace, in Dresden, you may meet, between two and four o'clock in the afternoon (the fashionable hour for a promenade), a man of about fifty. Grey-headed, and afflicted with gout, yet still handsome, he is elegantly dressed, and stamped with that air of good breeding which comes only of long association with elevated strata of society. That man is Paul Petrovitch. Having left Moscow for foreign parts for his health's sake, he has settled in Dresden for the reason that there he possesses the largest number of English and nomad-Russian acquaintances. Towards the former he bears himself with simplicity, and almost with modesty, but with a touch of *hauteur*; and, in return, the English look upon him as a trifle tedious, but respect him on the score of his being 'quite a gentleman.' In the presence of the Russian element, however, Paul Petrovitch is more free and easy – he gives rein unstintedly to his sarcasm, and rallies both his compatriots and himself. Yet from *him* such things come pleasantly, and with a gay *insouciance*, and in a becoming manner; while, in addition, he holds Slavophil views – views which (as we all know)

* i.e. the emancipation of the serfs, which was carried out in 1861.

invariably induce the great world to rate their holder a person *très distingué*. True, never by any chance does Paul read a Russian book; yet by way of compensation, there stands on his writing-table a silver ash-tray shaped like a *muzhik's* clog. Moreover, from some of our Russian tourists he receives considerable attention when they happen to be passing through the town; and even our old friend Matvei Ilyitch Koliazin, on finding himself 'in temporary opposition,' has paid him a visit while en route to Bohemia for a course of the waters. In fact, the only persons who show Paul no deference at all are the native Germans, whose society he does not greatly cultivate. Yet even they agree that, in the matter of obtaining tickets for the Court Chapel or the theatre and so forth, none is so clever, so dexterous, as 'der Herr Baron von Kirsanov.' In fact, always does he do 'the right thing' so far as he is able; and even yet he can create some stir, owing to the fact that he has once, and to good purpose, been a social lion. Yet life presses upon him not a little heavily – more heavily than he himself is aware. Merely need one look at him as, huddled against the aisle wall of the Russian church, he sits plunged in thought, with his lips bitterly compressed, and continues sitting there until, remembering his surroundings, he makes, almost imperceptibly, the sign of the cross.

In similar fashion. Madame Kukshin has gone abroad – in her case, to Heidelberg, where she is engaged in studying, not natural science, but architecture – a branch wherein she has, according to herself, 'discovered several new laws.' Also, still she is hail-fellow-well-met with students, more especially with some of those Russian physicists and chemists who swarm in Heidelberg, and who, though at first flabbergasting the simple-minded German professors with the moderation of their views, subsequently proceed to flabbergast those professors with the wholeheartedness of their sloth. In fact, it is of two or three of those chemistry students who, though unable to distinguish even oxygen from azote, are yet charged to the brim with conceit and the spirit of 'denial,' that Madame Kukshin's circle is chiefly composed.

Similarly, friend Sitnikov is preparing to become a great man. For which purpose he is flaunting it in St Petersburg, and (to quote his own expression) 'carrying on the work of the late Bazarov.' True, rumour declares that someone has recently given him a second thrashing; as also that he (Sitnikov) has declined to face the music – rather, that he has preferred to hint in an obscure article in an equally obscure newspaper that his assailant is the coward; but to this report Sitnikov merely attaches the epithet 'ironical.' For the rest, his father continues to send him remittances, while his wife accounts him equally a *littérateur* and a fool.

Lastly, in a remote corner of Russia there lies a little country cemetery. Like most cemeteries of the kind, it is depressing of aspect. Over its fences dense masses of weed have grown, its drab wooden crosses are rickety and turning mouldy under their blistered, painted canopies, its stone paths have lost their alignment, and look as though someone has displaced them from below, its two or three ragged trees diffuse only the scantiest of shade, and sheep wander unhindered over its tombs. But among those tombs there lies a grave which no man molests and no animal tramples upon: only the birds perch upon it and sing as evening falls. For around that grave stands an iron railing, and at its head and foot are planted two young fir trees. It is the grave of Evgenii Vasilitch Bazarov. Occasionally from the neighbouring manor-house there come two aged and decrepit folk, a man and his wife. Supporting one another with a step which ever grows heavier, they approach the railing, sink upon their knees, and weep long, bitter tears as they gaze at the dumb headstone where their son lies sleeping. Then they exchange a word or two, dust the stone with assiduous care, lay upon it a sprig of fir, and offer a last petition. Yet even then they can scarce bear to tear themselves from the spot where they can draw nearest to their son, and to their memories of him.

But are those tears, those prayers, all fruitless? Is that love, that hallowed, selfless love, of theirs to be wholly unavailing? No, no, and a thousand times no! For, though the heart which lies within that tomb may have been passionate and wild and erring, the flowers which bloom in that spot contemplate us with eyes of naught but peace and innocence, and speak to us of naught but the eternal, mighty calm of 'unheeding' nature, as an image of the Eternal Reconciliation, and of the Life which shall have no End.

WORDSWORTH CLASSICS
General Editors: Marcus Clapham & Clive Reynard

JANE AUSTEN
Emma
Mansfield Park
Northanger Abbey
Persuasion
Pride and Prejudice
Sense and Sensibility

ARNOLD BENNETT
Anna of the Five Towns

R. D. BLACKMORE
Lorna Doone

ANNE BRONTË
Agnes Grey
The Tenant of
Wildfell Hall

CHARLOTTE BRONTË
Jane Eyre
The Professor
Shirley
Villette

EMILY BRONTË
Wuthering Heights

JOHN BUCHAN
Greenmantle
Mr Standfast
The Thirty-Nine Steps

SAMUEL BUTLER
The Way of All Flesh

LEWIS CARROLL
Alice in Wonderland

CERVANTES
Don Quixote

G. K. CHESTERTON
Father Brown:
Selected Stories
The Man who was
Thursday

ERSKINE CHILDERS
The Riddle of the Sands

JOHN CLELAND
Memoirs of a Woman of
Pleasure: Fanny Hill

WILKIE COLLINS
The Moonstone
The Woman in White

JOSEPH CONRAD
Heart of Darkness
Lord Jim
The Secret Agent

J. FENIMORE COOPER
The Last of the
Mohicans

STEPHEN CRANE
The Red Badge of
Courage

THOMAS DE QUINCEY
Confessions of an English
Opium Eater

DANIEL DEFOE
Moll Flanders
Robinson Crusoe

CHARLES DICKENS
Bleak House
David Copperfield
Great Expectations
Hard Times
Little Dorrit
Martin Chuzzlewit
Oliver Twist
Pickwick Papers
A Tale of Two Cities

BENJAMIN DISRAELI
Sybil

THEODOR DOSTOEVSKY
Crime and Punishment

SIR ARTHUR CONAN
DOYLE
The Adventures of
Sherlock Holmes
The Case-Book of
Sherlock Holmes
The Lost World &
Other Stories
The Return of
Sherlock Holmes
Sir Nigel

GEORGE DU MAURIER
Trilby

ALEXANDRE DUMAS
The Three Musketeers

MARIA EDGEWORTH
Castle Rackrent

GEORGE ELIOT
The Mill on the Floss
Middlemarch
Silas Marner

HENRY FIELDING
Tom Jones

F. SCOTT FITZGERALD
A Diamond as Big as the
Ritz & Other Stories
The Great Gatsby
Tender is the Night

GUSTAVE FLAUBERT
Madame Bovary

JOHN GALSWORTHY
In Chancery
The Man of Property
To Let

ELIZABETH GASKELL
Cranford
North and South

KENNETH GRAHAME
The Wind in the
Willows

GEORGE & WEEDON
GROSSMITH
Diary of a Nobody

RIDER HAGGARD
She

THOMAS HARDY
Far from the
Madding Crowd
The Mayor of Casterbridge
The Return of the
Native
Tess of the d'Urbervilles
The Trumpet Major
Under the Greenwood
Tree

DISTRIBUTION

AUSTRALIA
& PAPUA NEW GUINEA
Peribo Pty Ltd
58 Beaumont Road, Mount Kuring-Gai
NSW 2080, Australia
Tel: (02) 457 0011 Fax: (02) 457 0022

CZECH REPUBLIC
Bohemian Ventures spol s r o
Delnicka 13, 170 00 Prague 7
Tel: 02 877837 Fax: 02 801498

FRANCE
Chiron Diffusion
40, Rue de Seine, Paris 75006,
Tel: 1 43 26 47 56 Fax: 1 45 83 54 61

GREAT BRITAIN & IRELAND
Wordsworth Editions Ltd
Cumberland House, Crib Street
Ware, Hertfordshire SG12 9ET

SCOTLAND
Lomond Books
36 West Shore Road, Granton
Edinburgh EH5 1QD

INDIA
OM Book Service
1690 First Floor
Nai Sarak, Delhi – 110006
Tel: 3279823-3265303 Fax: 3278091

IRAN
World Book Distributers
26 Behrooz Street, Suite 6
Tehran 19119
Tel: 9821 8714622 Fax: 9871 50044

ISRAEL
Timmy Marketing Limited
Israel Ben Zeev 12
Ramont Gimmel, Jerusalem
Tel: 02-865266 Fax: 02-880035

ITALY
Magis Books SRL
Via Raffaello 31/C
Zona Ind Mancasale
42100 Reggio Emilia
Tel: 1522 920999 Fax: 0522 920666

NEW ZEALAND
Allphy Book Distributors Ltd
4-6 Charles Street, Eden Terrace
Auckland,
Tel: (09) 3773096 Fax: (09) 3022770

PHILIPPINES
I J Sagun Enterprises
P O Box 4322 CPO Manila
2 Topaz Road, Greenheights Village
Taytay, Rizal
Tel: 631 80 61 TO 66

PORTUGAL
International Publishing Services Ltd
Rua da Cruz da Carreira, 4B,
1100 Lisbon
Tel: 01 570051 Fax: 01 3522066

SINGAPORE,
MALASIA & BRUNEI
Paul & Elizabeth Book Services Pte Ltd
163 Tanglin Road No 03-15/16
Tanglin Mall, Singapore 1024
Tel: (65) 735 7308 Fax: (65) 735 9747

SLOVAK REPUBLIC
Slovak Ventures spol s r o
Stefanikova 128, 94901 Nitra
Tel/Fax: 087 25105

CYPRUS
Huckleberry Trading
3 Othos Avvey, Tala Paphos
Tel: 06 653585

SPAIN
Ribera Libros, S.L.
Poligono Martiartu, Calle 1 - no 6
48480 Arrigorriaga, Vizcaya
Tel: 34 4 6713607 (Almacen)
         34 4 4418787 (Libreria)
Fax: 34 4 6713608 (Almacen)
        34 4 4418029 (Libreria)

DIRECT MAIL
Redvers
Redvers House
13 Fairmile, Henley-on-Thames
Oxfordshire RG9 2JR
Tel: 01491 572656 Fax: 01491 573 590